T0244775

DECEIVED
BY
THE
LIGHT

ALSO BY DAMIEN BOYD

DECEIVED BY THE LIGHT

A DI BOB WILLIS NOVEL

DAMIEN BOYD

Text copyright © Damien Boyd 2025

Published by Thomas & Mercer, Seattle

www.apub.com

Amazon, the Amazon logo, and Thomas & Mercer are trademarks of Amazon.com, Inc., or its affiliates.

ISBN-13: 9781662524707
eISBN: 9781662524691

Cover design by @blacksheep-uk.com
Cover image: © Magdalena Russocka / Arcangel

Printed in the United States of America

For Shelley

Prologue

She'd always hated driving aft night. It wasn't just the lights of the oncoming cars dazzling her. It was the idea of breaking down, getting stuck in the middle of nowhere, in the middle of the night.

All alone.

There'd been those reports on the news, women being attacked. Her mother had seen them; never given her a moment's peace after that.

'Why did you have to take that job?'

'Do you have to do the late shifts?'

'Why can't you find a job in Yeovil?'

Her mother had paid for her breakdown cover, full AA membership no less, which made them both feel a bit better, but not much. Not that she'd dare let on. She'd never hear the last of it.

It was the shift patterns, and there was no getting around it. Two till ten on lates, one week on, one week off; driving home after dark, unless it was high summer, of course.

A short run along the A303 to Yeovil, a deserted A-road, some of it dual carriageway, no street lighting. No one to hear you scream, her younger brother had said, with a mischievous grin.

Her father had filled a can of petrol, left it in the boot of her car, just in case. Not that she'd ever run out of fuel before. She was far too careful for that. A toolkit too, not that she'd know what to do with it.

The problems had started not long after she'd left Ilminster. She should have turned around, gone back to the hospital and phoned the AA. But, you never know, do you? Thomas was her pride and joy – her first car – and he'd never let her down yet. Besides, she had a full tank of petrol and he hadn't long been serviced. The engine was running well too.

The cassette player had been the first thing to die on her, Bruce Springsteen slurring his words, before the bloody machine mangled her copy of Born in the USA. *She ejected the cassette, threw it on the passenger seat.*

She'd tried flicking the lights to full beam when they started dimming; she hadn't really noticed it in the streetlights on the edge of Ilminster. It wasn't until she got out into the country that it dawned on her, Thomas casting a shadow in the lights of the cars coming up behind her.

The lights on the dashboard had all but gone too, and the fan had stopped working.

Maybe she should pull over somewhere? There'd be a telephone in the lay-by the other side of Ilchester, if she could get that far.

Then the engine cut out.

She tried turning the key, bump starting it too. Nothing.

Hazard lights on, she coasted into a field gateway on the nearside by the lights of a passing lorry, the steering getting heavier as the car slowed.

Praying that the lorry driver didn't stop.

Locked the driver's door.

There'll be a phone somewhere, she thought, peering out into the darkness. That's what those white posts are for, they tell you which way to walk. Not that she fancied that – along the grass verge of a dual carriageway. At night.

She remembered the torch in the glovebox, leaned over and fished it out, sending the vehicle service book and a bundle of receipts into the passenger footwell, sitting up just as a car was pulling in behind her.

Flashing blue lights on top.

Thank God for that.

Chapter One

Saturday 25th May 1985

'Let's talk about what happened.'

I'd known that one was coming. It was our third therapy session, after all, and she'd mentioned it before. The elephant in the room.

What happened.

I looked around her office, playing for time. Trying to work out whether I should trust her. There'd been all the usual promises of patient confidentiality, of course there had, but she was being paid by Avon and Somerset Police – my employer, for the time being.

Long term sick leave, although retirement on medical grounds has been mentioned more than once. It was the direction of travel, they said, and I've nearly done my thirty years anyway.

I'm guessing that all consultant psychologists have a treatment room that looks much the same as this, although I'd have gone for red leather on the desk. Actually, it's green. Lots of books on shelves. A fireplace. There's even one of those skulls with the areas of the brain mapped out on it.

No couch for me, oddly enough, but it's quite a comfy armchair, all the same. Green leather to match the desk; winged, with studs.

It's funny the things you notice when you're nervous. I'm fine talking about cricket, but there was always going to come a time when the conversation became . . . uncomfortable.

What happened.

It's been coming back to me over the last few weeks. Slowly. She said it would.

Actually, that's a lie. Sorry.

I remember everything. From the first moment I woke up in Yeovil Hospital.

She picked up a piece of paper. 'You went to see Superintendent Sharp. Told him it was a different car that hit you, so you must remember something.'

Close, but not quite. What I actually said was that the second car hit me . . . wait for it . . . deliberately. And you and I both know what that means.

His response was classic Sharp: 'Bollocks, mate. You stepped out into the road and it was a simple hit and run. Some bloke on his way home from work, probably. Anyway, we got the bloke who killed the girls. Case closed.'

I tried pressing the point – ended up banging my head against a brick wall.

'Have you found the car?'

'Probably never will. Not now.'

Then the bartender arrived and Sharp turned his back on me. More interested in getting a round in.

If I wait long enough, she'll change tack. She usually does; likes to keep the conversation flowing.

'Have you brought your scorebook?'

And there it is. Back to the cricket.

I slid the book across the desk. 'Two matches since last time. The away one was Glamorgan, so I went,' I said. 'There's a County Championship game going on at the moment, started yesterday. Home too.'

Nice of her to fit me in on a Saturday morning, but I'm missing the first innings.

'Who are Somerset playing?'

'Warwickshire,' I replied, with a heavy sigh. I knew what was coming. A few jokes to lighten the mood.

'Isn't that the team your namesake plays for?'

That old gem. The police do love a nickname. Everyone's got one. Some fun, some less so. At least mine is well-meaning, even though I'm only five foot ten on a good day. Bob is seven feet tall and bowls the ball at over ninety miles an hour. Sharing the same surname had been enough for it to stick, though.

'Yes, Bob plays for Warwickshire,' I said.

'Do you find scoring the games helpful?'

'It takes my mind off things. Keeps me busy.'

'That's the idea.' She tried a comforting smile.

I think I can trust her, but is that enough? She was flicking through the pages of the book, pretending she understood the dots. Come to think of it, maybe she did? I'd never asked.

'D'you understand cricket? I know it's not everyone's cup of tea.'

'It's a complete mystery to me, I'm afraid.'

That's a relief. A County Championship game. Four days at Taunton and I'd only been to one. I copied the rest of the scorecard from Ceefax. I could see her shaking her head, so it meant nothing to her, but it wouldn't stand up in court. Even a cursory check against the real scorecard would show it was mostly fiction.

'So, how do I know you were actually there and haven't made all this up?' she asked.

Bugger. 'You don't.'

'I'm going to have to start checking the mileage on your car, I think.' There was mischief in her voice, so maybe she was joking. 'How many times have you been out on the A303?'

She could tell from my hesitation.

'C'mon, Bob, how many times?'

'Every day.'

Sometimes honesty is the best policy. And she knows anyway.

'We talked about this.'

'We did.'

'I thought living above the post office in Blagdon was going to help. It's miles away from that damn road.'

'Thirty, if you go via Shepton Mallet and Bruton.'

'How are you getting on with your ex-wife and her husband?'

'Shirley's fine.'

She leaned back in her chair and folded her arms, making no attempt to hide her impatience. 'Is that it?'

'I don't see her much. They're downstairs in the post office before I wake up and I've got a separate entrance round the side . . .'

'And you're out all day driving up and down the A303.' Kind of her to finish my sentence for me. She was scribbling on the notepad in front of her, underlining whatever it was several times. 'What exactly are you looking for, Bob?'

The big sash window behind her gave me a grandstand view of Exeter Cathedral. I'd asked for a psychologist out of the immediate force area. Out of Somerset, basically. Not that she wouldn't be familiar with the case. It had made national news. Two murders, and then . . . *what happened.*

She was watching my eyes, so it was just a matter of time.

'Have you been to see Lizzie's family?'

So, that's it. She thinks I'm looking for forgiveness. Perhaps I am?

'It wasn't your fault, Bob.'

So everyone keeps saying.

'She made her own decisions that night. You were trying to stop her.'

'Was I?'

'Why don't you tell me what happened?'

A nice try. She nearly got me that time. Although maybe the time has come to tell someone? 'Why don't you tell me what you think happened?' I asked.

'I've only read the witness statements they sent me, but there was a killer operating along the A303, wasn't there? Two murders, single women who'd broken down late at night. Their cars were found where they'd left them and the bodies were found elsewhere.'

Elsewhere. It covers a multitude of sins.

'Lizzie went out one night, on her own, parked in a lay-by and waited. She'd done it several times, according to her flatmate.'

'She was my detective sergeant.'

'Are you saying you knew what she was doing?'

I'm not sure how to answer that one, if I'm honest. Not that I have been. Honest, I mean. Even with myself.

'When you found out, you went out to stop her and that's when you got hit by that car. The hit and run. You were found on the central reservation. A fractured skull. Broken ribs, punctured lung, left elbow shattered, broken leg. You're lucky to be alive.'

Thanks. Although I'm not sure *lucky* is the right word.

'Lizzie's body was found a week later in the boot of an abandoned car.'

'I was in hospital for her funeral,' I offered. Best to give the good doctor something to work with. However small. Otherwise, she'll just keep digging.

'Do you feel guilt, for missing her funeral?'

Among other things.

'Tell me about your physical injuries,' she said.

'I get headaches, shooting pains in my elbow, but I can move it and cast a fly, so I can't complain. I limp on cold days too; it's the plates and pins in my left leg. Like you say, I'm lucky to be alive.'

'And they got him three weeks later for driving with a defective brake light. When they pulled him over, he tried to make a run for it and fell from a bridge into the path of an articulated lorry.'

She's almost right. I made it to the inquest on crutches, sitting in the public gallery. The coroner actually recorded an open verdict; he couldn't be sure whether it was an accident or suicide, but the effect was the same. An appeal for witnesses, a cursory hunt for the hit and run driver who'd clobbered me, but otherwise, case closed. A killer apprehended reasonably quickly, compared to what happened in Yorkshire a few years ago, Sharp too busy patting himself on the back to worry about who had put me in hospital.

They like to keep victims of crime up to date with developments, even when there aren't any. Or is it still 'we'? I'm still getting paid, so I suppose I'm still a police officer.

A glance at the carriage clock on the mantelpiece. Five minutes left. I'll go home along the A303, I think. Just one more look. It's a bit of a detour, but . . .

'I see you clock watching, Bob,' she said. 'We're making progress now, so we'll keep going if that's all right with you. Strike while the iron's hot, and all that. My next appointment's not until midday, so we've got time.'

Bollocks.

'You still haven't told me what you're looking for out on the A303. Not the car that hit you, surely? That'll be long gone by now.'

A good point. A dark hatchback. A VW Golf, something like that. That was the best I could say. It would have been repaired or scrapped by now. Dumped in a barn or a lake, perhaps. There'd been no reports of burnt out cars matching that description anyway.

Flashing lights, the squeal of the brakes. I braced for the flashback, but it never came. It's happening less and less, these days.

Post traumatic stress disorder is the label she's given me. Some new thing, apparently. The flashbacks are usually at night now, though. I wake up sweating. Maybe I shouldn't have stopped taking the sleeping pills?

'Do you feel guilt for what happened to Lizzie?'

'I feel lots of things, but yes, guilt is one of them.'

'Because you couldn't stop her?'

'Because I didn't stop her.'

'Why don't you tell me what happened, Bob?' she asked. 'You have to tell someone at some point, so it might as well be me. And there is patient confidentiality. You do know that? Nothing you say leaves this room.'

There's a thing. Well and truly on the spot. Maybe the time has come? She poured herself a glass of water. Her turn to buy time; sensible enough to keep quiet and let me mull it over.

A deep breath.

'The first girl was twenty-one. We found her car in a field gateway east of Ilminster. Her body we found *elsewhere*.'

'Did you go to the scene?'

A slow nod. Purposeful. The images seared on to my brain.

'Do you want to talk about it?'

'No.'

'Another time then. You need to get it off your chest. Bottling it up is part of your problem.'

'The second girl was twenty-four. Her car was in a lay-by at Ilchester. Her body was found off the B390, just west of Chitterne on Salisbury Plain, which made it a Wiltshire case.' At least she knew not to ask about the scene this time. 'The press were starting to talk about the "A303 Ripper". Another murder and we had a serial killer on our hands, so . . .'

'Lizzie went out—'

'It was my idea. I went with her a couple of times and we waited out there all night, me hiding in the undergrowth. That night she went on her own. I knew she would. So, yes. I feel guilt, and I'm looking for forgiveness.'

'That doesn't make it your fault.'

'Yes, it does. I was supposed to go with her, but didn't get there in time and she went on her own. Workmen recovering a car dumped by the side of the road found her body in the boot a week later. The car even had police tape around it.'

'Why didn't you get there in time?'

One thing leads to another, doesn't it? An answer to the next question.

I didn't get there in time.

Why?

'It says in your medical records you've got a problem with alcohol,' she said, twisting the knife, almost apologetically.

'I haven't touched a drop since that night.'

'I understand the guilt, in that case, Bob.' Scribbling again; underlining whatever it was she'd just written down. 'Go and see her parents, make your peace with them, ask for their forgiveness. Maybe now is the time to lay these ghosts to rest?'

'Maybe it is.'

'But, whatever it is you're looking for, you won't find it out on the A303. Her killer is dead and the case is closed.'

Time to go.

'I was at his inquest, remember.' I stood up to leave. 'The case might be closed, but her killers aren't dead. Neither of them are.'

Chapter Two

Ilminster is a funny little place. I've never liked it. They should bypass it, do us all a favour. They keep talking about it, so maybe one day.

A small town, dreary on a sunny day.

It's only the A303 that keeps bringing me back. Actually, it brings everyone back, right through the town. A constant stream of vehicles going anywhere but here, drivers swearing at the traffic lights, trying to get to their holiday cottages in Cornwall.

A bottleneck in summer; traffic heading west on a Friday, and east – back to London – on a Sunday.

The killers never struck on a Friday or a Sunday. Too many people about. Simple, you might think, but Sharp was convinced the killer – singular – worked shifts.

Some of the lads call him Blunt; others a word that rhymes with Blunt.

To be fair to them, most of those travelling the A303 would be oblivious to what had gone on – *what happened*. Too busy driving, their passengers playing I Spy, children being sick in the back.

The only real sign anything happened at all is a bunch of flowers tied to a sapling on the bank behind Lizzie's lay-by. That's what I call it now. And I know the flowers are there.

I tied them to the tree myself.

I looked up at the council houses, a line of them on the edge of Ilminster; precast concrete slabs, metal window frames, railings and chicken-wire fences out front, the grass neatly mown on some.

I've still got my crutches in the boot of the car, so I'll use them. The sympathy might help.

The old man was watching me through the open window as I hopped up the steps to his front door.

'You'll be Bob Willis,' he said, a cat taking the opportunity to dart out.

'Actually it's Mungo, Bob's just a nickname,' I replied, leaning heavily on my crutches. 'After the cricketer.'

'You're nothing like him.'

'I think that's the joke.'

The old man smiled. He extended his hand, his fingers stained with nicotine. I'd spotted the overflowing ashtray on the windowsill too. 'What d'you want?' he asked.

'To talk to you about Martin.'

'Your lot stitched him up good and proper.'

A statement of fact I had no intention of arguing with. Best ignore it and wait.

'You'd better come in,' said the old man, with a shake of his head.

Baggy corduroys, carpet slippers, shirt open at the neck, and a cardigan – knitted by his late wife, probably. I already knew she was dead, but the photograph in pride of place on the mantelpiece gave it away.

I leaned my crutches against the back of the sofa and slumped down with an exaggerated grimace on to the small space in between the piles of newspapers. There wasn't much left of the sofa, the cat having shredded most of the fabric, the tassels lying on the coffee-stained rug.

I'm hoping it's coffee, anyway.

'You were at the inquest,' he said.

The old man had made an effort that day. Clean shaven, Sunday best. Let himself go since then. I can't really criticise him for that, I suppose. Shirley tells me I've done the same; let myself go since the *accident*, as she insists on calling it. I've made an effort today, though. I always do for the good doctor. Don't want to give her more ammunition.

'I wasn't there in an official capacity,' I replied. 'And I'm not here now. Officially.'

The old man nodded his understanding. 'They said my son killed three people, your colleague Sergeant Harper and those two women they found cut to ribbons. Not looking for anyone else, they said. Case closed, they said. No trial, nothing. When do I get a chance to clear his name?'

'He was a van driver?'

'They'd got boot prints, the soles worn by the pedals, so the killer was a driver, they said, just like that bastard from Yorkshire.'

There's more to it than that. The boot prints were found on my watch and were never of any real evidential value. I'd tried telling Sharp that. Not a line of enquiry worth pursuing – that is, until Martin Clarke was stopped and happened to be a van driver by trade.

'The boot prints were found at the scene of the second murder, on Salisbury Plain,' I said. 'An area squaddies trample all over on a regular basis. There were no tyre marks either, because a Chieftain tank had gone along the track and churned it to buggery.'

'That's what I told them,' protested the old man. 'Over and over.'

On their own, the boot prints wouldn't have been enough, but there was an elephant in this room too. 'They found the knives in the boot of his car.'

'They were planted there. Rope, gloves, two knives, all of it planted. They'd got someone they could pin it on, someone who couldn't argue because he was dead.' The old man thrust his hands into the sagging pockets of his cardigan. 'I have no doubt they genuinely believe my son was the killer, but he wasn't. No way.'

'Why did he run when he was stopped?' I asked. 'It was only a defective brake light.'

'We've only got their word for it that he did run.'

That's a surprise. I expected marijuana, or he was over the drink driving limit, possibly.

'All that crap he came out with at the inquest.'

'Who?'

'The officer who pulled him over. Police Constable Taylor. Said he couldn't be sure whether Martin was trying to jump on to the roof of the lorry to get away or jump in front of it to kill himself. That's why the coroner recorded an open verdict. Crap. All of it.'

'Have they returned his car to you?' I asked.

'It's in the garage round the back. D'you want to see it?'

'Can I see his room first?'

I followed the old man up the stairs. Slow going for both of us, although I was putting it on.

'Don't you need your crutches?'

'I'll be all right with the banister.'

The old man hesitated, holding the door handle, seemingly nervous to turn it. 'He was living with us temporarily; been kicked out by his wife. Turned into a bit of a lady's man had Martin, but the police used that against him too.'

A sink in the corner, dark wood furniture, a single bed that sagged in the middle.

'It's pretty much as he left it when he moved out ten years ago. Eighteen he was then, when he flew the nest.'

16

Queen posters on the wall, the corners curling, Freddie Mercury strutting his stuff. A toothbrush still sitting in a grubby glass by the sink. A Calor gas heater in the middle of the room, the back open, the gas bottle gone. Rugs on the floor, random bits of carpet that didn't match and didn't reach the skirting board.

Concert ticket stubs tucked into the edge of the mirror frame: Queen, Led Zeppelin, The Who.

'Did he have many girlfriends?' I asked, more to break the silence than anything.

'There'd only ever been Justine. That I know of anyway. They married too young, really, so I'm not surprised, to be honest, if he was . . . out and about. But there's no way he could've done what they said . . . killed those women. Just no way. He didn't have it in him.'

And there he was, kneeling down, grinning at the camera, the photograph leaning up against the lamp on the bedside table.

'I took that,' said the old man, with a sad smile. 'His first carp. Not huge, but that didn't seem to matter.' He picked up the photograph and held it up in front of me. 'Look at him. Look at that smile. Can you see my boy doing those things?'

'How old is he there?'

'Fourteen.'

'Let's have a look at his car, shall we?' Some fresh air wouldn't go amiss, either.

A set of keys from the cutlery drawer, then out through the back door. I followed, guessing correctly that the old man knew where the garden path was under the long grass.

'Mine's the end one,' he said. 'I'm not sure what to do with it, really. Justine doesn't want it, that's why it's here.'

The up-and-over garage door was a bit of a struggle, but he managed, me helping one-handed.

A black Capri.

'It's the three-litre one. I said it would get him killed, but it wasn't quite what I had in mind.'

I leaned my crutches against the wall and squeezed down the side of the car, popping open the boot with the key. I'd seen the photographs at the inquest, but it was empty now – cleaned too, that much was clear in the light streaming in through the window at the back of the garage.

The offside rear light was still broken; an MOT failure.

'You're looking at the light,' said the old man. 'He'd been in the Lord Poulett over at Hinton St George all night, so anyone could've done that. And I mean *anyone*.'

I know what he means.

'It's on-street parking in the village there.'

I'll have to pay it a visit.

'What happened to the car that hit you?' asked the old man.

'It's never been found,' I replied, slamming the boot.

'Sharp told me it was unconnected, a hit and run.'

'Sharp's full of shit.'

'Can I quote you on that?' The old man turned away, knowing he wasn't going to get an answer.

'I was deliberately run down by a second car, which means there were two of them.'

'They're both still out there.'

'They are.'

'And you're not here officially, you say?'

'I'm afraid not. I'm on long term sick leave, being shown the door on medical grounds.'

I held the garage door down with the end of a crutch while the old man turned the handle and locked it.

'I might sell it. Bloody thing's no use to me.' He was following me now, down the steps back to my car.

'Keep it, for now,' I said. 'It's evidence.'

18

'What of?'

'I don't know yet.'

'Maybe you should drive it, instead of this thing?' The old man was kicking the back tyre of my car. 'Look at the size of this bumper.'

I've never been one for cars. Provided it gets me there and back, it'll do.

'And yellow?' He squinted, pretending to be blinded by the glare. 'A yellow Volvo 240. What does that say about you, I wonder?'

'That I don't give a shit about cars.'

'I'm guessing you don't really need those things, either,' he said, watching me throw my crutches on the back seat.

'Not really.'

'So, what happens now?' His voice suddenly sombre, the moment of levity behind us.

'I find the killers. The men who killed your son, my sergeant, and two women who had the misfortune to break down on the open road. The same men who tried to kill me. As you say, they're still out there.'

'Doing what?'

'Waiting.'

'What for?'

'Me. They'll be waiting to see how much I know, how much I can remember, to see what I do; whether I come after them, or whether they can go on killing in peace.'

Sitting in the driver's seat now, winding down the window.

'What can you do about it? You're not even a serving officer anymore.'

'That just means there are no rules. And look at me. What have I got to lose?'

'Can I help?'

'You already have.'

Chapter Three

I used to enjoy driving. The open road, and all that, but there's far too much traffic these days. Boy racers in souped-up GTIs. Fuel injected this, sixteen valve that. They're a bloody menace.

A long queue westbound at the end of the short section of dual carriageway. South Petherton, a well known bottleneck. But then it is Friday afternoon, and merging in turn at a sensible speed is too much for some people. Some drivers pull over early and wait their turn; others blast down the outside and try to cut in at the last minute. Then you get the lorry driver sitting in the middle of both lanes like some sort of self-appointed lane-discipline guardian. The end result is chaos; huge tailbacks. Always has been and always will be, until they dual the whole thing.

Not in my lifetime, though. And actually the road would lose most of its charm.

Charm?

The wrong word, probably.

I sail past them, enjoying the sight of them drumming their fingers on their steering wheels, some of them leaning out of windows trying to see what the delay is. I like to watch the milometer ticking over as I speed past. Three miles; not bad, but it'll get worse before it gets better.

Most things do, in my experience.

Ilchester next, which is always bad because you pick up the Yeovil traffic. Lizzie's lay-by too. I think I'll stop and check her flowers, if *he's* not there.

Martin Clarke's father didn't say anything I don't already know, but it was what he *didn't say* that interests me. The unspoken inferences. The conclusions to be drawn. The biggest one being that Police Constable Sean Taylor was talking crap at the inquest.

I've always been able to tell when people are lying. I've had a lot of practice. Some do it for a pastime, and when they're talking to a police officer, they just can't help themselves.

Police officers have a particular way of lying too. Resorting to the notebook, lots of long words so what they're saying sounds official and beyond reproach. All that tells me is they've taken their time getting their story straight.

I've seen Taylor out and about several times in his patrol car, usually in a lay-by or on a bridge, waiting for someone to speed past. If he's on duty, he'll be watching the eastbound carriageway. No point watching the westbound side this afternoon; too much traffic.

And there he is. Based at Yeovil, so it's usually the Ilchester stretch. He rarely ventures too far from the kettle. Up on the bridge on the A37, looking down on everyone.

The last couple of times I've been on the other carriageway, doing over a ton by the time I've gone underneath him, and he's let me go. No pursuit. Nothing.

Let's see if he takes the bait this time, shall we?

Change down, then that click you get when you step on the accelerator. Pedal to the metal, as the saying goes, although it is a Volvo 240, so I shouldn't expect too much, perhaps.

Gently uphill going east, unfortunately, but I should get up to ninety by the time I go under the bridge. Surely enough to warrant a stop?

Watching the needle creeping up, I move into the outside lane, the more conspicuous the better.

He's sitting in the passenger seat this time, the patrol car parked right over the outside lane. I can't see the driver, but I look up as I go right underneath them. Eye contact almost.

No reaction.

A check in the nearside wing mirror for the big Rover flying down the slip road. Nothing. I've got the driver's window open, and no siren either.

I ease off the accelerator, dropping back to sixty, and pull in behind a 2CV. Missed Lizzie's lay-by in all the excitement too. Sod it.

That must be five times now Taylor has let me go. He knows it's me. He saw me in the car park at Martin Clarke's inquest, for a start, and he'd have run my number plate the first time I went past him. Yes, he knows it's me, so why does he let me go?

There'll be one of two reasons for that. Either he recognises a fellow police officer and is turning a blind eye, but then he doesn't strike me as the sort for that. An officious little twerp. The type for whom nicking a fellow officer for speeding would be an amusing anecdote to share with the lads in the pub. Might even be worth an extra round of drinks.

No, the second possibility is the more likely.

He knows that I know and he doesn't want to play the game; knows I'm baiting him and doesn't want to risk a confrontation.

What do I know?

Precious little, actually. It's more about what I suspect.

The boot prints. *Of little evidential value* was the phrase I used; they only became relevant because Martin Clarke turned out to be a van driver. He fitted the profile. What I suspect happened is that Martin was pulled over *because* he was a van driver. A defective offside rear brake light – not just a bulb gone, defective because it had been smashed by someone or something.

Hardly difficult to arrange. According to his father, Martin's Capri had been parked outside the Lord Poulett in Hinton St George for most of the evening.

Now for the elephant in the room. *I'll have enough for a bloody herd soon.*

If the murder weapons had been planted in the boot of Martin's car, as his father and I suspect, then it must have been done by Taylor at the time of the stop.

And, if that's right, where did he get them from?

Obvious questions, you might think. But the problem is I'm the only one asking them. For now.

I can feel a Little Chef coming on. I'll go as far as Camel Hill; an All Day Breakfast and a side order of beans.

Lovely.

I'm sitting in the window of the Little Chef at Camel Hill, watching the world go by, waiting for my Jubilee Pancake to arrive. You'll understand if you've ever had one.

Life has its compensations.

I had a lot of time to think when I was in hospital. About life, the universe and everything. I thought a lot about Lizzie, but spent most of the time feeling sorry for myself, to be honest.

The trouble with a career in the police is it sweeps you along. One case to the next, never a chance to draw breath, totally wrapped up in the job.

Then comes the divorce.

I noticed it after a while. Nobody asks *if* you're married. They ask how many times you've *been* married.

Most of us are divorced. The rate for male officers is seventy-six per cent, or something like that. Come to think of it, that might be America, but you get the picture I'm sure. It just sort of happens without you even knowing it. You're on some case. Working all hours, finally get a chance to open the post and there's the solicitor's letter.

We are instructed by Mrs Shirley Willis that the marriage between you has irretrievably broken down . . .

The next envelope had the divorce petition in it.

And there was me thinking she'd gone to stay with her sister.

I don't blame her. It wasn't as if my career was really going anywhere anyway. A journeyman. I made detective inspector by the skin of my teeth. I think they just felt sorry for me in the end. I kept applying, mainly because Shirley kept pushing me into it, and they probably thought they couldn't keep saying no.

Remarkably unremarkable, if I had to sum up my career.

Pub fights, fraud and a couple of murders, both of them domestic.

Not much to show for nearly thirty years on the force.

Thinking too much is a dangerous business. It's best if you don't do it at all, which explains why so many retired police officers go straight into a second career, or take up golf.

I've tried fishing on Blagdon Lake. Shirley's new husband, Alan, offered to take me out in a boat for a day, so I didn't have a lot of choice. It would've been rude to refuse, particularly when they're letting me live in the flat above their post office rent free. It was either that or a cardboard box in the Bearpit. That's an underpass in Bristol for those of you who don't know it.

It was a nice gesture, the fishing, and it is relaxing. I've been a few times since – Alan's lent me a rod – but there's too much time to think.

That's why the good doctor has got me scoring the cricket matches. I have to concentrate on that. Or at least I would if I did it properly.

Three months in a hospital bed, then the rehab. It was quite a shock.

Time to sit back, take stock, and find you don't like what you see. I don't recommend it.

Mediocrity.

Divorce.

Two daughters who don't speak to me.

A grandson I've never met.

I know what you're thinking, but sticking my head in a gas oven is not my style; too much of a coward for that.

So, here I am, recovering from injuries sustained in the line of duty that will keep me on sick leave until my retirement. Full pay until then too, so it's not all bad. Nothing else to do except watch the cricket, go fishing and relax.

Perhaps not.

I've got one case left. One chance, then maybe I can look back on my career and think it was worthwhile.

Four people are dead and the official line is that the police aren't looking for anyone else in connection with the murders.

They might not be.

But I am.

Chapter Four

I pick up the tail at Wincanton, still on the A303, but heading home. An unmarked car. Not very good at it, either. A couple of loops around the town and she's still there. In her little red Allegro.

I could outrun it. No bugger seems to want to stop me for speeding at the moment.

She doesn't look like police. Too young to be out of uniform. And she must know I've spotted her, but she's still there.

I'll pull in at the racecourse and see what she does. There's no racing today, and it'll be nice and quiet.

Well, there's a thing. Pulling in behind me.

I wind down the window and wait, watching her in my rear view mirror.

She looks a bit like Lizzie.

Of course she does.

Now, think, what's her name again?

Angela.

We've met before. Once. A long time ago. Lizzie had a party to celebrate her promotion to DS and her sister was there.

Best get out and face the music.

'Your wife said I'd find you in a Little Chef on the A303.'

'Ex-wife.'

'Doesn't surprise me.'

I see the movement, feel the sting. As slaps go, it's a good one; it has that crack sound to it. Probably hurts her as much as it does me, but neither of us are going to let that show. Besides, I deserve it.

'Remember me?'

'I do,' I replied.

'My parents don't blame you for what happened, but I do.' She's examining the fingers of her right hand, admiring the shade of red. 'They're sitting at home like a pair of wallies waiting for you to do the decent thing. I guess you're too much of a coward?'

There isn't much I can say to that. I should have been to see them long before now, of course I should.

'Still the snappy dresser.' She's on a roll. 'Lizzie always said it was like being partnered with an old scarecrow.'

I've made an effort today too. Smart trousers, a shirt and tie; granted, the collar is a bit frayed.

She's softening. Slowly. She clearly has more to say and is summoning up the courage, getting whatever else she has to say off her chest first.

'You were at school last time we—'

'I'm a journalist now,' she said. 'If you can call it that. It's hardly Fleet Street is it, the *Chard and Ilminster News*.' She shakes her head. 'Social and events editor. Coffee mornings. The highlights of the year are the agricultural shows and village fetes.'

'Someone's got to do it.'

'Fuck off.'

Just like Lizzie. Doesn't take any crap. She's sought me out for a reason, and there's likely to be more to it than a slap. All I have to do is wait.

Angela is small. Well, I say small, smaller than me. I'm not exactly Bob Willis, am I? I think we've established that. Dark hair, short. She's wearing a two-piece suit, heels, but they're not high. Come from work then.

They might make a detective of me yet.

'You don't believe Martin Clarke killed Lizzie and those two women, do you?'

'No.'

'You went to see his father.'

'How d'you know?'

'He rang me.'

I learned a long time ago to be careful what you say to journalists. Even the social and events editor. Not that I'm organising a bring-and-buy. You just never know when it's going to end up in print. Actually, I'm careful what I say to everyone these days, even the good doctor, who is always at pains to tell me she's on my side.

'We've had a date through for Lizzie's inquest. It's on Tuesday at Wells,' Angela said. 'You going?'

'Not been called to give evidence.' Hardly surprising, given my witness statement. 'But, I'll be there.'

She still hasn't got round to the real reason for tracking me down, but she's getting there.

'There's been another murder,' she said. 'The call came in to the news desk. We haven't got a crime reporter, so they're sending someone down from the *County Gazette* to cover the story.'

'Hello, Bob mate. I was sorry to hear about your accident.'

One advantage of a career like mine is that I haven't rubbed anybody up the wrong way. Well, not many people anyway. Everybody likes *good old Bob*. Almost everybody.

Accident again, though, but I'll let it pass.

I'm going to have to tell you what happened that night, aren't I? Tuesday, at Lizzie's inquest, I'll tell the coroner and you can listen in. That way I don't have to go through it twice. How about that?

28

The task in hand is trying to get past Police Sergeant Bromidge. A pain in the arse at the best of times.

'I thought you were off sick?'

I'd got through the road block at the top of the lane easily enough; the lads saw my car approaching and just moved out of the way. A big, yellow Volvo has its advantages.

'I am, Jim,' I replied.

'What are you doing here then?'

'Old habits. It would've been my case.'

'Would've been, but isn't.' He was standing in front of the police tape that criss-crossed the open front door, his arms folded. 'I've got Mr Sharp coming down from Taunton. Said he'd be about an hour and that was fifty minutes ago. I wasn't to let anyone in either.'

'A quick look, mate,' I said. 'For old times' sake.' Emotional blackmail, but it was worth a try. There'd been that time on Weston seafront when he got caught between the mods and rockers. Young officers, we were then, in need of 'blooding' according to our sergeant. The old git had been at Monte Cassino and thought everyone needed a baptism of fire.

I dragged Jim out, unconscious and suitably blooded.

Me? Not a scratch.

It's a favour I've called in a few times over the years, but I've got nothing to lose. One last try.

'Is it to do with those lasses out on the A303?' asked Jim. 'Rumour has it you don't think Clarke had anything to do with it.'

'He didn't.'

'And you were deliberately run down?'

'I was.'

'It can't be the same bloke,' said Jim. 'He always left the victim's car out on the A303. And the body, for that matter. This girl's got an orange VW Beetle and it's parked round the back.'

It's about trust. He's known me long enough to trust me. And my judgement. He knows I trust him and his.

'Five minutes,' he said, carefully peeling the end of the tape from the door frame. 'If I start coughing, Sharp's here and sneak out the back door. It's open.'

'Thanks, Jim.'

I thrust my hands into my trouser pockets – a reminder not to touch anything – and stepped into the porch.

'What's her name?'

'Faith Bennett.' Jim sighed. 'She's twenty-one. Only left home a few weeks ago. This is her first place. Her parents haven't been notified yet, so take it easy.'

'What about the pathologist?' I asked, over my shoulder.

'Said he'd be here about seven.'

Footsteps in the lane, someone running in heels. Angela must have got past the roadblock.

'Who the hell is that?' grumbled Jim.

'She'll tell you she's a journalist, but she covers social events and coffee mornings. Don't let her in.'

'I won't.'

A farm cottage, much the same as any other. End of terrace, two-up, two-down. The staircase is new, so there's been a refurbishment at some point. No cupboard under the stairs, either.

Kitchen first, mainly to check the back door really is open. I can't afford another run-in with Sharp. Not yet, anyway.

An old Ascot water heater over the sink, so there can't be any central heating. And that looks like an outside toilet in the yard at the back, a washing line hanging limply from the down pipe to the gate post at the far end. The gate is standing open and I can see the familiar shape of a Beetle.

Washing up done. Kettle sitting on the gas stove; one of those ones that whistles when it's boiling. I would pick it up, but I'm resisting the temptation to touch anything, so I lean over and check there's no light under it. Of course there isn't, but it's another old habit.

There are two mugs on the kitchen table, that familiar soup in the bottom of both of them: milk and coffee granules that have been left sitting for too long.

A jar of Maxwell House.

Making her killer a coffee.

Sitting room next, pushing the door open with my elbow. No sign of a struggle. No blood. A black and white television is sitting on a dining chair in the corner, the aerial perched on the end of the mantelpiece, next to her rent book. A gas fire. Two armchairs. A record player on a table in the front window, the speakers either side of it, *Brothers in Arms* on the turntable.

Her first home. It reminds me a bit of mine, when I left the police house. That was a cottage in Ilminster, right on the road. Always cold, even in May.

I'd be tempted to open the windows to get a bit of warmth in, but best not. I still haven't taken my hands out of my pockets.

She must be upstairs.

There's a smear of blood on the wallpaper at the top, just under the light switch. If I had to guess, I'd say she was unconscious and over a man's shoulder, her head brushing the wall as he turned on the landing. If that's right, she'll be in the front room.

I push open the door, elbow again.

And there she is.

Face down on the single bed. Naked. Blonde hair matted with blood.

I hear voices in the lane outside. No coughing yet, but I can't risk being seen at the window. There's not a lot they can do to me that I give a crap about, but there's Jim to think of.

A quick look around the room. Her clothes have been cut from her body and thrown into a pile at the base of the wardrobe in the corner. No sign of a knife or a pair of scissors, though, so whoever did it took them with them. I'll need to check the kitchen on the way out to see if they brought them as well.

I move the jeans with my foot, the telltale jangle of keys in the pockets. Door and car, probably.

No other apparent injuries, apart from the blow to the back of the head and blood soaking into the eiderdown underneath her.

Still no coughing.

I had hoped to avoid this, but I need to check for other injuries. The other victims had been cut to pieces – that's enough detail for now – and I need to see if a knife has been used on poor Faith. Sorry, young lady, I'm going to need to roll you over.

Gently, fleetingly.

If I'm right, there'll be stab wounds.

I roll down my sleeve and slide my hand up inside the material, taking hold of her left upper arm that's hanging over the edge of the bed. Then I lift, rolling her on to her right side.

I count seventeen injuries to her chest and abdomen, some cuts, others stab wounds. Very little blood, so they were inflicted post mortem. Dead bodies don't bleed; you don't need to be a pathologist to know that. Or even a police officer. There's gravity, of course, which explains what little blood there is.

I'm looking for a pattern cut into her flesh – don't ask – but it's not there this time. These look random. Angry.

That's not the image that will stay with me, though.

That'll be her eyes.

I lower her back down, careful to leave her arm in the same position. Then I roll up my sleeve again; wouldn't want to make Jim suspicious. Or, worse still, land him in the shit.

The coughing starts just as I'm opening the kitchen drawer with my car key. The cutlery's always in the top one. There's a pair of scissors, but I can't really tell if any knives are missing. I push it closed with my hip and slide out of the back door, taking the young constable watching the back gate by surprise.

'Who are you?' he asked.

'Jim Bromidge said it would be all right.'

'Oh, right, fine.'

'Don't tell anyone, though. You'll get him in trouble.'

'Yeah.'

I was looking in the window of her car, wondering why a girl shorter than me would have the driver's seat pushed back that far, when a man with a dog sidled up to me. A nosy neighbour, probably. Everyone wants to know what's going on when they see the police in their neighbourhood, don't they?

'You the police?' he asked.

'Yes.' Well, I am. Sort of.

'Is she all right?'

'I'm afraid not. She's dead.'

'Oh, God.'

'Did you know her?'

'I live a couple of doors down,' he replied. 'We'd pass the time of day, but she's not been here long.'

'Make yourself known to the constable there,' I said. 'They'll have some questions for you, I expect.'

'Only I'm not sure why she's parked here,' the man continued. 'This is my space. Hers is that one.' He turned around, jabbing his walking stick at one of those mustard-coloured Morris Marinas with the shit-brown fabric on the roof. 'I've had to park over there and it's very inconvenient. Can you get it moved?'

Now, I'm a fairly even-tempered sort of chap, but let me tell you, Jim Bromidge got there just in time.

'We'll take over, Bob, thank you,' he said, marching me around the side of the cottages, out of sight of the upstairs windows. He used to play second row for the police first fifteen, so there aren't many people Jim can't manhandle. 'Sharp's in there now, and he's seen your car, so he knows you're here. You didn't touch anything in there, did you?'

'Of course not.'

'I know you're past caring, but they're not having my pension away from me.'

'Well?' Angela was waiting by my car. I'd seen her from the upstairs window, pulling at the skin at the base of her nails.

'You don't want to know.'

'Is it the same killer?'

'Of course it bloody well isn't.' Sharp was standing in the open front door of the cottage. 'Clarke is dead. And what the fuck are you doing here, Bob?'

Bollocks. 'Just curious, sir, you know how it is.'

'I know how you are.' He turned to Jim. 'He hasn't been in here, has he?'

'No, sir.'

'I was just looking at her car, sir,' I said.

'You're pissing in the wind, Bob. This is something completely different. A blunt force injury to the back of her head. And her car's out the back, for God's sake. Everything is different about it.'

'If you say so, sir.'

'I do say so.'

Perhaps I'll have another go at that brick wall. 'I was run down deliberately, don't forget, which means there was a second person involved. They could have driven her car—'

'Let it go, Bob.'

'It's parked in the wrong space. And have a look at the driver's seat, sir,' I said. A sort of parting shot. For now. '*I* couldn't reach the pedals from there.'

♦ ♦ ♦

On the face of it, Sharp is right. There are obvious differences between the killings. Her car is at home, and so is she. Blunt force injury to the back of the head instead of strangulation. He doesn't know it yet, but the injuries were inflicted post mortem. It all points to a different killer.

Or to a killer or killers who have changed the way they do things. Killers who have got away with murder before and plan on doing so again.

I got rid of Angela shortly after leaving South Petherton; said I'd see her at Lizzie's inquest on Tuesday, which I will. I've not been called to give evidence for the simple reason that my witness statement doesn't contain any useful information, but I'll be there anyway. It was a little white lie – that I had no recollection of the events that night due to a head injury sustained in the collision.

A quiet word with the coroner beforehand and I'll get my chance.

Blow this thing wide open, I will.

You just watch me.

Chapter Five

Looks like it was a good day yesterday. And I missed it.

The batting collapsing all around him and Ian Botham ended the day on one hundred and forty-nine not out. Despite Bob's best efforts: nineteen overs, three maidens, four for seventy-one.

Now, I know some of you won't understand all that; suffice it to say it was a cracking day's cricket. I, on the other hand, spent the morning with the good doctor and the afternoon driving up and down the A303. That is until Angela caught up with me, and you know what happened after that.

It was Faith's eyes. I said they'd stay with me, and they have.

I could be wrong about everything, of course. Don't think it hasn't crossed my mind. The one thing I do know for sure is that if it was Martin Clarke all along, and the murder weapons weren't planted in the back of his car, then he had an accomplice.

The driver of the second car that hit me.

Everything I know about Clarke tells me it wasn't him, though. And that's enough to keep me going. For the time being.

Actually, the idea of having nothing to keep me going scares me shitless. I've spent nearly thirty years trying to catch somebody for doing something, and when this is over all I'll have left is catching fish and watching cricket. A sobering thought, if I wasn't sober already.

'Ah, there you are.'

I recognised the voice, stifled a grimace.

'I thought I'd come and see for myself. I asked if anyone knew where I might find Bob Willis and ended up in the players' pavilion.' The good doctor sat down next to me. 'Tall, isn't he?'

We're in the temporary stand, the River Tone off to our right. Well, I say temporary. It was put up in 1978 and has been here ever since. Plenty of empty seats, but it'll soon fill up. It's a Sunday, after all.

Thankfully, I had the scorebook open on my knee. A Thermos of coffee on the floor under my seat too.

'Would you like a coffee?' I asked.

'Thank you.'

'No sugar, I'm afraid.'

'That's fine.' She gave a wave of her hand. 'So, how are Somerset doing?'

'It's finely balanced,' I replied.

'Isn't everything?'

I couldn't really argue with that, so decided to let it pass. 'A strong start from Warwickshire on Thursday, Somerset hanging on by their fingertips yesterday. Two days to go and everything to play for.' I sounded like a commentator on local radio.

'Will I get to see Bob in action?'

'He'll be first on this morning, bowling to Ian Botham.'

Names she'd recognise. Everybody did.

'You'll have to explain it to me as we go along,' she said.

'Really?'

'No, not really. I thought it might be a useful setting to get you talking about . . . it . . . them. Concentrate on the cricket and just talk to me.'

'Oh, right,' I said, when what I actually meant was *Oh, God.*

37

The ripple of applause started in front of the players' pavilion and spread around the ground, Bob leading Warwickshire out on to the pitch. Polite applause for the away team; this is cricket, after all. Even the good doctor was clapping, although I'm not convinced she knew what for.

Then came Ian Botham, twirling his bat like a windmill, as usual. If I tried that, my arm would come out of its socket.

'Who's that with him?' asked the good doctor. Perhaps I should tell you her name? I can't keep calling her the good doctor, can I? Her name is Dr Caroline Mellanby. I can't remember the letters after her name, but there are plenty of them.

'That's Joel Garner, the West Indian fast bowler.'

'He's taller than Bob.'

'Not as fast though.'

'How fast is fast?'

'You'll see.'

I'll let her watch the first few overs in peace, I think. Perhaps she might forget what she's here for?

Bob steamed in from the River End.

'Fucking hell,' hissed Caroline. 'I didn't even see that.'

'Neither did Ian Botham,' I said. 'So, you're in good company. They call that one a *bouncer*, for obvious reasons.' Botham had tried to hook it. 'He missed it, no run, so I just put a dot in the book.'

'I wondered what all those dots were.'

'He won't like that,' I said. 'He'll put the next one in the river.'

It was a good effort, but Bob had the last laugh, Botham's middle stump spinning away into the outfield like a stick thrown for a dog.

'Tell me about the first victim,' said Caroline, when Botham's standing ovation was subsiding.

'Her name was Fiona Anderson. She was found on the morning of eighth of March last year by a dog walker at Cadbury Castle.

She was in amongst the first tier earthworks, well off the beaten track. It's a Bronze Age hill fort at South Cadbury, so quite near the A303. Dates from about 3500 BC. Neolithic, originally. The Romans occupied it for a time too.'

'Tell me about her, please, not the hill fort.' Caroline spoke quietly, the seats around us starting to fill up. 'Where were you when you got the call?'

'At Ilminster police station. It was a slow morning and the call came in just after eight: a body found on Cadbury Castle. North-west corner. Lizzie and I dropped everything and went. There were two patrol cars and an ambulance by the cottages at the bottom of the track when we got there. One of the paramedics had vomited, I remember that. They were sitting in their cab, staring into space. Jim Bromidge had got there just before us, thankfully. He'd sealed off the scene, closed the road. The only other car belonged to the dog walker who'd found the body. He hadn't got too close; lucky for him.' Bob was steaming in again now, so I paused to draw breath, much like the rest of the crowd, but for a different reason, of course. The ball sailed through to the wicketkeeper. Another dot. 'Jim was pale. I'd not seen him like that before, so I knew it was bad. And the look he gave me. I asked Lizzie if she wanted to take a statement from the dog walker, but she said she'd come with me, so that was that. Off we went, following the path around the side.' Another dot ball. 'The earthworks are in three tiers, they're the original defences, she was at the bottom of the first tier, lying in the ivy on the edge of the undergrowth, brambles and stuff like that. Two officers were there, stringing up blue tape.'

Caroline leaned across and tapped the scorebook in front of me. 'That was another dot,' she said.

I did the honours. 'They probably carried her up there from Folly Lane. It's suitably quiet; if they'd gone the way we went they'd have had to carry her right past two cottages. Anyway, she was lying on her back, naked. Posed, possibly, it was difficult to tell. Her throat had been cut, something carved into her chest too, although it was impossible to tell what that was because of all the blood. I tried counting the knife wounds but gave up at thirty.'

The soft click of leather on willow, but no run.

'What does "over" mean?' asked Caroline.

'Change of ends and a new bowler,' I replied. 'The post mortem report concluded there were forty-seven in total; thirty-one stab wounds and sixteen cuts. The cuts had been inflicted before she died. We never did get to the bottom of what had been carved into her chest, but it looked like a cross of some sort. Maltese, almost. Four rough triangles meeting in the middle. There were all sorts of theories for that.'

'He hit that one.'

I looked up, watching the ball speeding towards the boundary, only to be intercepted just in front of us by the fielder at square leg, sadly. 'They ran two,' I said. I was marking up the score, and continued without looking up. 'It was one of those cold March mornings. A heavy frost, but warm as toast by midday. You know the ones. A lovely spring day. Trouble is the ground had been frozen that night, so no footprints. No sign of her clothes, either. Probably kept as a trophy.'

'Why's he walking back to the pavilion?' asked Caroline.

'Oh shit, not another one.' I'd heard the thud of ball hitting pad. 'Must be an LBW,' I said. 'If the ball hits his pads and would've hit the stumps, then it's out, leg before wicket.'

'Where was her car?'

'In a field gateway on the A303, the stretch just before Ilchester where it follows the Roman road for a while; a place called Trent's Lease Farm. Nobody's heard of it. Most people race past and never even notice it, but she'd broken down and had to pull over there, so . . .' I shrugged. 'We had a motor engineer look at her car and the alternator had packed up. She probably stopped and couldn't get going again with a flat battery. Paid for it with her life.'

'Who told her family?'

'I did. With Lizzie, of course. Her parents live in Martock. Fiona was an only child. Somehow, it's not quite so bad when there are other children. Does that make sense?'

'It does.'

'I'll tell you what haunts me about Fiona,' I said. I was watching the bowler running in, but hadn't kept the score for several deliveries now. 'The look on her face, in her eyes. You'd think it would be fear, pain, all of those things, but actually it was disbelief. I saw it again yesterday.'

Caroline stuck it out until lunchtime, which was a good effort, I thought. She seemed pleased that I'd opened up about the first victim, her parting shot a promise that next time we'd talk about the second.

Something to look forward to.

I told her about Faith as well; no details though.

'Be careful. I'm concerned about the effect on your mental wellbeing, Bob,' was what she said.

You're not the only one flashed across my mind when she said it, but I resisted the temptation.

It's tea now, with Warwickshire on two hundred and one for two. All you need to know is that what had been finely balanced is no longer. And I'm off.

Home the long way round. The A358 to Ilminster, then the A303 as far as the Little Chef at Camel Hill for supper.

I think the waitress recognises me now. If she ever says 'Usual, is it, Bob?' when I walk in, then I'll know I need to start eating somewhere else.

Chapter Six

I don't get much sleep these days. Sometimes I go for a walk around the lake – on a moonlit night, of course, although I do carry a torch. A good three hours that is. Shirley says I should get a dog, and maybe I will one day. A feisty little terrier and I'll name her after Lizzie.

Other nights I sit up, staring at the wall in the spare bedroom. I haven't told you about the wall in the spare bedroom, have I? I'm sure you can picture it. There was a time I'd have had a glass of Irish whiskey in my hand, but not any more. I owe Lizzie that much. When this is over I might have a celebratory glass of something, but it's not over. And it's a long way from being over.

My spare bedroom has a lock on the door, which I've changed. It's useful, because Shirley creeps into the flat from time to time and does the washing up. Once a week, a pile of clean clothes appears on the end of my bed too, my shirts ironed and left hanging on metal coat hangers in the wardrobe. Food keeps appearing in the fridge, loo roll in the bathroom. I'd forget my own head, according to Shirley.

She wouldn't like the wall in the spare bedroom, though, leaving aside the Sellotape on the wallpaper. Photographs, maps, I've even hung a blackboard, arrows pointing here and there. It's my own incident room, and all of the arrows point to Police Constable Sean Taylor.

I had an idea overnight. It must've been gone two and I was sitting in the deckchair – the only piece of furniture in *that* room – staring at the picture of Martin Clarke. Poor sod. If I'm right, his only crime had been the old 'wrong place, wrong time'.

I have been to see the pathologist who conducted his post mortem, before you ask, and he showed me his report. The photographs too. They were pretty grim. Martin had been struck by an articulated lorry on the dual carriageway, after all. I knew the answer to my question, but I had to ask it, all the same.

'Is there any evidence to show that he might have been thrown from the bridge by a person or persons unknown?'

I added the 'person or persons unknown' bit to muddy the waters for him.

'It's impossible to tell. You've seen the photos.'

I had. Won't forget them in a while, either.

So, back to my idea. If I'm right then Martin was targeted by Sean Taylor *because* he was a van driver and fitted the killer's profile, not that the killer had a profile at that stage. Just a boot print. So, how did Taylor know Martin was a van driver? My guess is he'd stopped him before, out on the A303. There was no mention of that in either Taylor's witness statement or in the evidence he gave to the inquest, but that's hardly surprising. If I'm right.

First thing on Tuesday, after Lizzie's inquest anyway, I'm going to see Martin's employer, B & D Light Haulage in Ilminster. If he'd got a ticket for speeding, or there'd been an accident perhaps, he'd have to have told them. Don't know why I haven't thought of it before, really.

It's Monday morning now and the traffic is light, as you might expect. A few cars westbound, but very little heading east. That'll start to build after lunch with the bank holiday weekenders going back to London.

It must be nice to have a cottage in the country, but then I live in the country, so what do I care?

'He's out on the A303 again,' I hear you say. And you're right, I am. Only this time I'm driving Martin's black three-litre Ford Capri, with the go-faster stripe down the side and the broken brake light. His father was happy to lend it to me, although I didn't tell him what I wanted it for in case he insisted on coming along for the ride. We had to push it out of the garage and jump start it off my Volvo, but the battery's fine now.

I'm not sure I like the driving position, to be honest, although that might be because I'm not tall enough to see over the steering wheel. It's almost like sitting in my deckchair, if that makes sense. I've got the seat forward as far as it will go, but I need to sit on a cushion, really. Still, it's not about that. It's about the top speed. My old man used to do a bit of rally driving after the war, and he'd have described it as *purposeful*.

There's a cassette sticking out of the tape machine so I push it in: *A Night at the Opera*, Freddie Mercury belting out 'Bohemian Rhapsody' as I step on the accelerator off the roundabout; a little too early as it turns out, the car snaking. I ease off. Did I mention it rained in the night and the roads are wet? Shame.

There's a short stretch of dual carriageway at South Petherton, so I'll see what it can do there. Ready for Ilchester.

Rewinding the cassette, dual carriageway in one mile. I press play, halfway through the song, rewind a bit more.

Change down, hanging on the petrol cap of the car in front; a Mini Metro.

Press play again. Perfect.

Floor it.

No police cars about, which is disappointing.

Martin's father said the top speed is one hundred and thirty. So, we'll see.

◆ ◆ ◆

Roadworks, on a Bank Holiday Monday? Piss off.

The queue is short, mercifully. Only three cars in front of me. I'm on the single lane stretch near Stoke sub Hamdon now; a hole in the road and nobody working on it.

I eased off at a hundred and twenty, in case you were wondering. It was only a short stretch of dual carriageway and someone up ahead pulled out to go around a caravan.

Smooth as silk, flying along. I couldn't hear the engine over Brian May's guitar solo, though. I wonder how much Martin's father wants for it? Not that a Capri is really *me*, I suppose.

My old bus would've been rattling like I don't know what.

Ilchester next, and the bridge on the A37.

Funny isn't it, how you always drive that little bit faster when the music is right, and loud. Rewinding the tape again. I'm sure it's a great album, but 'Bohemian Rhapsody' is the only song off it I know.

Dual carriageway, one mile ahead.

Press play.

Change down, revs up. I move over to the offside, ready to go, letting the cars in front know I'm coming, assuming they check their wing mirrors before they pull out. I'm going first and that's all there is to it.

The A37 bridge is up ahead and I'm hoping there's a police car on it.

Change down again, third gear this time. I can hear the engine now, even over the orchestral bit.

There's a Golf GTI up ahead, but he's seen me and moves back over to the nearside.

Hammer down, across the white lines and I'm away.

The Golf comes out into the outside lane behind me, but quickly starts falling back as I get above ninety miles an hour.

I'm watching the needle creep round to one hundred and ten when movement up on the bridge catches my eye. A police car, pulling away; a big Rover.

This is going to be good.

One hundred and twenty as I go past the end of the slip road. I glance in my wing mirror, and here he comes around the loop, lights flashing. I can't hear the siren, but then I've got Brian May at it again and a three-litre engine almost redlining it in front of me.

I check the rear view mirror, watching the Rover gaining on me. Slowly.

He'll run my number plate, then shit himself. Assuming it's Taylor.

The Rover is dropping back a bit, so I ease off the accelerator; dab the brakes, just to remind him I've got a light out.

He's closing on me again now and it's Lizzie's lay-by next up on the nearside.

Seems fitting somehow.

◆　◆　◆

'Why don't you just fuck off, Bob?'

The Rover had pulled in behind me. Taylor was driving, but it was his passenger who got out. I was watching in my rear view mirror, quickly climbing out of the driver's seat when I saw him coming.

Police Sergeant Brian Druce.

'What is your fucking problem?' he continued, striding towards me.

I've known Brian a few years now and he seems a decent sort. He runs the traffic team out of Yeovil; a fairly rapid promotion to sergeant too. He only joined the police when he left the army five years or so ago. A company sergeant major, or something like that. Three tours of Northern Ireland under his belt.

Our paths first crossed at a retirement party, oddly enough, when he drank me under the table. Then there was that fight at the Golden Fleece in Ilminster. Pool tables should be banned in pubs, they really should; they cause arguments and provide the weapons. Anyway, Brian single-handedly broke up the fight, so we had nine people charged with affray and one with grievous bodily harm for glassing another in the face. And there was Brian in the middle of it all, knocking seven bells out of them.

He was at the scene of Fiona's murder too; traffic management was a nightmare that day. We had to close the A303 for nearly twelve hours, in both directions.

He'd stopped in front of me now, and was leaning over, his nose a few inches from mine.

'What the bloody hell d'you think you're playing at?'

This wasn't quite what I had in mind, but at least it shows Sean Taylor still won't face me himself.

'Have you got permission to be driving this vehicle?'

'Of course I have.'

'Do you know how fast you were going?'

I'll give that one a miss, I think.

'You were doing one hundred and twelve miles an hour.'

'Really? It said on the speedometer I was doing a hundred and twenty-one. You can't rely on the things, can you?'

'Don't fuck with me, Bob.'

I can imagine him towering over a new recruit on the parade ground.

'I could have your licence for that,' he continued. 'I bet you've been drinking too. And if you haven't, you'll still be pissed from last night.'

'I haven't touched a drop since that night, Brian.'

He knows what night I'm talking about. Everybody does. Every police officer, anyway. And he'd have been there after the event, managing the traffic. The road was closed for eighteen hours that time.

'Let it go, Bob.'

'I can't, mate,' I said. He wasn't really a *mate*, but then who is?

'Taylor's told me what you've been doing. He's already let you go four times, and then we find you've borrowed Clarke's Capri. There's only so long that being one of us will protect you.'

'Have you ever wondered how the murder weapons got in the back of Clarke's car the night that Taylor pulled him over?'

'No, I haven't. They were in his car because they were his weapons and he was on the prowl, looking for another victim.' Druce took a step back. 'What are you saying? That Taylor planted them?'

I nodded. Slowly. 'Where did *he* get them from?'

He reminded me of a strip light, flickering into life; that few seconds before the light takes hold and shines brightly.

'Oh, fuck off, Bob. Sean's a good copper. Conscientious. And Clarke fitted the profile. He was a professional driver and there was the boot print.'

'What does Sean Taylor do for a living?' I asked.

'He's a traffic . . .'

'Spends his time behind the wheel of a car.' I glanced over at Taylor, sitting in the driver's seat of the big Rover. It was an automatic, but then it had been a right boot print, worn on the heel and toe – heel resting on the floor, toe for the accelerator and brake.

I've never liked automatics. Not real driving at all.

'Can't be.' Druce shook his head. 'He was with me the night Lizzie was killed and you had your accident.'

'It was no accident. There were two of them there that night and I was deliberately run down.'

'You're barking up the wrong tree, mate. I'm telling you, he was with me that night. We were out on patrol together. It's all in the logs, if you want to check them.'

I'd been watching the motorists speeding past the lay-by with smirks on their faces, the twerp in the Capri getting his comeuppance, the bloke in the Porsche thanking his lucky stars it was me and not him.

'Do me a favour then, Brian,' I said, not holding out much hope, to be honest. 'Check where he was the night of Fiona Anderson's murder. She's the one we found at Cadbury Castle. And the night of Alice Cobb's.'

'No, I won't, Bob. The case is closed. Those murders were committed by Martin Clarke.' Druce was softening. 'Look, mate, it's good to see you up and about, but you've got to let this go. Have you spoken to someone about it?'

'Like who?'

'They said you'd had a breakdown. Are you getting help from a trick cyclist?'

A sharp intake of breath. I haven't told you about the breakdown, have I? You might have guessed, of course, from my conversations with the good doctor. They're therapy sessions. I'm sure I mentioned that right at the start. And, yes, I had a nervous breakdown, but that's not for today.

'Maybe you're becoming a bit obsessed with all this?'

'I'm seeing a consultant psychologist, if you must know. Not a psychiatrist.'

'What's the difference?' asked Druce, with a mischievous grin.

'No idea,' I replied.

'Me neither,' he said. 'Look, take that fucking thing back where you got it, get your old Volvo, and go and sit in the Little Chef, if you must, but you've got to stop pissing about on this road, or I'll tell the lads to nick you next time. You could cause a nasty accident.' He put his hand on my shoulder. 'This is your last chance, mate. Have you told your psychologist what you've been doing, because you need to. Maybe he can help?'

'I have told her, yes.'

'And what did she say?'

'Stop it.'

'There you are then.' Druce smiled. 'And I haven't even got letters after my name.' He turned back towards the patrol car.

'Will you check those dates?'

'If it helps you sleep at night, then yes, I'll check them. Now, go home.'

Chapter Seven

I know what you're thinking. You're wondering why I never mentioned the breakdown before and I should've done. Of course I should. I'm guessing you feel cheated? You're beginning to think I'm imagining the whole thing. I'm right, aren't I?

Don't answer that.

Yes, I had a breakdown. And, no, it's not why Shirley left me. She was gone long before that. Actually, it was Shirley who saved me. Rescued me.

It started when I came out of hospital, and I know exactly what caused it.

The guilt – the good doctor is right about that.

I was living in my car at the time. Another advantage of a big Volvo, I suppose. Shirley and Alan found me parked in a lay-by at the top of Cheddar Gorge and took me home. I stayed with them for a few weeks while they tidied up the flat above the post office, and I've been there ever since.

Shirley got me in to see her doctor too, and he prescribed a course of Valium, which helped for a while. I had a bit of trouble coming off it, though. I started accusing Alan of all sorts, but it's a common thing with Valium withdrawal, apparently, and I'm fine now. We didn't come to blows or anything, I wouldn't want you to think that. I just had to manage the withdrawal more slowly. It was

Shirley who organised the referral to the good doctor, or Caroline as we call her now; even got the police to pay for it.

I'll tell you what helped more than anything, though, and that's deciding to do something about Lizzie's death, rather than just feeling sorry for myself. Hours, I'd spend, sitting in a boat out on the lake, a fishing rod in my hand. Sometimes I wouldn't even bother tying a fly on the end of the line. I'd just sit there, staring into space. That's why Caroline's got me scoring the cricket matches; it gets me *doing* something, rather than just sitting there, thinking.

I suppose I should tell you how long all this went on? I was discharged from hospital at the end of November and I just shut down, really. I hadn't paid my rent in months and I lost my bedsit in Chard just before Christmas – I hate Christmas at the best of times, to be honest. It wasn't long after that Shirley found me, a couple of weeks, maybe. Cold, it is, sleeping in a car in winter, but I did buy myself a sleeping bag; managed to think of that.

So, now I'm fine and here we are, doing something about Lizzie's death. I'm not sure whether I'm doing it for me or for Lizzie, but I'll worry about that later. At the moment, it's giving me something to cling to, and that's enough.

The sound of tapping on glass dragged me back to the present and I looked up to find Angela standing beside the driver's door of my Volvo.

I'm parked in the market square in Wells, right outside the town hall, the venue for Lizzie's inquest this morning. I got here bright and early to get a space, but as you know, I don't get much sleep these days so it was no great hardship.

'Are your parents here?' I asked, winding down the window.

'They're inside,' replied Angela. 'I said I'd have a look around, see if you were here. Gives me a chance to have a ciggy.'

I should've been to see Lizzie's parents long before now. Did I mention that I'm a bit of a coward? Shirley always says if there's an easy way out, I'll take it.

Well, no more.

Today is the day I set the cat among the pigeons, and any other cliché I can think of.

'There was a piece on the news last night about Faith,' said Angela. 'Did you see it?'

'Don't watch the telly.'

'It didn't mention her name; just that a body had been found at a house in South Petherton.' She was following me across the square, furiously pulling on her cigarette, before dropping the butt down a drain. 'My parents don't know I smoke,' she said.

I opened the door. There's no going back now, Bob.

'They're over here.' Angela was gesturing towards a seating area on the left; dark oak benches, where an older couple were sitting, holding hands.

Lizzie's father looked up at the sound of our footsteps on the stone floor. He stood up and turned to face me, his hand out-stretched. 'We want you to know, Bob, we don't blame you for what happened that night.'

I've got to tell you, my legs nearly went from under me when he said that.

'Lizzie knew what she was doing,' he continued, my hand clasped firmly in both of his. 'It was her decision to go on her own. Her risk.'

'I blame myself.' A mumble was the best I could muster. 'I should've been there.'

'We heard you've not been well. You really need to let her go. Guilt does terrible things to you.'

'I'm getting help,' I said.

'Good.' He finally let go of my hand. 'We've instructed a solicitor. We've got questions about what happened in the week she was missing, until her body was found in that car. He'll be here in a minute.'

Lizzie's mother was standing beside her husband now. 'He's not happy with the police investigation, but I just want it all over and done with. I want Lizzie to be able to rest in peace.'

I can sympathise with that. I'm just not sure she can, with her killers still out there.

'Our solicitor warned us we may not get to ask what we want, but he's going to have a go. Useless buggers. Why wasn't that car checked again, that's what I want to know?' Lizzie's father was holding his wife's hand now. 'There were serious flaws in the police investigation. No reflection on you, of course. You were in hospital. We know you'd have left no stone unturned.'

'If you'll forgive me,' I said. 'I need to have a word with the coroner's officer. That's him there with the clipboard. I'll need a word with your solicitor as well, please.'

Ex-police. Coroner's officers usually are. I managed to catch up with him before he disappeared into the court. 'Hello, John,' I said.

He looked at me, then checked his clipboard. 'You're not giving evidence, are you, Bob?'

'I haven't been called,' I replied. 'Mainly because when I gave my statement, I couldn't remember a thing about what happened. Now I do.'

'I'll speak to the coroner.'

'Thanks, mate.'

◆ ◆ ◆

A crowded court, the press gallery full. No surprises there. I was at the back, behind Lizzie's parents, who were sitting either side of Angela, all of them holding hands.

There were plenty of people I recognised. The pathologist, several police officers; Sean Taylor was avoiding my gaze, DCS Sharp was glaring at me.

The coroner was looking at me over his reading glasses. We've met before. I say *met*, I've appeared in front of him before. I can't say he left a lasting impression, but then I shouldn't think I did either. Inquests are not usually confrontational.

We've done the 'be upstanding in court' bit and the murmuring has died down now we're all seated again.

'This is the inquest touching the death of Elizabeth Margaret Harper, known to her friends and family as Lizzie. I am the coroner, Ian Harrow, and I will be conducting this inquest. I see legal representatives in the front row, if you would kindly identify yourselves, please.'

Lizzie's family solicitor was first to his feet. 'My name is Brendan Freer, sir, and I appear on behalf of the deceased's family. I'm from Freer and Garfield Solicitors in Somerton.'

'And I'm Simon Somerfield, sir, police solicitor.'

The coroner took a slow breath, although it could have been a sigh. 'I would remind all those present that this is an inquest. It is an inquiry into the death of Lizzie, if I may call her that, and it has four distinct purposes: to determine who she was, how, when and where she died. We are not here to apportion blame. Is that clear?'

'Yes, sir.' The two lawyers in unison.

'Nor are we here to raise questions about the efficiency or otherwise of the police investigation into her death.'

Freer turned in his seat and raised his eyebrows at Lizzie's father, the 'I told you so' unspoken.

'Now, we have with us today a witness not warned to give evidence, the reason being that the statement he gave at the time was simply that he had no recollection of the night in question. I am told that is no longer the case, and I therefore propose to call him to give evidence before this inquest. My view is that it would be remiss of me not to hear from him, and unless anyone has any strong objections . . .'

The police solicitor was leaning over the back of his chair, whispering with Sharp, who was still glaring at me.

'No, sir,' he said, turning back around to face the coroner.

'Is that you?' asked Angela, over her shoulder.

I gave her a knowing smile. I thought that would be enough, for now.

Sharp was mouthing something at me. I'm no lip reader, but it looked like 'What the fuck are you playing at, Bob?'

'We'll start with the pathologist, I think,' continued the coroner. 'Dr Paul Cartwright conducted Lizzie's post mortem at my request and I have here his report, which I am proposing to admit in evidence. Dr Cartwright is also here, should anyone have any questions for him?'

'I do, sir.' Freer again, on behalf of the family.

'Otherwise, I propose to read the summary into evidence, being conscious that Lizzie's parents and sister are present.' The coroner seemed determined to finish his sentence, if only to make the point that Cartwright would be giving evidence at the family's insistence. He cleared his throat. 'Call Dr Cartwright, please.'

I switched off for much of his evidence, but I can summarise it for you, having seen a copy of his report. Cause of death was strangulation, with multiple knife wounds inflicted pre mortem. What that means, though, is that things are going to get very uncomfortable when I give my evidence, but we'll see what Cartwright says when he's being questioned by the family solicitor, Freer.

'Mr Freer, you may ask your questions now, but with a reminder of the purpose of this hearing.'

Freer stood up. 'You said in your report, Dr Cartwright, that Lizzie was almost certainly unconscious when the knife injuries were inflicted. How can you be sure of that?'

'There were no defensive injuries and no sign of restraint to her wrists. Her hands hadn't been tied, for example. There was bruising, so her wrists had been held at some point during the struggle, but that was most likely when her killer was overpowering her, in my opinion.'

'There was no evidence of blunt force trauma to the back of her head?'

'Not to the back, no. There was an injury to the front, over her left eye, which may have rendered her unconscious, but it's possible to strangle a person to the point of unconsciousness, don't forget.'

'Might your findings be equally consistent with her being conscious but with a second assailant holding her down, perhaps?'

A gasp from the seats in front of me.

Cartwright looked flustered, his eyes darting around the room. 'Yes, that's possible. As I say, there was bruising to her wrists, so they could have been held.'

'Moving on then,' said Freer. 'You gave a time of death as between five to seven days before she was found, so between the eleventh and thirteenth of August last. Is that correct?'

'Time of death is never easy. And it gets more difficult the longer it is,' replied Cartwright. 'My view is that the condition of her body was consistent with her being in the boot of that car for between five and seven days. It was hot, remember. August.'

'We know she was abducted from the lay-by on the night of the eleventh and was found on the evening of eighteenth of August, so according to your evidence, it's possible she was alive for two days after she was taken.'

'That is my view, yes.'

'It's possible she was still alive in the boot of that abandoned car?'

'Of course there's a chance. It's not an exact science—'

'I know where this is going, Mr Freer,' interrupted the coroner. 'If you have questions concerning the efforts made by the police to find Lizzie, they are best put to the officer in charge when he gives evidence. Dr Cartwright has given you his opinion on the time of death.'

Freer sat down.

'You may go Dr Cartwright,' said the coroner. 'Thank you. Now I'll call Detective Inspector Mungo Willis, please.'

Chapter Eight

Lizzie and me? No, there was nothing going on. My marriage broke up long before I was teamed up with her, and anyway, I was old enough to be her father, for heaven's sake. She was just starting out and I was at the other end of my career. There was a connection, though. Of course there was. And if I hadn't been twenty-five years older, then who knows?

Four years we had together. Working, as I said. It took a while to get to know her, to get used to her. Most of the lads thought she was trouble, but that was just because she was better than they were. She gave as good as she got when it came to police station banter too, and they didn't like that. Some of them anyway.

A dyke, they said, but that was just the idiots she'd turned down. Everybody tried it on, even the married ones. 1985 it is and some of them still behave like it's the Stone Age. The police is just a gentlemen's club to some, a working men's club to others.

I said *everybody tried it on*, but I wouldn't want you to think I did. Never. I had too much respect for Lizzie for that. And we got on too well to risk mucking it up. I've never been very good at that sort of thing, either. Shirley made all the moves when we got together, so it's not as if I've ever had much practice at reading *the signs*.

I do sometimes wonder whether we would have got together in the end, but truth is, it doesn't matter. It's not about that. It's about a respected colleague and friend.

And, yes, I loved her.

In my own way.

◆　◆　◆

'Are you all right, Inspector?'

Actually no, I wasn't. A ten-minute adjournment, and the pathologist had left a set of post mortem photographs on the witness stand.

I needed to see them, I suppose, but it's not how I wanted to remember Lizzie, stuffed in the boot of a Ford Fiesta. Stolen probably, abandoned in a lay-by westbound on the A303 at Chicklade; Wiltshire again, to confuse things. The photographer must have stepped back and taken several photos of the car, the boot standing open. An unpleasant shade of brown; you have to wonder who in their right mind would buy a car this colour. Wrapped in blue tape, with 'Police Aware' stickers on the windscreen. Bits had been pinched in the time since it had been abandoned, the windows smashed, stereo gone, number plates, that sort of thing.

Someone must've stolen the parcel shelf before Lizzie's body was dumped because she'd been covered with a blanket; naked, curled into the foetal position, blood everywhere.

That same look of disbelief. Shock.

I'd imagined it, but seeing the real thing was worse. Far worse.

Her eyes were wide open. So was her mouth. Blood was coming from both nostrils and there was a cut above her left eye. Her short bleached hair was matted with blood, so a blow to the head at some point too. There were several stab wounds to the left side of her chest.

There's a picture of her at home, drinking a glass of champagne, beaming at the camera. We'd got a conviction for something or other and were in a restaurant in Taunton, celebrating. Just the two of us. That's the Lizzie I shall remember.

When all this is over.

I made the mistake of turning the page and now she's lying on the slab in the mortuary. There was a pattern of sorts to the cuts on her chest. If you knew what you were looking for. The first lines of a cross being cut into her flesh, possibly.

'Shall I take those?' asked John, the coroner's officer. He was standing in front of me with his hand outstretched.

'Better had,' I replied, closing the album and passing it to him.

'Do you need a minute, Inspector?' asked the coroner.

'No, sir.'

'In your witness statement you said that you have no recollection of the events that night after leaving your home in Ilminster. Is that correct?'

'It was, at the time I gave the statement, sir,' I replied, fingers crossed in my pocket. 'I was still in hospital at the time, recovering from my injuries; I'd only regained consciousness a matter of hours before I gave that statement. I didn't even know Lizzie was dead at that point.'

'And now you remember what happened?'

'I do, sir. I've been having trauma counselling and it's helped.' *Trauma counselling* sounds better than seeing a psychologist because I had a breakdown, don't you think?

'Well, I think we can dispense with that,' said the coroner, placing my original witness statement to one side on his desk. 'When you're ready, Inspector.'

A deep breath. 'My name is Mungo Willis and I am a detective inspector with Avon and Somerset Police based at Ilminster. I am currently on sick leave. Detective Sergeant Lizzie Harper and

I were working on the investigation into the murders of Fiona Anderson and Alice Cobb. Both victims had been murdered in strikingly similar circumstances and the working hypothesis was that the same killer or killers had committed both murders. Both women had broken down on the A303 – Fiona had pulled into a farm gateway, Alice into a lay-by – where their vehicles were later found. They had also suffered similar injuries. Fiona's body was found below the earth ramparts at Cadbury Castle and Alice was found on Salisbury Plain just west of Chitterne.'

I've been rehearsing this in my head for weeks now, over and over, and know exactly what I'm going to say. It might sound a bit formal, but then I'm a police officer with nearly thirty years under my belt, so it's bound to, I'm afraid. What I should do is give a revised witness statement, of course I should, but that wouldn't land with the same splash, would it? Look at the press gallery; it's full to the rafters and I'm going to make the most of it.

'We were making very little progress, so I came up with a plan for a sting operation. I pitched it to the chief superintendent, but he refused to authorise it.'

'Why?' asked the coroner.

I could see Sharp squirming in his seat. 'Cost, sir,' I replied. 'It would've needed myself, Lizzie and four other officers on an open-ended operation. The murders had been committed months apart, so it was thought there was very little chance of success within a reasonable time frame and that the resources would be better tasked elsewhere.'

'Why six officers?'

'The lay-bys on the 303 are long, with paving between the parking area and the carriageway. That provides an entrance at one end and an exit at the other, giving motorists the opportunity to build up speed before rejoining the carriageway. There's no turning straight out of the lay-by into the nearside lane. I wanted two officers hidden at either end, covering the entrance and exit. I would've been in the undergrowth adjacent to Lizzie's car. That was the plan, anyway.'

'So, what happened?'

'We did it anyway. Just me and Lizzie. Always the same lay-by at Ilchester. It was the one where we found Alice Cobb's car. Fiona Anderson had pulled over in a farm gateway further west.' I poured myself a glass of water and took a sip. 'We'd tried it three times before that night,' I said. 'Always after dark, and we sat it out until about three in the morning.'

'What happened that night?'

'We planned to go out about nine. I can't remember the exact time of the sunset, but it was there or thereabouts. The arrangement was that we'd meet at her place about eight-thirty and go in the one car.' Now it's going to get a bit difficult. Another sip of water. 'Only I never got there. I was drinking in a pub in Ilchester. I thought I'd ring her and we'd arrange to meet somewhere else, but I forgot. And Lizzie decided to go on her own. I only realised about eleven o'clock and rang her place, but her flatmate said she'd gone out. I knew exactly where, of course, and got out there as fast as I could. Too late as it turned out.'

'Were you drunk?' asked the coroner.

'No, sir. I was not.'

It's surprising how quickly you can sober up.

'Go on.'

'It was a quiet night; very little traffic about, and I was westbound. It must've been about half eleven and I can see the lay-by up ahead, on the other side of the dual carriageway. There were two cars, one in front with its hazard lights flashing, and the other parked directly behind it. I stopped on the grass verge opposite and ran across, jumped over the Armco barrier on the central reservation. Then I was just crossing the eastbound carriageway when I had to wait for a car in the nearside lane. I didn't know where it had come from, but I managed to stop on the white line. There was plenty of room for it to pass by, but it suddenly swerved at the last minute and hit me. It wasn't overtaking anyone or anything in the nearside lane and there was no reason for it to change lane whatsoever, other than to hit me. It was accelerating too. I remember the engine noise quite clearly.'

'Just to be clear, are you saying it hit you deliberately?' asked the coroner.

'Quite deliberately, sir. It's my belief that it had been parked at or near the entrance to the lay-by with its lights off. There are no streetlights there and there was no other traffic about either, otherwise I would have seen it. These lights suddenly appeared in the nearside lane, so I stopped.'

'Was the car already moving when the lights came on?'

'Yes, sir.'

'And what happened then?'

'I was thrown in the air, and the next thing I remember is a week later in Yeovil Hospital. I regained consciousness the same day they found Lizzie's body.'

'Can you remember anything about the car that hit you?'

'It was small, dark, accelerating hard; a Golf GTI, possibly. I didn't see the driver.'

'What about the cars in the lay-by?'

'Lizzie's was in front, obviously. I could see her car clearly enough in the lights of the car parked behind. There were two figures behind it too, by the bins there, so one of them must've been Lizzie, but apart from that it was all happening too fast and it was dark.'

'And the second car?'

'All I can say with any degree of certainty is that it was not a Capri. They have a very distinctive shape.'

'So, what you're in effect saying is that there were two people involved in the disappearance of the deceased. The person you saw standing with her in the lay-by and the driver of the vehicle that struck you. Is that correct?'

'It is, sir. The figure in the lay-by was taller and thicker set than the smaller figure I believe to have been Lizzie. So, an unidentified male.'

'Have you brought this to the attention of the investigating officers?' asked the coroner.

'I have tried to bring it to the attention of DCS Sharp, sir, and been told simply that the case is closed.'

'Do you have any information about the police investigation into Lizzie's disappearance? What efforts were made to find her, for example?'

'I was unconscious throughout that whole week, sir, and haven't returned to work since.'

'Of course. My apologies.' The coroner looked up. 'I believe the police solicitor, Mr Somerfield, may have some questions for you, if you would stay there for a moment.'

Fingers holding the lapel of his jacket. I stifled a sneer. Another one who thinks he's Rumpole of the Bailey. A long pause too, for dramatic effect.

'Inspector Willis, were you drunk that night?'

I'd known that one was coming. 'No.'

'How much had you had to drink?'

That one too. 'I don't recall.' And I really don't.

'Do you have a problem with alcohol?'

'No.'

'You've had a mental breakdown, though, haven't you?'

'I have been diagnosed with post traumatic stress disorder, and am receiving treatment from Dr Caroline Mellanby, a consultant psychologist.'

'Do you think that might render your evidence unreliable?'

'No.'

'So, you remain convinced the second car hit you deliberately?'

'I do. There was more than one person involved in the kidnap and murder of Detective Sergeant Lizzie Harper.' I'd stake my professional reputation on it, if I had one. 'And given that neither vehicle was a Ford Capri, I'd go further and say that Martin Clarke was not involved.'

'Oh, come now, Inspector. What makes you say that?'

'They've killed again. Another body was found yesterday,' I replied, solemnly. 'Faith Bennett was found in her cottage at South Petherton. She was twenty-one.'

It took the coroner a few minutes to calm everyone down after that; the press, the public gallery. I wouldn't call it uproar, but there was some shouting. I hadn't spotted them before, maybe they'd crept in once the inquest had got going, but Fiona Anderson's parents were there. Alice Cobb's mother and brother too. I'd got on well enough with them before, not that family liaison was really my thing.

'Ladies and gentlemen, I'm going to adjourn this inquest to enable further enquiries to be made. I'm conscious, of course, that the family might wish this matter to be resolved sooner rather than later, but it is incumbent on me to ascertain *how* Lizzie died, and given this new evidence from Inspector Willis – which, I might add, I find compelling – it is only right that I ask the police to reopen the investigation and look again at what happened. I shall be writing to the chief constable accordingly and, in the meantime, adjourn this inquest to a date to be fixed in due course.'

I could never have done that a couple of months ago. I couldn't have faced it; wouldn't have faced *them* – my demons, that is. I'm beginning to think that might have been the easy bit, though, facing them in open court. Now, I've got to get to my car in the market square, and no doubt DCS Sharp will want to share his opinions with me. Fiona's and Alice's families too. I hope Lizzie's parents will be fine about it. And Angela.

The courtroom had cleared and I was still sitting in the witness box when Sharp came steaming back in.

'You fucking prick!'

Oddly enough, I felt ready for him this time. 'When a police officer's first thought is covering his own arse, it's time to go,' I said. 'And it's time for you to go.'

And with that, I picked up my coat from the chair and walked out into the foyer.

I counted three tape recorders thrust under my nose on the way out. 'Do you have any comments for the *Gazette*,' or whatever local rag it was.

'No.'

'If Clarke wasn't involved, where did he get the murder weapons that were found in his car?'

'No comment.' It felt odd saying that; suspects used to say it to me often enough in interview, though.

'Is there police corruption here, Inspector?'

I kept walking, letting the double doors slam behind me. The answer to that one was . . . *nuanced*. A good word; almost spot on. I can't remember where I read it, but it was fairly recently. Yes, there was some corruption, and Sean Taylor knows now, if he didn't before, that I'm coming for him. Plenty of incompetence too. I'm putting Sharp in that category. For the time being. If he's covering anything up, it'll be his own backside.

Now for the families.

'Can we have a word, Bob?'

It sounded ominous. Alice's mother was standing in a small group by my car; Fiona's parents, Alice's brother, David, all of them blocking the driver's door, so I didn't have a lot of choice. 'Yes, of course.'

'You'd better be right about this,' she said. 'Clarke had the murder weapons in the boot of his car, for God's sake. We thought we had the closure we needed and now you've gone and opened it all up again. Alice's death, everything—' Tears started flowing.

'And Fiona's,' interrupted Ralph Anderson, finishing her sentence for her. 'What are you going to do about it?'

'Find them,' I replied. 'Think about it, even if I'm wrong about Clarke, he had an accomplice.'

'You'd better keep out of my mother's way as well.' Angela had crept up behind me and was listening to the conversation. 'The last thing she wanted was Lizzie's inquest being adjourned.'

'She'll be all right.' Lizzie's father had followed Angela and was standing behind her. 'We're not sure about Clarke's innocence, but if there's the slightest chance there's someone responsible for our daughter's death still out there, we want them found.'

'Amen.' Fiona Anderson's father gave an emphatic nod.

'That's all we had to say,' said Alice's mother. 'If it really wasn't Martin Clarke, find who killed our daughters.' They were holding hands now, Fiona's father and Alice's mother. 'Please.'

Chapter Nine

B & D Light Haulage. They're on the trading estate on the edge of Ilminster. Well, I say *trading estate*, there are a few prefabs and an old barn. A timber merchants too, and that's about it; apart from the caravan in the lay-by selling tea, coffee and bacon rolls. He throws the salmonella in free, I'm told.

I know B & D, or rather I've seen their vans out and about often enough on the 303. Large Transits and a few flatbed lorries.

Someone has taken the trouble to fill the potholes in the yard with gravel. It's a large area, high fencing all around, the stuff with the spikes on top. Barbed wire too. The yard is empty, apart from one box van parked on the far side.

I parked next to the pile of gravel and managed to catch my driver's door on the wheelbarrow. Sod it.

There were no puddles to dodge as I walked across the yard to the office, but there was that mustard-yellow dust that sticks to everything. It won't show on my car, though, so that's something to be grateful for.

The receptionist looked surprised when I walked in, but I'm guessing they don't get many visitors. 'Can I help you?' she asked, before I reached the top of the folding metal steps, a breeze block to keep them steady. The door was standing open, a fan on the corner of her desk moving slowly from side to side.

She was small – petite, I think they call it these days – with a sort of downtrodden look to her.

'Detective Inspector Willis,' I replied. 'I'm making some enquiries into the death of Martin Clarke.' The two offices on my left were both empty, the doors open.

'They're both out.' She spoke over a sigh, as if it was all too much effort.

'Who are?'

'Bruce and Derek. The "B & D" of B & D Light Haulage.' She trotted it out like the well-rehearsed line it probably was.

There was a large whiteboard on the wall behind her; names, routes, times. You can imagine it, I'm sure. One column was blank, the name rubbed out. Martin's, probably.

'Did you know Martin?'

'I already gave a statement.'

'I was in hospital then, I'm afraid.' My best disarming smile. There was a hollow sound as I walked around the prefabricated office, and the floor was slightly springy. I looked at all the certificates mounted in frames on the wall. Small Business of the Year 1984, that sort of thing. Insurance certificates, crap like that.

'Are you the one that got hit by that car?' The sigh had gone now.

'That's me.'

'Yeah, I knew Martin. I was with him the night he died, in the Lord Poulett. He was the only decent one around here. The rest are . . .' She hesitated, craning her neck to look out of the window. 'Always trying it on; dirty old men, some of them. *Most* of them,' she said, when she was satisfied she wouldn't be overheard. 'Even the married ones. Martin was nice, respectful. He'd always step in when the boys got a bit carried away, the jokes got a bit . . . crude. He asked me out properly, nicely, so I went and we had a nice evening in the pub. He paid for my scampi and chips and then dropped me home.'

'Where's that?'

'Martock.'

Eastbound on the 303 to get home. That explained why he was out there that night.

'I remember when we came out of the pub, he found his brake light had been smashed. There was glass in the road behind his car and everything. The road's wide in the middle of the village there and you park nose in to the pavement, so he reckoned someone had been walking past and just whacked it. He was bloody furious.'

'Had there been any incidents involving Martin in the weeks or months before that night?' I asked. 'Had he been stopped for speeding, had an accident, anything like that?'

'Let me have a look.' She stood up and walked over to a filing cabinet against the far wall. She took a file from the top drawer and began flicking through the various documents. 'Yeah, it looks like someone rear-ended him at the roundabout at Podimore. He's filled in the insurance claim form. I didn't think it would've been his fault, he was a good driver. Never got done for speeding, either, even in his Capri, although he had been stopped a couple of times.' She shrugged. 'A young lad in a car like that.'

'When was this?'

'September.'

'What else is in that file?'

'His tachographs, driving schedule, overtime records, what's left of his personnel file too. And there's the insurance stuff about that claim. You've got copies of everything. I sent them over at the time.'

'Can I see it?'

'I don't know.' She glanced out of the window at a car arriving in the yard, the sound of gravel crunching under wheels carrying through the open door. 'I'll need to check with Mr Jackson,' she said, quickly closing the file and replacing it in the cabinet. 'He's here now.'

Heavy footsteps. A big lad then. Shame, Maxine and I had been getting along so well. Yes, Maxine. She was wearing a name badge, in case you're wondering how I know her name.

'Who's this?' Jackson had stopped at the top of the metal steps, blocking most of the light that had been streaming in.

'Bruce, this is Detective Inspector Willis, Avon and Somerset Police,' Maxine replied. 'He's asking about Martin.'

He turned to me, looked me up and down. 'Have you got a warrant?'

'I don't need one to ask a few questions,' I replied.

'Let's see your warrant card then.' He stepped into the office and dropped his briefcase on Maxine's desk with a loud clunk.

'I don't have it with me.' And that's true, I haven't got it with me. Actually, I haven't got it at all, but he doesn't need to know that.

'How do we know you're a real police officer then?' Jackson was squaring up to me now.

Not invading my space, you understand, just making sure I know he's far bigger. And he is. Second row to my scrum half.

'You'll have to take my word for it,' I said, more in hope than expectation.

'No we don't. No warrant card, no answers. Now get out.'

A hasty retreat, they call it. I wouldn't say my tail was between my legs, but near enough. I didn't stop to put my seatbelt on until I'd got clear, put it that way.

It's a shame because Maxine was being very helpful. In fact, she told me what I needed to know. That Martin had been involved in a road traffic accident in the weeks before his death. Jackson arrived before I got the chance to find out whether the police had attended the scene, but she also told me he'd been stopped several times in his Capri anyway.

I wonder if PC Taylor ever pulled him over out on the 303?

I'd dearly love to have seen Martin's personnel records too. There might very well be copies of everything on the police file, but that's no bloody use to me, is it?

'I thought I'd find you skulking here.' Angela sat down opposite me.

We're in the Little Chef at Camel Hill. There are a couple of spaces around the back so I can park my car out of sight, although I suppose if it didn't fool Angela, it won't fool anyone else. Sitting in the window might have had something to do with it. I like to watch the world go by.

'How are your parents?' I asked.

'They'll be fine. I dropped them home and popped into the office,' she replied, turning in her seat and waving at the woman by the till. 'They just want it over; want to know who killed Lizzie. You'd better bloody well be right about this.'

'What d'you think?'

'I don't think it was Clarke, but if it was then he had an accomplice; must've done. That's what I told my folks anyway. Stood up for you, I did.'

'Thanks.'

'You've caused quite a rumpus. Ray, our crime reporter, nearly shat himself. He's doing a whole feature on it. On *you*. The murder of Faith Bennett too.'

I stifled a grimace, instead pointing at Angela when a figure appeared next to our table.

'Oh, tea, please.'

'Nothing to eat?'

'No, thanks.' Angela didn't stop to draw breath. 'I passed a film crew from the Beeb out on the dual carriageway at Ilchester. You know, where they found the dead girl's car. The bloke off the telly, I can't remember his name, he was doing a piece to camera.'

I blame the good doctor. What was it she said? *Maybe now is the time to lay these ghosts to rest?*

Maybe it is.

What's that other phrase off the telly? You know, that quiz show.

'So, what happens now?' asked Angela.

Well, *several things* is the short answer to that, but I'm buggered if I'm involving her in any of it. And this is where I step over the line, good and proper. I haven't done anything illegal up to now; impersonating a police officer, perhaps, but then I am one, for the time being, so I doubt I'd get convicted even if they bothered to pursue it. No, it's what comes next that I'm talking about.

I need another look around Faith Bennett's cottage in South Petherton, preferably without DCS Sharp breathing down my neck this time, so that'll be burglary. Then I want Martin's personnel file out of that cabinet in the office at B & D Light Haulage, so that'll be a second count of burglary, albeit non-residential. Then there's going equipped too, that's if they find the toolbox in the boot of my car.

If I'm caught? Probation, probably. Hopefully. You really don't want to go to prison, not if you're a police officer.

The question is what do I do with Angela in the meantime? Something that will make her feel useful and yet keep her out of the way.

'I want to help,' said Angela, firmly. She'd have stamped a foot, if her legs hadn't been under the table. 'Lizzie was my sister.'

There's some research I need to do. Easy enough for a serving police officer, not so easy for one on sick leave. It needs to be done discreetly. I can't risk it getting back to Taylor. Or Brian Druce for that matter. He'd tell Sharp and that would be that. No, a journalist is the next best thing. It'll keep her out of trouble too.

'I need you to do something for me.'

'What is it?' she asked, her eyes darting from side to side.

'Fiona Anderson and Alice Cobb both had a cross carved into their chests. Lizzie had the beginnings of it. Faith Bennett too. It looks something like this.' I was drawing four triangles on the edge of a Little Chef serviette, the points meeting in the middle. 'We thought it was a Maltese cross. You get the picture.'

Angela snatched the napkin and was staring at it, breathing deeply.

'You think this is what those cuts were on Lizzie's breasts?'

'We looked for a similar pattern in other murders, solved and unsolved, but found nothing. Presumably you can look back at other cases at the newspaper?'

'Yes, of course we can, but if the crime reporter finds out, he'll want to know what I'm doing.'

'Make sure he doesn't find out.'

'And what do I do if I find a case?'

'Tell me.'

'Is that it?'

'It may not sound much, but it's the most important job of all,' I replied, with a stern look to emphasise the point.

'Oh right.' Angela waited while a small tray of tea was placed in front of her. 'What will you be doing?' she whispered, when the coast was clear.

'The less you know, the better,' I replied. 'It's going to be a bumpy ride, and it might very well get bloody, very quickly. At the moment, you can say "all he asked me to do was a bit of research", so let's keep it that way, shall we?'

'Bloody?'

'What have I got to lose?' I could feel a knowing smile creeping across my lips. 'I fired the starting gun this morning at the inquest and there's no going back now.' I've remembered that phrase off the telly, that quiz show.

I've started, so I'll finish.

Chapter Ten

It's dark now. Always best when you're planning a burglary. Actually, it'll make for a very interesting legal argument, if I do get caught. Burglary is defined as entering a building as a trespasser – can't argue with that – *and* with intent to steal, inflict GBH on any person therein, and of doing unlawful damage.

The *and* is all important there, because I don't intend to do any of those things. Just have a look around. Still, I'll probably have to break a window to get in, and there's the damage, I suppose. Let's hope someone's left a door unlocked.

I've parked my car in the village and walked along the lane to the terrace of old farm cottages. It's a dark night, no moon to worry about, but there's a car outside Faith's, which I didn't expect, and a light on inside.

Her parents, possibly. There's no sign of a police presence, and Scenes of Crime will be long gone by now. Still, I've come all this way and it seems a shame to turn back now.

What's the worst that can happen?

I hadn't intended the knock on the door to be quite so tentative, but it was. Unconvincing, but then maybe I'm not entirely convinced I should be doing this? That might explain it. Disturbing her parents at a time like this. It feels a bit insensitive. Maybe even *very* insensitive. That's assuming it is her parents, of course.

'Who are you?'

'Detective Inspector Willis,' I replied.

A tall man, pale, with red eyes behind thick glasses. About my age. My daughters are about Faith's age, so he could well be her father. The maths works. There's a woman sobbing in the front room too.

'Detective Chief Superintendent Sharp told us not to talk to you; said you've had a nervous breakdown and are on sick leave, that you're not part of the investigation.'

'Can I come in?'

'Why?'

'To talk to you. Explain.'

'Let him in, Fred.' A woman's voice, calling from the living room.

'That's my wife, Gwen,' said Fred, quietly. 'She's very upset, as you might imagine. The doctor's given her something to calm her down.'

'I understand.' Know it well, as it happens.

'What was it you wanted to explain?' she asked. She was perched on the arm of one of the chairs when I followed her husband into the front room.

The room was much as it had been on Saturday, although someone had put the Dire Straits LP back in its sleeve.

'Was she an only child?' I asked.

'Does it make a difference?' Fred was standing with his back to the gas fire, his arms folded.

'Forgive me, it was a clumsy way of trying to confirm you're Faith's parents without actually asking the question.'

'Yes, we are.' Gwen was pulling a paper tissue out from the sleeve of her cardigan. 'And we have a son. He's in the army.'

'What was it you wanted to explain?' asked Fred.

'Do the names Fiona Anderson and Alice Cobb mean anything to you?'

'They were the girls murdered out on the A303,' replied Gwen. 'But they got him, didn't they? Pulled him over and he was hit by a lorry when he tried to make a run for it.'

'That's what DCS Sharp will tell you, yes. But I'm not so sure.'

'Faith was at Yeovil College with Alice,' said Fred. 'Knew her quite well, went to the funeral.'

'There was a police officer killed as well, wasn't there?' asked Gwen. 'And another one got hit by a car.'

'That was me,' I said, trying to ignore the sudden stabbing pain in my leg. Any reminder of that night will do it, and the pain shoots. Sometimes the leg, sometimes my elbow.

'A hit and run, they said.' Fred was looking me up and down for any sign of injury, probably.

'It was no hit and run. There was a second car and that means two people were involved. My view is they're both still out there, but even if I'm wrong about that and Martin Clarke was involved, that still leaves one of them out there.'

'And you think they killed our daughter?'

I cleared my throat, ready to answer, but nodded instead. The easy way out again. 'The official line is case closed and I suspect they won't even look at the possibility of a connection with Faith's murder. There are obvious differences, of course there are. Faith, and her car, were both found at her home, for a start, but that's hardly surprising, is it?'

'Change confuses people,' said Fred.

'Some people are easily confused,' I said, quickly regretting it. It's hardly the time for flippancy, after all.

'What are you doing here?' asked Gwen.

I was wondering when someone was going to ask me that; the follow-up question will be more difficult to answer. 'I was hoping to have a look around.'

'What if we hadn't been here?'

And there it is. How am I supposed to answer that?

'How were you going to get in?' Fred was staring at me.

I must've looked guilty and decided the best course was to change the subject. 'Is there anything out of place?' I asked.

'Not really,' replied Fred.

'Oh, come on, Fred,' said Gwen. 'Just about everything is out of place. You know how untidy she was.'

'It looks like someone has tidied up, but I just thought that was your Scenes of Crime lot,' he said, turning to me. 'And there's this grey powder everywhere.'

'That's the fingerprint stuff,' I said.

And it was everywhere. The record player, television, mantelpiece, door knob, the arms of the chairs, even Fred's trousers where he'd sat in it.

'I'll run the hoover round before we hand it back to the landlord,' said Gwen. 'It's the same in the kitchen.'

'Do you mind if I . . .' I let my voice tail off as I headed for the kitchen.

More grey powder, this time on the fridge door, kettle, drawers, windowsill, door handle, the two mugs, the chairs, light switch. Some of the cutlery had been laid out on the table and dusted for prints too, gaps in the line-up where items had been kept by the Scenes of Crime team, perhaps.

I checked the cutlery drawer, just to be on the safe side, but there were no prints in the powder. I'd used my key to open it, of course, but you'd have expected to find some prints on it, even if they were just Faith's. That there were none, anywhere, told me the place had been wiped clean.

That's right. Not a single print in any of the powder, anywhere on the ground floor.

'May I go upstairs?' I asked, poking my head around the door of the living room.

'Go ahead,' said Fred, with that 'what bloody harm can it do now' tone of voice. 'She was in the front room.'

I knew that, but thought it best not to let on.

Yet more powder on the white-painted handrail, and no prints.

The bedding had gone, as had the pile of clothes. All that was left was a single bed, an empty wardrobe, the doors standing open, and more grey powder. I checked for fingerprints, but there were none.

It seemed oddly sparse for a girl's bedroom. Maybe it was the spare?

Across the landing, I pushed open the door to the back bedroom with my elbow; touching it would've left my prints in yet more grey powder.

This was more like it. Posters on the walls, makeup on the small dressing table. Clothes dumped on the floor, the duvet in a heap in the middle of the bed. I looked out of the back window and her car was still parked in the neighbour's space.

'I was always telling her to tidy her room,' said Gwen. I'd heard footsteps on the stairs but had thought it would have been Fred.

'Did she have a boyfriend?' I asked, when Gwen appeared in the doorway.

'Not that we know of. No one special anyway.'

'Where did she work?'

'She was training to be a nurse at Yeovil Hospital. In the casualty department.'

'Her route home?'

'The A3088, then along the . . .' Fred's voice, out on the landing. 'Oh my God.'

Gwen was sitting on the edge of the bed now, her face buried in Faith's duvet, breathing deeply through her nostrils.

'"Just think of it, Mum. No more shouting 'Tidy your room!'" It was the last thing she said to me when she moved out.'

'You said everything was out of place downstairs. What did you mean by that?' I asked.

'I'll show you.'

It looked much the same as it had on Saturday, but here was someone who'd know what it was like *before*.

Gwen sighed. 'I don't know, it just appears too perfect, too tidy, for Faith anyway. Look at the mantelpiece.' She was gesturing with both hands. 'We gave her that clock, but it was never in the middle like that. It's dead straight too. She'd have just plonked it there. Anywhere would do as long as she could see it.'

'The aerial was usually on top of the telly,' offered Fred. 'We tried it on the mantelpiece when she moved in but there was no signal. On top of the telly, at an angle was the best.'

'Someone's straightened that rug too,' continued Gwen. 'It moved on the carpet and she never bothered, just let it ruck up. The antimacassars have gone too. White lace they were. I got them in Honiton.'

'Could they be in the wash?' I asked.

'No.'

'How do you know?'

'She brings it home for me to do, that's how.'

Chapter Eleven

There was a light on in the B & D Light Haulage office and I could see a figure moving about inside. A security van was doing the rounds of the industrial estate too, so I decided against it. Thinking about it, Martin couldn't have had alibis for the murders anyway. If he had, and they'd checked out, then the case wouldn't be closed, would it?

Assuming that's right, then all his personnel file will tell me is that he was probably working those nights. Out and about in his van, with no one to vouch for him.

And his alibis would've been checked. Not all police officers are corrupt; I wouldn't want you to think that. There will have been a thorough investigation of Martin's whereabouts at the times Fiona Anderson and Alice Cobb were murdered. Lizzie too.

No, the only officers I'm suggesting are in it up to their necks are PC 1068 Sean Taylor and his accomplice, whoever that might be. It was Taylor who pulled Martin over, Taylor who planted the murder weapons in the boot of his car, and Taylor who threw him from the bridge into the path of that lorry. I could be wrong about that last bit, but you get the picture. If it wasn't him, it was his accomplice.

Taylor was also first on the scene the night Lizzie was murdered and I had my mysterious hit and run. Funny that, wouldn't you say?

So, I've decided to give burglary non-residential a miss tonight. Not worth the risk. I got lucky with Faith's parents being at her cottage, and now I'm back out on a deserted 303, lights on full beam, heading home. I'll go as far as Ilchester and pick up the B3151; go home via Glastonbury tonight. I could do with some sleep, not that I'll get much, I shouldn't think.

Roads you know well have a special feel to them after dark, especially country roads. Familiar landmarks zip by, lit up fleetingly by my headlights; the occasional deer on the nearside grass verge, or sometimes the central reservation. A fox maybe.

I hate seeing roadkill.

It's gone midnight and there are few lights on anywhere. Even the Little Chefs will be shut.

I can see that comforting orange glow of streetlights up ahead, so that'll be the junction with the A37. Lizzie's lay-by is just beyond that, then I'm off across country at the next roundabout. Podimore, they call it. I might even go home over the Mendips for a change.

There's a car parked in the lay-by. The blue light on the roof comes on just as I dip my headlights. Then the driver's door opens and a figure in uniform steps out into the nearside lane, waving a torch, directing me into the lay-by.

I wonder.

◆ ◆ ◆

Yes, it's him. Police Constable 1068 Sean Taylor. We've all got numbers. Mine's 732, in case you were wondering. Uniformed officers wear them on their shoulders – chrome badges clipped to the epaulettes – so they can be identified by members of the public, although we always took them off and stuffed them in our pockets when the mods and rockers were at it on Weston seafront.

Happy days.

I've pulled in behind the patrol car, switched off the engine and wound down my window a crack. Now I'm watching him walking towards me, shining his torch at my tyres.

'Do you know what speed you were doing, sir?' he asked, avoiding eye contact. Suitably officious, of course, but then he's the type.

'Yes.'

'And what speed was that?'

'Sixty-eight,' I replied. It had been there or thereabouts.

'And may I ask where you're going at this time of night?'

'Home.'

'Have you been drinking tonight, sir?'

Like that, is it? 'I don't drink, Constable,' I said. 'Haven't done for some time.'

'Would you mind stepping out of the car, please, sir?'

He's in uniform, as you would expect. About six foot two, maybe, although the spiky blond hair makes him look taller; younger than me, bigger too, and perfectly capable of throwing me off a bridge. Boxed at some point, now I see his face up close, although the light's not great. His nose has definitely been broken, probably more than once. A big man, with big features. Mid-thirties, possibly.

Four inches doesn't sound much, but he towers over me when I step out of my car.

'Would you mind breathing into this, please, sir?'

I'm old enough to remember when these things were introduced. 1967, although I was already in CID by then, so we skipped the training. The biggest thing we had to worry about was not getting on the wrong end of one.

Taylor is holding the breathalyser in front of me, pointing at the small tube. 'Just breathe into this and hold it for as long as you can.'

'I know the drill.'

'Of course you do.'

The last time I had to breathe into one of these things, I bloody well failed, didn't I? Over the limit. Only just, mind you, and the officer gave me a lift home. Somehow I don't think Taylor would be quite so obliging.

'Negative,' he said, no hint of disappointment in his voice. 'Can I see your driving licence?'

'I don't carry it on me.' This isn't a police state. Yet, anyway.

'What about your MOT and insurance?'

'At home.'

He should issue me with a Producer at this point. Driving licence, MOT and insurance documents at a police station of my choice within ten days. Ilminster. At least there's a car park outside.

Instead, he walks back to the patrol car and picks up a torch from the passenger seat. 'I'll need to check your vehicle as well, if you wouldn't mind waiting by the patrol car, please, sir.'

'Fine.' I'm doing my best to stay patient.

'Where are the keys?'

'In the ignition.'

Thoroughly professional, so far. I was expecting a good kicking, to be honest. Give him time.

I'd left the lights on, so he can see they're working. The bugger checks the glovebox, door pockets, even the tread on my tyres. The boot too, my toolbox rattling. Then he straightens up and slams the lid. 'What is the purpose of the tools?' he asked, shining his torch in my face.

'I don't have a garage, so I keep a few tools in the boot of my car.'

He opens the driver's door of his patrol car.

'Is that it?' I'm curious, you understand. He surely knows I'm accusing him of planting the murder weapons in Martin Clarke's car?

'Yes, that's it. Your nearside rear tyre is on the limit. You'll need to get it changed in the next month or so,' he replied. 'There are no hard feelings, Bob. You don't mind if I call you Bob, do you? They told me about your mental health problems, and I was sorry to hear about the breakdown. It's always a shame when a respected officer's career ends like that.' He climbs into the driver's seat and winds down the window. 'I'd appreciate it if you stopped telling everyone I planted the murder weapons in Clarke's car, but if it helps you get through the day, then . . .' His voice tails off into a shrug as he turns the key. 'I've been accused of planting evidence before. We all have, and I never take it personally. It goes with the territory.'

Then he accelerates away, swinging out of the lay-by at the far end and on to the dual carriageway, his lights soon disappearing into the distance.

Seemed perfectly reasonable, didn't he? Perfectly professional.

I know what you're thinking; that I've become fixated on Taylor. That he's got nothing to do with it. You're starting to doubt me.

Make no mistake, I'm starting to doubt me too.

Really?

No, not really.

Taylor had a fair point about police officers being accused of planting evidence, though. It's happened to me a couple of times, usually when the suspect had no other defence open to them;

tell the jury the police planted the drugs and hope for the best. Sometimes it worked, sometimes it didn't.

It depends on how the police officer comes across in his evidence as much as anything, and I'm pleased to say those who tried it on with me were always found guilty. I should clarify that I didn't plant the drugs. Never did. Never needed to, actually.

I'm left wondering two things.

Firstly, how Taylor knew I was out on the A303. Make no mistake about it, there was nothing random whatsoever about that stop. 'By the book' it may have been, but he knew it was me when he pulled me over. I'm under no illusion about that. All he would've seen from that lay-by is a pair of headlights approaching along the dual carriageway, but he knew.

The second thing that's worrying me is whether he thinks I was born yesterday.

I'm parked in a field gateway on the top of the Mendips. It's a narrow lane, a bit of a grass verge both sides, then dry stone walls. It's pitch dark, and I can see for miles in each direction; a light moving across the fields a mile or so away – someone lamping for rabbits, probably. A clear sky too, stars by the billion. There was a time I'd have stopped just to gaze at them, but tonight I'm more interested in what Taylor left in the boot of my car.

Planted, if you'd rather.

He's done it to Martin Clarke and he's just tried it on with me.

It's a good, big lay-by, with two gates. Nice and wide and I've got all four doors and the boot of my car open. I knew that torch would come in handy.

The floormats are on the dry stone wall and I've checked under the seats, even under the carpet; Taylor rummaging in the boot could have been a diversion, couldn't it? Nothing behind the armrest between the back seats, either. Glovebox is clear, as is the ashtray and the fuse box under the dashboard.

The boot then.

It took me about ten minutes, but I've got my toolbox out and the tools are all laid out neatly on the grass. The box is definitely empty and I've tipped it upside down several times to make sure. I've checked the side panels too, the jack one side and a first aid kit the other; never knew that was there to be honest.

Next it's lift the carpet and check the spare wheel.

Interesting. I expected drugs in a little plastic bag, silver foil perhaps, but there's a small towel wedged in behind the tyre. It looks clean, but I'm more concerned by what's in it.

A towel is clever, I suppose, because there's no chance of fingerprints. Taylor hadn't been wearing gloves, and probably thought doing so would look odd, which it would have done. That explains the towel, but what's wrapped in it?

A knife, probably. If I had to guess. And that means that someone else is dead, although it could be the weapon used to murder Faith Bennett.

I lift the towel out from behind the spare wheel, holding it tightly in a pair of pliers. Then I place it on the ground behind my car and unfold it. I still haven't touched it, and have no intention of doing so.

Yes, it's a knife. A small kitchen knife, maybe five inches long, with a wooden handle; looks very much like mine, from the cutlery drawer in my kitchen.

Blood on the blade.

Fresh blood by the looks of things, so someone has died tonight.

Someone else.

Chapter Twelve

The kitchen knife from my flat. It looks like it. It could be, it just could be. Wooden handle, two studs, serrated, like any steak knife. Common enough.

I've only lived in the flat a few weeks, remember. And it's not as if I do much cooking either, so I can't be sure whether or not it's mine. Well, I say *mine*, it actually belongs to Shirley. As does pretty much everything else in the flat, except my clothes and the deckchair.

That said, it could just as easily have come from Faith Bennett's cottage.

Anyway, I'm not taking any chances, and it's buried under loose stones at the base of the wall opposite the field gateway, and yes, I'll be able to find it again, before you ask. I even had the spare tyre out of the boot of my car to check for blood and it's clean.

Now, I'm on my way home, dropping down off the Mendips towards Compton Martin.

Frame me for murder. At best it would discredit me; not that I've got a lot of credit, as you might have noticed. At worst, it would have had me in custody. I didn't expect that; didn't think Taylor was bright enough. I know he's not working alone, though, so whoever is behind him is the one pulling the strings, but that's for another day.

What concerns me more right now is whose blood it is on that knife. I can see blue lights ahead, on the slate roofs of the cottages in Blagdon, and there's that sinking feeling in the pit of my stomach.

◆ ◆ ◆

Two patrol cars are blocking the road outside the Seymour Arms. I'm guessing the road will be blocked at the other end of the village too, and the post office is right in the middle.

I'm watching the driver of the car in front of me arguing with the police constable, not that it'll do him any good. It's a bollocks of a long way round too.

All I hope now is it's not Shirley. I couldn't bear that. I've got a horrible feeling it'll be somebody at the post office, though, so that's either Alan or the part-timer who helps them out. Tanya, or whatever her name is.

God, I hope it's not Shirley.

PC 1068 Sean fucking Taylor had better hope it's not Shirley.

I've stopped at the roadblock and wound down my window, not that the constable is interested in talking to me. He's on his radio.

'He's here, guv.'

'Let him through.'

There are two plain-clothes officers I don't recognise standing in the road as I drive down towards the post office. It's on the bend at the bottom, on the right where the lane goes off to the lake. There's a shop too; every village has got one. Newspapers, bread and milk, spuds, that sort of stuff. Open all hours, just like the sitcom.

I usually park around the back, but not tonight. There are several vans, and an ambulance.

What day is it today? Tuesday. Shuts at ten, post office counter shuts at five-thirty. Shirley and Alan would've gone home then.

I've left my car in the middle of the road, simply because there's nowhere else to park.

'Mr Mungo Willis?' asked one of the detectives, walking towards me as I climbed out of the driver's seat.

'*Detective Inspector* Mungo Willis,' I replied. 'What's happened?'

'There's been a stabbing, sir. I'm Detective Sergeant Jones and this is DC Ash.'

Lights on everywhere, curtains twitching. You'd never know it was two o'clock in the morning.

'Fatal?'

'Yes, sir, I'm sorry to say.'

'Who?' It's like pulling teeth.

'A Mr Alan Carpenter. He was stocktaking and confronted someone trying to break into the upstairs flat by the looks of things.'

'My flat.'

'So we understand.'

'Do we have a time of death?'

'The pathologist thinks between ten and midnight, and we have to ask, can you account for your whereabouts during that time frame?'

I should be outraged, but I know it's just procedure. Poor Alan. Poor Shirley. 'Where's Mrs Carpenter?' I asked.

'She found the body, I'm afraid, sir, but she's at home now. One of her daughters has come over from Bristol to be with her.'

That'll be Christine. It must be; Joanne lives in London, unless she's moved without telling me.

'Your whereabouts, sir?'

'I was in the Little Chef at Camel Hill until it closed at ten. Then I met with Faith Bennett's parents at her cottage in South Petherton; left there just after midnight. I was stopped by PC 1068

Sean Taylor on the A303 at Ilchester at about half past midnight, passed a breathalyser and here I am.'

'Did he issue you with a Producer?'

'No.' And now I know why. Date, time and place of issue would've put me miles away, given me an alibi.

'Do you mind if we have a look in your car, sir?'

'Be my guest,' I replied, handing the keys to Jones, who passed them to DC Ash.

Tipped off, they must've been. Anonymous, probably. It will be interesting to see if Ash goes straight to the boot of the car.

There's a surprise. Straight to the boot and lifting the carpet. It's a bloody good job my alibi isn't burgling the offices of B & D Light Haulage.

'It's clean, Andy.' Ash looked disappointed.

He didn't even bother to check the rest of the car, which ordinarily I would take him to task about, but on this occasion it tells me all I need to know.

'Is the pathologist in there now?' I asked.

'Yes, sir.'

'I'd like to have a word with him,' I said, pushing past Jones.

'We can't allow that, sir. Standard proced—'

'Come with me then, if you're worried I might tamper with evidence.'

Footsteps behind me, so they were doing just that.

The front door of the shop was closed, but the lights were on inside, piles of boxes next to the shelves; McVitie's this and that. Shirley always leaves a packet of biscuits in the flat.

'The post office counter is all locked up, but the back door is open, sir,' said Jones. 'So, we reckon he heard a noise and went to investigate. The body is just inside your front door.'

Up the metal staircase at the side of the building; the old fire escape before the upstairs was converted into a separate flat. My front door is open, light streaming out into the darkness. I've got my hands in my pockets but my fingerprints will be everywhere, of course. I live here, after all. The problem I've got is I don't know the Bristol pathologist, so won't get to see his report or the photographs. That makes it now or never.

'Detective Inspector Mungo Willis,' I said, standing just outside the front door. Jones and Ash had squeezed on to the landing behind me.

The pathologist looked up. He was kneeling at Alan's head, which was furthest from me, the body lying face down in the narrow corridor, blood soaking into the rug. 'I told your colleagues, between ten and midnight. Death would've been quick, there's a stab wound penetrating the heart so that would've killed him on its own.'

'How many are there?'

'Seventeen,' he replied. 'There's a lot of anger here, some of these injuries have been inflicted after death – he or she just kept stabbing – which makes me think it was personal. The wife's ex-husband, something like that.'

'I'm the wife's ex-husband.'

'Oh, sorry.' He gave an embarrassed laugh, as if that made it all right. 'I had a quick look in the kitchen drawer and there's no sharp knife. Everyone's got one, haven't they? That's your murder weapon, I expect, but he's taken it with him as far as I can see. I can give you a better idea of the blade when I open him up.'

I was looking down at Alan, feeling like shit, to be honest. I hadn't killed him, but then again he'd still be alive if I'd just let it go, let all of it go; stuck to cricket and fishing. I can't do that, though, can I? Not when I know there's a pair of serial killers out there – *still* out there – and they've killed again, not that Sharp can see it.

It was personal before because of Lizzie, but now it's doubly personal. Poor old Alan. One of life's bloody good blokes. Far better than me, and far better for Shirley than I ever was. How will I ever face her after this?

'Do me a favour, will you?' I said. 'Just try that door over there, tell me if it's still locked.'

'Yes, it is,' replied the pathologist. 'I checked it earlier. Why?'

'No reason.' That's my incident room, with the wall and the deckchair. Taylor, or whoever it was, obviously hadn't found that. 'Thanks,' I said, turning for the stairs, my path blocked by Jones and Ash.

'Like I said, a lot of anger. Personal, I reckon.' The pathologist was still kneeling at Alan's head.

'Or made to look personal.'

'Yes, there's that, I suppose.'

'This had better not be anything to do with you, Dad.'

Christine answered the door. As you might have guessed, I'm not taking the easy way out this time and have come to see Shirley.

I won't be mentioning the knife in the boot of my car, though.

I haven't seen Christine for at least three years; at her grand-mother's funeral, it was, which makes it well before my breakdown. She didn't even visit me in hospital, come to think of it. Still, I suppose I should be grateful she called me Dad. Last time it was 'you little shit'. It doesn't help that she's taller than me.

Children tend to side with one parent or the other in a divorce, depending on who they blame for it. Called life, it is, and I accepted it a long time ago. Probably because it was my fault.

'How is she?' I asked, to break the ice and change the subject.

Christine had been crying. Her eyes were red and I could smell wine on her breath too. She's had her hair cut even shorter than last time, if that's possible.

'She's in bits, what d'you bloody well expect?'

I was trying to appear understanding. And I did understand, of course I did. 'Who's looking after Rufus?'

'I brought him with me. He's on the bed in the spare room, asleep, and we haven't told him his Grandad Alan is dead.'

I haven't met him yet – my own grandson – and he's got a Grandad Alan. I try to stay philosophical about these things, I really do. And there's a time and a place. Just not now.

'Where is she?'

'In the living room.'

I followed the sound of the sobbing, although I stayed here for a while and know the way. It looked much like any other living room, or sitting room; whatever you choose to call it in your house. The only difference here is that my ex-wife was sitting on the edge of the sofa, crying her heart out. There was a box of paper tissues on the seat next to her and two empty wine glasses on the mantelpiece.

She looked up. 'You find who did this, and you kill them. You do that for me.'

Well, that's a relief. It was set up to look like I did it, but Shirley's smarter than that. Thank God.

'Tell me what happened,' I said.

'He was stocktaking,' she replied. 'Said he'd be home about ten; wasn't answering when I rang, so I walked down there about eleven.' She shrugged. 'You can imagine the rest, I'm sure.'

'Is this anything to do with that case you're working on?' asked Christine. She had followed me along the corridor and was standing in the doorway. 'Mum said you think the A303 killers are still out there.'

'I'm off sick at the mo—'

'Don't treat me like an idiot,' snapped Shirley. 'I've seen the wall and your deckchair.'

'Yes, they're still out there,' I replied. 'My guess is I was the target and Alan was just in the wrong place at the wrong time. So, they killed him and made it look like I did it. In my flat, with a knife from my kitchen; multiple stab wounds to make it look personal.'

'How d'you know about the knife?'

'The pathologist said the sharp knife was missing from the kitchen drawer.'

'So, where were you?' asked Christine. She made no effort to mask the hatred in her voice; loathing almost.

'South Petherton. Thirty-five miles away.'

'Of course he didn't do it,' said Shirley. 'They got on well, for heaven's sake, Chris. Even went fishing together.'

'We did.'

'If I find out—'

'Rufus is crying,' interrupted Shirley. 'You'd better go and see to him.'

Saved by a young grandson I haven't even met yet.

Shirley stood up, put her arms around me and started to sob.

'I'm so sorry, Shirley,' I mumbled. 'I really am. He was a lovely bloke.'

She quickly regained her composure when Christine appeared in the doorway, carrying a little boy in her arms. 'Rufus, this is your grandfather.' He was too busy waking up to take much notice of me; rubbing his eyes furiously.

'Where's Grandad Alan?'

'This is Grandad Mungo,' said Shirley, stepping forward with her arms outstretched, taking the boy from Christine. 'Come and say hello. You haven't met him before.' Then she plonked him in my arms.

I forced a smile, bounced him up and down, as you do. 'Maybe I'll take you fishing one day, when you're a bit older,' I said. 'I really need to be . . .'

'Yeah.' Christine took Rufus from me and carried him back towards the bedroom, while Shirley showed me to the door.

'I'm going to shut the shop for a while and go and stay with Joanne in London. Will you be all right?'

'Me?' I frowned. 'I'm more worried about you.'

Shirley was holding the open front door. 'You remember what I said,' she whispered. 'I don't want to find myself sitting through a bloody trial at Bristol Crown Court.'

We'd been married nearly twenty years when she left me, and there's a certain understanding that survives between a husband and a wife, even after a divorce – especially a divorce like ours; sad rather than acrimonious.

I nodded, then made for the comparative safety of the darkness.

Chapter Thirteen

It was a long night, but then it was always going to be.

They'd opened the road through the village by the time I left Shirley's, although getting in to my flat was out of the question and would be for at least another twenty-four hours.

I spent the night in my car down at the fishing lodge, parked in the trees behind it. It's a quiet spot, until the anglers start arriving, of course. A lovely old building it is too, more like a cricket pavilion on the edge of the lake there.

I said *spent the night in my car* quite deliberately. I didn't get much sleep.

There are a couple of lads tackling up in the car park now, a few others climbing into boats at the small jetty. I've made myself a coffee and am sitting on the veranda, watching the world go by, not that there is much here, compared to a Little Chef, for example. A few ducks, the odd trout rising. It looks like being a nice day, but I can't get rid of that sick feeling in the pit of my stomach.

Shirley knows Alan's death was my fault and the anger will follow soon enough. She was too upset last night.

My fault?

I thought about this a lot overnight – thought about nothing else, in fact – and it is and it isn't. If that makes sense. I didn't kill him – obviously – but he's dead because of me. That said, could I have foreseen it? Not really, in fairness. I thought they'd come after me; I was expecting that, but killing someone close to me and trying to frame me for it . . .

Could I – should I – have seen that coming?

I don't know, you tell me.

And here's another question for you. Could I – should I – just let it go? Forget about Lizzie, forget about the driver of the car that ran me down. Forget about Alan.

I could forget about Martin Clarke, perhaps. But not the others.

Not then, and certainly not now.

Polish Water is right in front of the lodge. Shallow, weedy, and there's an angler into a fish. He's in a boat about thirty yards off the bank. An idyllic scene, although I'm more interested in the two people walking towards me along the veranda.

Definitely not here for the fishing. They'll be police officers, although I don't recognise them.

'We're looking for Bob Willis,' said the male officer in the suit and red tie.

'The County Championship game at Taunton finished yesterday, so he'll have gone home by now.'

'Sorry, Mungo Willis.'

'I'm Detective Inspector Mungo Willis,' I said, emphasising my rank. He hadn't used it, quite deliberately, so I did; just so they're clear who they're talking to, you understand – that I outrank them, judging by their ages.

'I'm DC Tom Field and this is DC Helen Webster. We're looking again at the murder of DS Harper.'

'And the attempted murder of me, I expect.'

'Yes, sir.'

DCS Sharp really is as thick as pig shit. The smart move would have been to have appointed someone who outranked me, rather than two officers who look like they're straight out of kindergarten. Still, he's really only interested in keeping the coroner happy.

'We called at your flat,' said Field. 'I gather the owner of the post office has been found dead.'

'Murdered,' I replied.

'Do you think the two cases are connected?' asked Webster.

Staying patient is going to be the challenge this morning, I think. 'Of course Alan's murder is connected. I was the target, and if I wasn't, then it was an attempt to frame me for his murder.'

'Because of what you said at the inquest?'

'The cat's out of the bag now; it's in amongst the pigeons, whichever way you choose to describe it. The genie's out of the bottle. No one who knew him seriously believes Martin Clarke killed those girls and DS Harper, or that I was run over by accident.'

'We've looked at the file,' said Webster, 'and he had no alibis.'

'He was selected precisely because he had no alibis. Because he was a driver. The murder weapons were planted in the boot of his car by Police Constable 1068 Sean Taylor.'

'Where did he get them from?' asked Field.

'Do I really need to answer that?'

'Just for the avoidance of doubt.'

'We know there are two killers working together. Taylor is one of them. I don't know who the other is. He had the murder weapons because they belonged to him and he had used them to kill.' I let out a long, slow sigh; exaggerated it a bit, if I'm honest. 'Is that clear enough for you?'

'We've got no evidence of that.'

'Yes, you do. You have a witness statement from a senior police officer; a detective inspector, no less.'

'You?'

If he mentions my nervous breakdown, I'm going to lose my rag. 'Sit Taylor down in an interview room and ask the question,

101

execute a search warrant at his house. Put some pressure on him. You know the drill, surely?'

'We do.'

'Who else is on your team?' I asked.

'Just us,' replied Field.

Sharp has excelled himself this time. 'Look again at Martin Clarke,' I said. 'Speak to his father and the receptionist where he worked, Maxine somebody. Do it with an open mind; ask yourselves if he really was capable of what is being alleged – that he killed and mutilated three women, one a police officer.' I looked at Webster. 'Have you ever let a man overpower you?'

'No, but then I'm trained in self—'

'So was Detective Sergeant Lizzie Harper, and there was no way Martin Clarke was overpowering her.'

'Anything else?' asked Field.

'Speak to the bloke driving the lorry that hit Clarke. He said he saw two figures on the bridge. Clarke and another running towards him. Everybody thought that was Taylor in pursuit, didn't they, but what if there was already someone standing behind Clarke and Taylor was running to help that person throw Clarke off the bridge?'

'The driver probably wouldn't have seen that from where he was, down on the dual carriageway, at night.'

'Well, ask the bloody question, because you can bet no one has. Give me his name and address and I'll do it myself. I bet no bugger has bothered to try and find the vehicle that hit me, either.'

'How would we . . . ?'

'Check local garages, body shops; they might have been asked to repair it. Car breakers' yards. Use your imagination.'

'We've been told to be discreet,' said Webster, curling her lip. 'And DCS Sharp wants us to run everything past him first.'

'That's fine, if you want to get in his good books.' I stood up, emptying the dregs of my coffee into the flower bed. 'If you want to solve the case, don't.'

Field handed me his card. 'How can we get hold of you?' he asked. 'There's no phone in your flat and the post office will be closed.'

'Leave a message at the Little Chef, Camel Hill, and I'll call you.'

◆　◆　◆

I'm not holding my breath. Maybe they will, maybe they won't, but I can't wait for Field and Webster to sort it out. Not after last night.

Field had been right about the post office, though. I noticed the large sign in the window as I drove up through the village.

CLOSED UNTIL FURTHER NOTICE.

Can't say I blame her.

There was still a Scenes of Crime van parked around the back too, and the front door of my flat was open. Not that I'll be sleeping there until further notice, mind you. I'll be finding a bed and breakfast from now on. Never the same one twice, either.

I said it would get bloody, didn't I?

Chapter Fourteen

Interviewing a witness is a fine art that most of us get wrong, most of the time. I know I did. Instead of asking them what they know – everything they know – we look for answers that confirm what we think we know. I'm guessing the officers who took the statements slanted their questions like that.

There was the bloke who was first on the scene the night Lizzie died, and then the poor sod of a lorry driver who hit Martin Clarke a few weeks later. I can hear it now.

'So, you saw the man we now know to be Martin Clarke on the bridge?'

Answer: 'Yes.'

'And you were in the nearside lane?'

'Yes.'

So the interviewing officer writes down: *I saw Martin Clarke on the bridge as I approached in the nearside lane.*

'Did he fall or jump in front of your lorry?'

'I don't know.'

The end result is a statement that says *I couldn't tell if he fell or jumped*, and that's why the coroner recorded an open verdict. He had no choice.

I bet the witness wasn't even asked if Clarke might have been pushed. Was there anyone else standing behind him on the bridge? Did you see a scuffle? Questions like that.

Well, he's bloody well going to be asked now. I can't rely on Field and Webster to do it properly, so I'm going to have to do it. And the questions are going to have my slant on them. I'm looking for confirmation of what I know.

Don't expect an apology for that, because you won't get one.

I had breakfast in the Little Chef.

I know, I know.

Now I'm sitting in my car outside a thatched house in Kingsbury Episcopi. Paul Spalding, and he's a veterinary surgeon. That's all I could remember, but I managed to trace him to a practice in Somerton – God bless Yellow Pages – and it's his day off, apparently. There's a local BT phone book in the Little Chef as well, so it hadn't been difficult to find an address after that.

A Land Rover in the drive, so I'm hoping he's at home. It's the sort of car a vet would drive, isn't it, and they advertise the practice as 'agricultural and domestic' so he'd be out and about on farms. Actually, I see it now I'm walking up the gravel drive. There's a spare wheel mounted on the back door with a sign on the cover: *Spalding and Lee Veterinary Surgery – Domestic, Agricultural and Equine.*

A nice house too, timber framed, dormer windows set into the thatch, a solid oak front door with one of those handles you pull to ring the bell. I couldn't hear anything when I tried it, but it must've worked because dogs started barking.

'I know you, don't I?' He was holding the collar of a bulldog in one hand and the front door in the other, but I'm more interested in the three retrievers sniffing my legs. 'They'll be fine, don't worry,' he said. 'It's this one you've got to worry about. I'll shut him in my office.'

An internal door slammed, then the bulldog appeared in the leaded window to my right, standing on the back of an armchair.

'Sorry about that.' He was stroking his beard. 'I've got it now. You're the chap I found lying in the road that night.'

'I never got the chance to thank you for what you did,' I said, my hand outstretched. 'I'm Mungo Willis.'

'Paul Spalding,' he replied, shaking my hand vigorously. 'Come in, come in. I know it's a bit early but you must have a drink.'

'Thank you.'

I know what you're thinking. It was a shameless trick, but needs must. And I do need to thank him; I would have bled out before the ambulance arrived if someone with medical training hadn't been there.

'I thought your name was Bob?' asked Spalding, shutting the front door behind me.

'That's a nickname,' I replied. 'I bear a striking resemblance to the cricketer, apparently.'

'They call that "irony", don't they?'

'Something like that.' It's always a good icebreaker.

'I'm through here,' he said, walking towards an open door at the end of the corridor. I followed, admiring the oil paintings mounted on the oak panelling; a lovely old stone floor too. 'I was very sorry to find out later about your colleague, DS Harper.'

'Lizzie. She was my friend.' We were in the kitchen now. 'Coffee for me,' I said. 'If that's all right.'

'Are you sure you won't have something stronger?'

'It's a long story.'

He understood. 'Coffee it is then.'

'They told me I'd have died that night, if you hadn't been there, and I wanted to thank you.'

'There's no need. Really. Standard stuff for a vet, clamping an artery, although I usually do it on cattle and horses. I'm just glad to see you up and about. I did wonder if you might lose your leg.'

'It's got pins and plates in it. My elbow too. God knows what will happen if I ever try to get on a plane.' Another old joke. The old ones are the best, and all that.

'My wife's gone shopping,' said Spalding. 'She will be sorry to have missed you.'

'Would you mind if I asked you a few questions about that night? I'm struggling to get it all straight in my head.'

He was filling the kettle. 'Yes, of course. Fire away.'

I'm going to try this without asking a leading question, see what he remembers for himself before I start putting words in his mouth. Lawyers make a big deal out of leading questions. *Did you see a car?* As opposed to: *What did you see?* Basically, if you can answer 'yes' or 'no' then it's a leading question; easy when you get the hang of it.

'Where were you going at that time of night?' I asked.

'I'd been to a calving over at Spring Farm, between West Camel and Marston Magna. Just like you see on the telly, James Herriot with his arm up a cow's backside. I was on my way home. Quickest way is along the 303. Sugar?'

'One please.'

'I saw a car on the nearside verge. A big yellow Volvo with its hazard lights flashing, so I slowed a bit, as you do. Then I saw something in the road on the eastbound side, in the middle of the outside lane. You, as it turned out.'

'What did you do then?'

'I pulled in behind your car, ran across the road and jumped over the crash barrier. You were still breathing – you were a bit of a mess, mind you – and there was blood coming from the artery in your thigh, so I got my kit from the back of the Land Rover and clamped it. Someone else had come along by then and I sent them off to dial 999. There's a garage on the A37.'

'What else did you see when you arrived on the scene?'

'There was a car in the lay-by, but apart from that, nothing else. Nobody else either, if that's what you mean. Then a lorry arrived. He was eastbound, coming straight towards us, so I'd run along the central reservation, waving like a mad thing, and he saw me, thank God; parked his lorry at an angle, blocking both lanes. I dread to think what would've happened if he'd gone over you.'

'What about on your approach to the scene, maybe two or three minutes out? Longer even.'

'Not a lot, from memory,' replied Spalding. 'Traffic was light at that time of night, although I did see a car with only one headlight. Didn't think much of it at the time, to be honest. It was eastbound, waiting at the roundabout at Podimore as I came around heading west. I indicated left and off he went. It's in my statement. It only occurred to me later it might have been the car that hit you.'

'Make, model?'

'Dark hatchback. A VW Golf, possibly.' Spalding frowned. 'It was the car that hit you, wasn't it?'

'Sounds very much like it.'

'I don't know which way it went, I'm afraid.'

Time for a few leading questions. 'Did you see the driver?'

'No, sorry.'

'D'you remember a second car? Some distance behind the Golf.'

'Not really.' A pensive frown. 'There was a police car behind it, now you come to mention it. I remember seeing it on the approach to the roundabout, the lights on the roof. There are streetlights there and I could see them over the top of the barrier. He didn't seem in much of a hurry, to be honest, so I don't think he was in pursuit of the Golf.' He placed a mug of coffee on the table in front of me. 'Bloody well should have been.'

'Could you see into the passenger compartment of the patrol car?'

'No, sorry.'

'How far behind the Golf was it?'

'Not far. A couple of hundred yards, maybe.'

'Did the Golf stop at the roundabout?'

'No, he was creeping forwards, waiting to see which way I was going. That's why I indicated, I think, and off he went.'

A patrol car pulling out of the lay-by would have been just about that distance behind the Golf. I don't remember seeing lights on the roof of the car behind Lizzie's, but it would make sense. What better cover could there possibly be? A police officer in uniform stopping to help a young woman in a broken-down car. The immediate trust that follows the blue light wherever it goes. Even Lizzie would have been off her guard.

Until it was too late.

'You look a bit pale, Bob,' said Spalding. 'Are you sure you won't have anything a bit stronger?'

'No, I'm fine, thank you.'

'D'you think your colleague was in the Golf?' he asked.

'No,' I said. 'She was in the boot of the patrol car. Unconscious probably – hopefully.'

Chapter Fifteen

There's one phone box in the village and it takes a sodding card, doesn't it? I've got plenty of change in my pocket but no phone card. I really should get one next time I'm in the post office, not that I'll be going in there for a while.

It's funny how you can forget things, even just for half an hour or so, and then it all comes roaring back.

Poor Alan.

Poor Shirley.

It was nice to meet Spalding at last, though. I knew he'd saved my life by clamping my femoral artery, but I didn't know he'd risked his own life to do so, stopping that lorry before it went over me.

Field and Webster really need to go and see him, get a fresh statement, but I'll have to ring them later.

Terry Greenslade is an owner-driver, which means he could be anywhere. I've seen the lorry out and about on the 303, *Greenslades Transport* emblazoned on the side. You could be forgiven for thinking there was a whole fleet of them, but actually it's just him. Probably lives in it too.

I've got an address in Stocklinch – Yellow Pages, again – that sounds more like a residential address than an office, but what are the chances of finding him at home? Let's hope he's semi-retired. Or better still, bone idle.

Greenslade didn't appear at Martin Clarke's inquest, the coroner having simply read his statement into evidence, so I've got no idea what he looks like. All I know is he drives an articulated lorry for a living and saw bugger all that night.

Still, it's about the slant of the questions, isn't it?

Greenhayes, Stoney Lane, turned out to be a brand new bungalow; clad in that yellow hamstone with a new wall to match, around the front garden. All they needed now was some grass and a few roses around the bay windows either side of the front door; instead they'd got a skip and flattened cardboard boxes leaning up against the wall. Two cars in the drive, though, so maybe he was at home.

The front door was open and I could hear the sound of a drill. There was a hoover going in the front room too, although the woman had her back to the window and hadn't seen me picking my way through the crap in the garden.

It didn't sound as if the doorbell had been wired up yet and knocking hadn't done any good, even on the window, so I edged into the hall.

'Hello?'

There was a plug, the cable going through the open living room door, so I switched it off. That got her attention.

'Hello?'

'What the bloody hell's wrong with this—'

It sounded like she was kicking the hoover, so I poked my head around the door. 'Sorry, that was me,' I said. 'The front door was open; I'm looking for Terry Greenslade.'

'He's in the kitchen, love. And switch that thing back on, will you?'

'Sorry.' A cheery wave and a flick of the switch, the hoover spluttering into life again.

There were a few framed photographs mounted on the wall in the hall, more in the corridor. Some older black and white photographs of a young man in military uniform – old enough to have done his national service then, like me – and more recent ones of an older man, on a Greek island, possibly. Looking up from his newspaper and smiling at the camera. That'll be him.

'I'm looking for Terry Gr—'

'That's me. Give us a hand with this will you, mate.' Greenslade was pushing a dishwasher into position under the kitchen worktop. 'She's been asking for one of these for months,' he said, his voice hushed, even with the hoover still going in the front room. 'There's cardboard underneath, so it won't rip the lino.'

'Sorry, my left elbow's been smashed up,' I said, pushing with one hand.

'No problem.' Greenslade tipped the dishwasher back and pulled out the cardboard from underneath. 'There, that'll keep her happy. For a few days, anyway. Now, what can I do you for?'

He was my age; a bit older, perhaps. Balding and his beard's greyer than mine would be if I let it grow. Bit of a beer belly too. Mine's almost gone now, even with the breakfasts at the Little Chef.

'I wanted to have a chat with you about the incident out on the A303 when Martin Clarke went under your lorry.'

'Oh, that.' Greenslade sighed. 'What are you, police?'

'Detective Inspector Willis. I was the officer struck by the car a few weeks before.'

'Which explains your elbow.'

'It does.'

'Well, look, there's not much I can say, really. I gave a witness statement at the time and it's all in that.'

'I just wanted to understand exactly what you saw on the bridge as you approached.'

Another sigh. 'Let's go in the garden,' he said, gesturing to the open back door. 'I can have a smoke then, without getting earache.'

The back garden had been turfed. I could still see the lines. 'How long have you been here?' I asked. It was certainly long enough for him to have given the address to Yellow Pages.

'Fourteen months. We were in a caravan before that, so we moved in a bit earlier than we should. I've been finishing it off bit by bit; not easy when you drive for a living.'

'I see you out on the A303 from time to time.'

'I do a regular route, Bodmin to Tilbury. Let me tell you, I can't bloody wait for the new M25 to open. It'll take hours off that run.'

'And you own your own lorry?'

'It seemed like a good idea at the time.' Greenslade was sitting on a low wall around a raised flower bed. There were two either side of a path. No flowers in them; not even any soil for that matter. That said, there was a wheelbarrow leaning up against the side of a garage, and a shovel sticking out of a mound of soil on a patch of bare earth behind it, so perhaps that was next on his list.

'Tell me about that night,' I said, watching him lighting a cigarette with a Union Jack lighter.

'Coffee anyone?' A woman's voice from the kitchen.

'Yes, please,' I replied, knowing that he wouldn't be able to get rid of me until I'd drunk it.

'It was the Tilbury run. Later than usual, and I'm out on the A303, eastbound, in the nearside lane. There's a police car in the lay-by beyond the bridge and it looks like he's pulled someone over, the blue light's flashing, you know. Then I see movement up on the bridge. Next thing I know this bloke's falling right in front of me. I didn't even have time to hit the brakes. I went right over him.' Greenslade's eyes glazed over. 'You hear about it happening and I know blokes who've had jumpers in front of their lorries, but fuck me, it's a different kettle of fish when it actually happens and you go over them. You don't feel much, mind you, just a bump really, but you know what it is. They come right down in front of the windscreen.'

'Here you go, love,' said the woman, handing me a mug of coffee. 'Sugar?'

'One, thanks.'

'Where's mine?' asked Greenslade.

'You never said.'

'Marvellous, isn't it.' He looked at me and rolled his eyes.

I could hear the kettle boiling again so thought it best to get the difficult questions in before his coffee arrived. 'Did he jump, or was it an accident and he slipped?'

'They asked me that at the time,' replied Greenslade. 'Whether he jumped in front of my lorry or was trying to jump on to the roof, and I really don't know. I say *at the time*; it was a week or so later when I gave my statement.'

'Really?' I'd not picked up on the date, or maybe the coroner hadn't read it out.

'Yeah, the police officer at the scene had seen everything, he said. Knew I wasn't at fault, so he issued me with a Producer and sent me on my way. That was after the bloke had been pronounced dead at the scene.'

'What did you do then?'

'I went back to the depot, then came home. Rang the Tilbury lot and told them it'd be a few days too. They understood when I explained why.'

'Depot?'

'I keep my rig over at a yard in Ilminster.'

His wife appeared with his coffee, so I waited until she'd gone. 'So, going back to the bridge, what exactly did you see as you approached?'

'Movement, that's all, really. It looked like a figure climbing over the railings. I'm sure I saw a leg coming over, like he was stepping over them, you know.'

'Was there anyone standing behind him?'

Greenslade frowned. 'What d'you mean?'

'Right behind him; pushing him, perhaps.'

'Pushing him?'

'Yes.'

'No, I never saw anything like that.' Greenslade shook his head. 'There was just the bloke climbing over the railings and the police officer further along, running towards him, but he hadn't reached him when he fell.'

'No scuffle on the bridge before he fell?'

'Nothing like that, no. Like I say, I saw movement, and the bloke fell. As for whether he was trying to kill himself or jump on to the roof of my lorry, I really don't know.'

'Which station did you produce your documents at?'

'Ilminster. That's when I gave my statement, within the ten days you've got. I rang and some inspector was waiting for me and I gave the statement at the same time.'

'That should've been me, but I was in hospital, unfortunately.'

'Yeah, I heard about that.' Greenslade took a swig of coffee. 'It sounds a bit of a shitty thing to say, to be honest, but I felt better about it when I found out who he was; what he'd done. Killing those girls like that. Helps me sleep at night, you know.'

'What did you do after the impact?'

'I stopped and ran back, like you do. There's street lighting there, but it's not great. Even so it was obvious he was dead. He'd been under my twelve-wheeler, hadn't he.'

'Who else was there?'

'The police officer had run down the slip road, so he was there, radioing for an ambulance. I seem to remember cars stopping on the other carriageway and a few people milling about, but the officer kept them away. He reversed his patrol car back beyond the scene and parked it across both lanes, lights flashing, but it wasn't long before we heard sirens. They closed the road in both directions, all night, I think.'

'Where were you while all this was happening?'

'He told me to wait in my cab, which I did, until he gave me the Producer and told me to go home. I got to sleep about three in the end, once I'd hosed my lorry off. Slept in the cab, rather than wake her up,' he said, nodding in the direction of the kitchen.

'How long was it until other people started arriving on the scene?'

'A few minutes, maybe. It was late and there wasn't much traffic about.'

'And until then there was just you and the one police officer?'

'Yeah.' He stubbed his cigarette out on the wall and dropped the butt into the bottom of the raised flower bed. 'My next job is to fill this thing.'

'And you're sure there was no one else up on the bridge?'

'I didn't see anyone.'

'Right, well, thank you for your time.'

Mrs Greenslade was leaning against the back door frame, her arms folded. 'Thank you for the coffee, as well,' I said, handing her my empty mug.

'I'll show you out.' Once in the hall, Greenslade tapped me on the shoulder and whispered, 'Is there a problem? I get the impression you think he was pushed, or something?'

'No, it's just me, trying to get my head round it all,' I replied. 'You been away?' I was looking again at the picture of him on holiday somewhere reading a newspaper. 'Looks like a Greek island, possibly?'

'Corfu. You been?'

'A long time ago.'

'I wouldn't want you to think I read the *Guardian*, though.' Greenslade gave a lopsided grin. 'I'm more of a *Sun* and *News of the World* man myself, but it was all they had.'

Chapter Sixteen

We get feelings about people, do police officers. Hunches, you might call them.

I know we're not supposed to, and it leads to exactly the sort of slanted questions that we've talked about already. We *think* a person's guilty, so we slant our questions looking for evidence of that guilt. I like to think I don't do it, but I do.

I've been doing it deliberately this morning, as you know, but I can't get rid of the feeling that somebody has been lying to me. Ask me how I know and I couldn't tell you. I can't tell you who it is, either. I just have that feeling.

The reality is that it's likely to be Greenslade, because I can't believe Paul Spalding would lie about that night. Not to me. But what would Greenslade lie about? And why?

The short answer is I don't know, but I will find out.

One way or the other.

I'm parked outside Sean Taylor's cottage now. Yes, I know where he lives, but only because I've followed him home before. Twice, actually, although I think he saw me the second time. It's a bit of trek from Yeovil and the 303, but we often live outside the area we police, for obvious reasons.

It's a small cottage, just along from The Albert in Street, which is convenient because I can sit outside the pub and watch what's going on. And there *is* something going on.

There's a search team in there, which means Taylor is probably being interviewed right about now.

Maybe Field and Webster aren't as hopeless as I thought. Not all coppers are. Have I said that before?

Leigh Road, Street. Taylor rents it, probably. I know that he stays in the Yeovil police house during the week when he's on duty.

I walked past on the other side of the road, trying to look casual, and the front door is just visible behind a box hedge that could do with a cut. There's parking around the back, by the looks of things. I can see a police van in there. More on the pavement outside. The door of the cottage is standing open and it's tempting, but I mustn't. Really, I mustn't.

I'll just sit here with my Coke and watch all the comings and goings, everything crossed that they actually find something.

How did I know a search warrant had been issued? Don't ask. Suffice it to say, I still have friends.

I've been here two hours and only seen two bags being carried out to the van. There could've been more, I suppose, being optimistic. I'm on my third pint of Coke and have been in and out to the loo.

Now DCS Sharp has arrived though, which doesn't bode well. I can see the front door of the cottage from here and he's leaning in, shouting. I can hear the bellowing, but can't make out what's being said.

Then Webster appears in the front door, looking ashen faced. You can imagine it can't you? *What the fuck are you doing? I told you to clear it with me first.* I thought Webster was handling it quite well, until she pointed at me sitting outside the pub.

Bollocks.

I'll stay put, I think. Even a prick like Sharp won't want a blazing row outside a crowded pub.

'What the fuck are you doing here, Bob?' he demanded, appearing at my table in the small beer garden.

'Would you like a drink, sir?' I asked.

'I thought I'd made it abundantly clear, Bob. Martin Clarke killed Fiona Anderson, Alice Cobb and DS Harper. The case is closed. Which bit of that do you not understand?'

'I don't understand how you can be so fucking stupid.'

'Be very careful, Bob. Your pension is on the line here.'

'I don't give a shit.'

'You're bloody lucky you're not in custody yourself,' said Sharp. 'We had an anonymous tip you were seen in Blagdon at the time Alan Carpenter was murdered. Your ex-wife's new husband.'

'An anonymous tip from Sean Taylor. He framed Martin Clarke and got away with it, so he's got form on that front.' I'll keep the knife he planted in the boot of my car to myself, I think. 'And what about Faith Bennett?'

'We've found no connection with—'

'You've found no connection because you haven't been looking for one,' I said. 'Faith phoned the AA the day she died. And what's the first thing the AA do when a woman alone breaks down by the side of the road?'

'They ring the police for a welfare check,' replied Sharp.

'Her body and her car were both found at home, so it's not connected as far as you're concerned. But it is. Only, her killers drove her car home to make it look different and you fell for it.'

'Have you phoned the AA?'

'Yes.' Actually, just between you and me, that's a lie. I'm taking a bit of a flyer here, guessing that Sharp will check and I'll be proved right. I haven't had a chance to ring the AA yet, or the RAC. It'll be one or the other. If I'm right. 'Whoever killed her knew enough

119

to tidy her house too. I spoke to her parents. And what about the injuries on her chest?'

'Random cuts and stab wounds. It was a frenzied attack.'

'Really.'

Sharp was losing momentum. I've got him on the back foot, but I'm still not telling him about the knife. No way. That's our little secret.

'Have another look at the statement from Paul Spalding,' I said. 'Speak to him again. He was first on the scene the night I got run down. He told me there was a police car behind the car that hit me, he passed them at Podimore. It was about two hundred yards back, not in pursuit. Ask yourself why that might have been.'

'Well, it might've—'

'It would have to have driven past me lying in the road or left the scene to get where it was.'

'A marked police car?'

'A marked police car,' I repeated, for emphasis. 'What about the search?'

'They've found nothing,' replied Sharp. 'We've had Taylor in for most of the afternoon. His story checks out and we've had to let him go. There's nothing. His federation rep is doing his nut.'

'I'll bet he is.'

'You're not going to let this go, are you?'

'No.'

'What am I going to do with you, Bob?'

Chapter Seventeen

It was dark by the time I got back to my flat. All the lights were off and there were no vans when I turned into the yard behind the post office. Blue tape was tied across the railings at the bottom of the steps and I'm guessing there's a 'Crime Scene – Do Not Enter' sticker on the front door.

I'm not entirely sure why I want to go in, really. I should've found a B&B for the night, but forgot. Perhaps it's just that I've got nowhere else to go? It's either that or another night in the car down by the lake. They do rooms at the Seymour, so maybe I'll go up there, park my car around the back.

Pyjamas and a toothbrush it is, then.

I ducked under the tape and tiptoed up the metal steps, just in case a nosy neighbour dialled 999.

Yes, there's a sticker. I'm not sure it applies to me though. I am the resident after all, and nobody's told me I can't go in. Key still fits too.

A cream carpet with flecks of oatmeal in it. Nice. New. The wallpaper was new as well. I closed the door behind me and flicked on the light, stepping over the bloodstain. Actually, there were several of them, one big, the others smaller. There was blood spatter on the wallpaper, more on the right-hand side as I went in, which meant the killer was right-handed; most of the injuries had been to the left side of Alan's chest.

The join is outside the living room door, so I could just roll up the hall carpet and throw it out. I'm sure Shirley won't want to see it. A lick of paint on the wallpaper too. I could even do that myself.

The door to my incident room was standing open, so SOCO have had a good rummage in there. I wouldn't be surprised if Sharp hadn't been for a look too. You can imagine it, can't you?

You need to come and see this, guv.

I've always hated 'guv', although that might be because I've never risen to a rank high enough to get called it, of course.

Lots of grey powder everywhere. Plenty of fingerprints in it, although they'll all be mine. Some might be Shirley's, come to think of it. She popped in and did the washing up the other day.

Poor Alan. I can picture the scene: stocktaking downstairs when he hears a noise in my flat, checks the car park, no Volvo, so he goes to investigate and . . .

Either that or he was deliberately lured upstairs, but the end result was the same.

There was a knock at the door.

Keep calm, Bob. If it was Taylor coming to finish the job, he'd hardly announce his arrival, would he? It's a bit late to switch off the lights too.

I peered around the corner, trying to see who it is out on the landing through the frosted glass.

A deep breath, relief as it happens.

'I know you're in there, Bob. Your car's here,' said the good doctor, knocking again.

Nothing for it.

'Shirley rang me,' said Caroline, when I opened the door. 'Told me what happened.' She was staring at the bloodstains on the carpet behind me. 'She's worried about you.'

'Me?'

Sounds like Shirley, though. Her husband's been murdered and she's worried about me. Yes, I know what I've lost, thanks.

Caroline stepped into the hall, nervously. 'Are we supposed to be in here?' she asked. 'There's a sticker on the door.'

'That doesn't apply to the resident,' I replied. 'And besides, nobody's told me I can't be in here.'

'Apart from the sticker on the door.' Caroline was stepping over the bloodstains. 'Is it safe?'

'While you're here it is. I'm just picking up some stuff, then I'm going to find a B&B.'

'How are you feeling?'

That question again. Everyone wants to know how you're 'feeling' these days. How do you *feel* about this, how do you *feel* about that? I don't. I just get on with it, is the short answer. That is, until I don't get on with it and have a breakdown, I suppose.

'I'm past the point of no return,' I said.

'What's that supposed to mean?'

'Laying my ghosts to rest. It was your idea.'

'And what happened to Shirley's husband is part of that?'

'The ghosts came after me, got him. There was even an attempt to frame me for his murder.'

'How?'

'Don't ask.' I'm starting to trust her, but not that much.

'Grab your stuff and we'll go and have a drink in the pub,' she said. 'I'll feel safer if there are more people around.'

Seems there's no getting out of it, sadly. I've got a Tesco carrier bag in the back of the car with a pair of pyjamas in it – clean, as it happens – a toothbrush, toothpaste and a change of clothes.

Now I'm sitting in a quiet corner of the Seymour Arms, watching Caroline getting the drinks.

'There are no rooms available,' she said, placing a Coke on the table in front of me. 'I think the girl behind the bar may have got the wrong idea, but I soon put her straight, don't worry. You could always come back to mine.' She hastily tagged: 'I've got a spare room' on the end, to see to it I didn't get the wrong idea as well.

'I'll be fine.'

The car park down by the lake it is, then.

'So, tell me what's happened.'

'I gave evidence at Lizzie's inquest,' I replied. 'And the coroner's ordered a fresh investigation. Someone doesn't like it and you know the rest.'

'You were going to tell me about the murder of Alice Cobb,' said Caroline. 'The second girl.'

'I feel a lot better. In control, now I'm actually doing something about it, although the situation is totally out of control. I'm in control of me, if that makes sense.'

'It does. You're clearly in danger, though.'

'That hardly matters.'

'Have you spoken to Lizzie's parents?'

'I have. At the inquest.'

'And what did they say?'

'That they don't blame me at all for what happened. They're furious the inquest was adjourned, mind you, but they don't blame me for her death.'

'There you are then.' She took a sip of her drink. 'Alice Cobb? You need to talk the whole thing through, Bob, even if it's just bit by bit.'

'There's not a lot to tell, really. We got a call from the military police. I went with Lizzie. The body was lying in a rut on a dirt track north of the B390 at Chitterne Down. It's a wild and open part of Salisbury Plain and they'd driven about half a mile off the road. There was a convoy of military vehicles on exercise and the driver of the lead tank had spotted her, thank God.' I folded my arms. 'Do we really have to do this now?'

'Yes.'

'She was lying face down, naked. Forty-one stab wounds this time. The same pattern to them; inflicted before she died. Turned out she was the spitting image of my daughter Joanne.'

'Is she the one who doesn't speak to you?'

'Neither of them speak to me.'

'When this is over you need to sort that out.'

'I know.'

'Go on.'

'We found her car later that day in the lay-by east of the A37 junction.'

'Lizzie's lay-by?'

'It's only a couple of miles from where we found Fiona Anderson's car, so the same hunting ground.'

'Tell me about the boot print.'

'Meaningless. It was a military training area, squaddies trampling everywhere in boots. I said so at the time.'

'And now you're doing something about it?'

'Still haven't got a shred of evidence, though. All I've really learned so far is that I'm not the only one who thinks Martin Clarke had nothing to do with it.'

'Shirley is worried you might be suicidal,' said Caroline, with that concerned look on her face. 'And so am I.'

'I'm not suicidal. I'm going to pursue this to the bitter end, and I don't care what happens to me along the way, but I'm not going to do it myself. They're going to have to kill me.'

Come to think of it, Shirley knows me better than that. At least, I thought she did.

I thought Caroline did too.

◆ ◆ ◆

I know what you're thinking. It's all in his head; he's imagining it.

After Caroline left, I tried ringing Shirley from the payphone on the wall by the gents, but Joanne put the phone down as soon as she heard my voice.

Suicidal?

Shirley knows I'm too much of a coward for that.

I'm starting to wonder now; think all sorts of things. Where did all that crap about being suicidal come from?

Not Shirley. I'd bet my house on it, if I had one.

The number of people I can trust is shrinking fast. Shirley's gone. I'm having my doubts about Caroline now. That leaves . . . no one. Except, maybe, Angela. Coffee mornings and fetes, God help me. I wonder how she's getting on finding similar murders.

Maybe I should go back to work? Then I'd have access to all sorts of databases and records. Sharp would block it, of course; say that I'm not physically fit enough, which is probably right. And if they checked with the good doctor, she'd tell them she thought I was suicidal as well.

That makes my mind up for me about one thing, though. The good doctor and I are done. Finished. Whatever problems I had are behind me, now I've taken control. And that's the way it's going to stay.

I sat it out in the Seymour Arms until last orders and then drove down the lane to the lake. The last anglers are long gone and the lodge is all locked up and dark. Shame that, I could've done with the loo.

It's a clear night, moonlit, and the black and white timber-framed building seems to glow in the dark. The lake is calm, not a ripple to be seen. No fish about either, nothing rising.

I'm sitting in my car in the far corner of the car park, under the trees, the engine ticking over to keep the heaters going without draining the battery. It may look nice out there, but it's oddly cold for late May.

I can hear an owl hooting in the trees behind me, a fox barking in the distance. He's on the other side of the reservoir, I reckon. Apart from that, there's not a soul about.

I've got the doors locked, to be on the safe side. You know how it is. The window is open a crack too, otherwise I get terrible condensation. Sleeping in a car is all well and good, but it's bloody uncomfortable. I should've got the estate version, then there'd be room to stretch out in the back if I put the seats down.

It's no good, I'm going to have to pee. Too much bloody Coke. People keep telling me I've reached that age.

I'm watching a badger down by the lake. He came out of the trees behind the lodge and is rooting about in the long grass at the water's edge. More appear, until there are two large and three small; parents and cubs. It's that time of year, after all.

Sorry, but I'm going to have to ruin your evening.

I switched on the headlights and opened the car door, sending them darting into the undergrowth.

The bush behind my car will do. Needs must, and all that.

I was mid-stream when I saw the movement, heard the thud, pain exploding across my forehead. I fell backwards, on to the boot of my car, pissed myself. I could feel the warmth on my leg.

Then it all went black.

Chapter Eighteen

I'm sitting in water. My trousers are soaked. My head hurts. I'm alive, though, so that's something.

I can't see anything, but it takes me a moment to realise my eyes are closed. I can't open them for some reason, so lift my hand to check for a blindfold.

That's right. It's coming back to me now. Someone or something hit me. Or someone hit me with something; that'll be it.

My hands are cold. Wet. My legs are cold too.

I pissed myself. I remember that.

I can hear running water now, trickling; my senses slowly returning one by one.

There's a gash on my forehead. Feels a nasty one – deep – so that'll be congealed blood in my eyes. I cup my hands and bring water up to my face, rubbing my eyelids with my fingertips. They still won't open, so I try again. And again.

What the fuck is this water? And where is it coming from?

It's dark. There's a steering wheel in front of me. A familiar shape, so I'm in my car, sitting in the driver's seat. Must be.

Think, Bob.

I reach for the door handle and try to open it. Won't budge, even with my shoulder to it. I fumble for the popper; it's up, so why the fuck won't the door open?

Fighting the panic that's rising in the pit of my stomach.

Breathe, Bob. Breathe.

The water's up to my belly button now, so it must be rising too.

I can see my hand in front of my face, but not a lot else. Squinting into the darkness, there's a strange glow above, shimmering. It's moving too, swirling. And there are bubbles, rising.

Fuck, fuck, fuck.

I'm sitting in my fucking car under water. I knew they were coming for me, those bastards, and this is it.

Taylor.

You'll have to do better than this.

The passenger compartment is filling up and I can't open the door.

Blagdon Lake, most likely. It's fresh – I know, I've tasted it – so it must be, and I was parked fifty yards from the water's edge, for fuck's sake.

It took me a minute, but I got there in the end. Now, I've just got to get out.

Keep calm and think, Bob. There's time. At this rate, perhaps five minutes.

Everyone will think it was suicide, won't they? Poor old Bob couldn't take it anymore and drove his car into the lake; drowned himself. The gash on my forehead will be where I hit the steering wheel, which explains why they didn't put my seatbelt on. A nice touch that.

Think!

Rainbow Point is the obvious spot to get a car into the water; a gate and then a grass bank down to the edge of the lake. I probably floated a few yards out before I sank, which means I'm in about ten feet of water. The reservoir was full the last time I went fishing and it's rained since then. Crystal clear, which explains why I can see moonlight above, flickering on the surface, the ripples coming from the air bubbles escaping.

My watch is still working. Good old Timex. I got it free with Green Shield Stamps.

It's just before two. The first boats won't be out until just after eight, but bank anglers sometimes arrive before dawn and Rainbow Point is a popular spot. Sunrise is about five at the moment, so three hours at best.

I haven't got that long, have I?

What it does mean though is that Taylor is probably long gone. I hope so, because if he's watching from the bank, I'm in deep shit.

I wonder who else. There's no way he could have done this on his own.

So, here I am. Sitting in my car in Bristol's water supply. I apologise in advance if I crap myself.

It's up to my chest now, but there's still time and I'm going to wait it out. That's right, until the last minute. Just in case they're still waiting out there. I don't want them to see me bobbing up, gasping for air, do I?

Is that Bob, bobbing up?

Fuck off.

Funny, the things you think of at a time like this. Fucking Green Shield Stamps!

I just have to hope they're long gone. I would be. After all, as far as they're concerned, I'm unconscious and the old bus must've sunk fifteen minutes ago at this rate. Yes, they'll have run back to their cars and got the hell out of here, probably when my car hit the water.

Nice and calmly does it, Bob. You know you can get out when the time comes, so take a deep breath and wait.

I can remember the conversation with the salesman as if it were yesterday.

'It's a very nice car, sir,' he said. 'Low mileage. One owner; full service history. There's this one though, it's just a little bit more expensive. But it does have electric windows.'

'I don't want electric windows,' I replied. 'It's just more to go wrong, isn't it?'

The key's in the ignition, so I try the windscreen wipers. Nothing. The electrics are the first thing to go when a car goes into water.

You can always open manual windows, though. Just crank the handle and away you go.

Electric windows, my arse.

That said, finding myself under water wasn't exactly top of my list. It was more about the cost of putting the bloody things right if and when they went wrong.

I'm breathing deeply now, getting ready for the last one, the big one, when I go for it. I'll have to be nice and quiet, just in case. No splashing about. I should be able to open the door once the pressure has equalised inside and out, but I can slide out of the window, if not. You never know with this newfangled central locking business.

The bubbles have stopped rising now.

If they had waited then they'd go now, surely? Now they think all the air is out of the car.

And I'm dead.

Actually, there is air left. An inch or so trapped in the top of the passenger compartment. I'm kneeling on the driver's seat, my head tipped back, face pressed to the inside of the roof, sucking in the last of it.

Time to go, I think.

A deep breath, hold it, then I duck down and begin winding down the driver's window. It's already under water so no air escapes to alert anyone on the bank.

I roll on to my back, both hands on the roof, and pull myself out into open water. A couple of kicks with my feet and I'm rising. I might even be able to stand on the roof of the car, if I'm lucky.

I break the surface gently, just my eyes at first and I can't see anyone there. I can see the bank of Rainbow Point, tyre tracks in the grass down to the water's edge.

Now inhale. Silently. Not that my lungs are bursting. I couldn't really claim that. It's only been a few seconds, after all.

I'm reaching down with my feet trying to find the roof of the car, but can't. Sod it. The real Bob Willis could, I bet, but then he's a good deal taller than me.

Swimming now, towards an area of gravel where I can climb out without leaving tracks.

Taylor thinks I'm dead. So, let's keep it that way, shall we?

My left leg hurts like buggery, and my left elbow. It's the cold water, I think, although kneeling on the seat didn't help. I bloody well felt that. My head hurts too.

I've run my fingers over the gash in my forehead and it feels deep. There are flaps of skin, so it'll probably need stitches, knowing my luck. The bleeding's stopped though, which is something, but I had hoped to avoid a hospital visit.

I'm guessing Taylor has headed back over the Mendips. That's the way I'd go if I were him, less chance of being seen. So, I'm going in the opposite direction and I'm following the footpath around the lake, heading north. Getting across the dam at the bottom of the lake was a bit nervy; nowhere to hide and I'm not exactly light on my feet these days. It's more of a hobble than a run, but there was no one about, no lights anyway, so I was soon across and back into the trees on the far side.

I've never walked this path before, but I've seen plenty of dog walkers using it when I've been out on a boat. It's narrower than I thought, with tree stumps in dark and unlikely places.

I've got to get clear before dawn, assuming my car is found then, which makes stopping for a rest not really an option.

I'm heading for the village of Butcombe. There's a phone box by the church and one person left I can call.

Chapter Nineteen

There's a brand new bench in the churchyard at Butcombe, but I'm sitting on the old one. It's been dumped around the back, out of sight.

Ideal.

I can hear sirens in the distance, away to the south. I'm guessing my car's been spotted. The first anglers of the day at Rainbow Point would've seen the tyre tracks in the grass, wouldn't they? Not difficult to guess the rest.

Oddly enough, I was largely dry by the time I reached Butcombe. Thankfully the phone box was working and now I'm waiting for Angela to get here. That's right, Angela was the one call I could still make, although it was a bit of a struggle getting past her father. He seemed keen to know why a man of my age would be ringing a girl of her age at this time in the morning.

It was just before six, so perhaps that's fair enough. And I do have a track record of getting his daughters killed, don't I?

Anyway, Angela's on her way and I'm struggling to stay awake, although the pain is helping with that. My left leg is banging after all that walking. And then there's my head. I got no sleep at all last night, although I must've been unconscious for about an hour. Does that count?

I tried the church, but it's locked, which is a shame. Stretching out on a pew sounds lovely right about now, but I'll have to make do with this mouldy old park bench. At least it's not raining.

'Are you all right?'

Someone is prodding my shoulder. A girl's voice.

'Bob?'

I must've nodded off, but it's Angela, thankfully.

'Not really.'

'There were fire engines and all sorts going down to the lake. What's happened?'

I gestured to my forehead. 'They knocked me out, sat me in my car and pushed it into the lake.'

'How did you get out?'

'The cold water woke me up, the manual windows let me out.'

'That looks nasty,' she said, reaching out to touch my forehead, although I recoiled before she was able to. 'You should get that checked out at hospital.'

'No hospital. We can get some of those butterfly things at a chemist and put a dressing on it.' I puffed out my cheeks. 'I'm more concerned about getting some headache pills, to be honest.'

Angela sat down next to me. 'Who was it?'

'Never saw them,' I replied.

You and I both know who it was; one of them anyway.

My eyes are closing and she's prodding me again.

'Don't go to sleep,' she said. 'Not here. At least get in the back of my car.'

'There are some B&Bs on the seafront at Burnham. There'll be a chemist too.'

There were no boats out on the lake when we crossed the dam ten minutes later; fishing cancelled for the day, probably. In the distance, there was a fire engine down by the water's edge at Rainbow Point; several vans and an ambulance; putting divers in the water, I expect, looking for a body.

My body.

Then they'll get a local farmer to tow my car out with a tractor.

No doubt they'll check with the good doctor too, and be told I was suicidal.

Police cars in the middle of Blagdon again, officers at the top of the steps to my flat, banging on the door for a welfare check. *I'm fine, thanks*, I thought, as I ducked down in the passenger seat of Angela's Allegro.

It's got manual windows, in case you were wondering. That was the first thing I looked for.

We got some strange looks when we checked into the B&B. I did, anyway. I think the bloke thought I'd done well for myself.

'She's my daughter,' I said.

'Oh, right.' He looked almost disappointed; didn't notice Angela stifling a chuckle either.

'I'm just going to nip to the chemist,' she said.

'Butterfly stitches, the big plasters or dressings, and some antiseptic.'

'And headache pills, I know.'

I looked at the bloke, tried a guilty smile. 'I had a few too many last night and fell flat on my face.'

I gave a false name, paid cash. It was a good job Angela had some; mine would have to dry out on the radiator. First on the right, at the top of the stairs. I left the door on the latch, slumped down on to the bed and closed my eyes.

◆　◆　◆

TCP. She bought TCP.

The bloody smell will follow me around for days. And it stings like I don't know what.

Turns out she's squeamish too, so I had to do the butterfly stitches myself in the mirror. I mustn't grumble, though. Angela remembered the painkillers and some big plasters.

'I got you a toothbrush and toothpaste, some disposable razors and a can of shaving foam. Doughnuts too,' she said. 'There's a bakery just round the corner. Some with jam and some without.' She's standing by the window, waiting for the small kettle to boil, the string of a teabag hanging over the side of each of the two mugs on the tray. 'It's that UHT milk, I'm afraid.'

'I'll have mine black in that case.' I'm sitting on the bed, eyes closed, waiting for the headache pills to kick in. It's a moment to take stock, which is never a good idea at the best of times.

I'm beginning to think I've bitten off a bit more than . . . you get the picture. Not that I had a lot of choice. Faith Bennett's murder was connected. I can see it, even if that fucking idiot Sharp can't. It's not about me and my ghosts anymore. It's about stopping killers who are still out there.

Still killing.

Actually, it would have been far easier to have walked away; let someone else sort it out. Alan would still be alive if I'd done that. I know that much and will have to make my peace with Shirley when this is all over. That's assuming I live through it, which at the moment seems to be anyone's guess.

Next time they might be less worried about making it look like suicide.

Funny that the good doctor popped up when she did, worried that I might be suicidal. Don't you think?

It's been a long night and I've thought a lot about that, as you might imagine. I'm going to give her the benefit of the doubt. Someone put the idea in her head and she came to look for me out of genuine concern for a patient.

Or am I a client? I never know. Hardly matters.

What matters is that the alternative is too horrible to contemplate – that she's part of a wider conspiracy to get rid of me. Kept me up all night, that did.

Among other things.

So, Taylor and his accomplice are still out there, thinking I'm dead, and you and I both know what that means.

They'll let the dust settle and then kill again.

And again.

Until someone stops them.

'What's it like when a car goes into water?' asked Angela, just as I was drifting off to sleep.

'Frightening,' I replied.

'Does it float to begin with?'

'Do you mind if we change the subject?'

'No, sorry.' A nervous laugh. 'I am a journalist,' she said.

Social events and coffee mornings, I know, but I resisted the temptation to remind her. Everyone's got to start somewhere, haven't they?

'How are you getting on looking for similar murders?' I asked.

Angela placed a cup of tea on the bedside table next to me and then retreated to the seat in the bay window overlooking the seafront. I say *retreated* – that's what it looked like. As if she wanted to be out of reach.

'Yeah, not very well, I'm afraid,' she said. 'Ray found out; wanted to know what I was looking for, and why.'

'Who's Ray?' I can guess, but asked anyway.

'Ray Keenan. He's the crime reporter on the *County Gazette*. I rang him when I nipped to the chemist and he's over at Blagdon, covering the story of the car in the lake.'

'There can't be anything interesting going on at Bristol Crown Court today then.'

'He had a tip it was your car, so . . .'

'What did you tell him?'

'Just that you'd asked me to look for similar cases, the pattern in the stab wounds; the Maltese cross thing. He said he'd have a look, maybe ring round a few contacts, and let me know.'

'Has he found anything?'

'Not sure. I haven't spoken to him.'

A sip of black tea. Disgusting. 'See if you can get hold of him,' I said, gesturing to the phone on the bedside table while I rummaged in the bag for a doughnut. Not exactly a slap-up lunch, but it would have to do.

I watched her dial the number on the push-button phone. All mod cons in this B&B, which explains the four stars. It'll soon be time for the *News at One*, which we'll be able to watch in colour.

'Hi Ruth, it's Ang. Has Ray rung in yet?'

I'm only getting Angela's end of the conversation, but it's not hard to fill in the blanks.

'When he does, can you get him to ring me?' She put her hand over the mouthpiece. 'Can I give him this number?' she whispered.

I nodded.

'Yeah, the number is . . .'

I was drifting off at that point. We might get a call, we might not. He might have found something, he might not. I won't know until he rings back, and until then there's nothing else to do except catch up on lost sleep.

'He's what?' Angela clicked her fingers at me. 'He's just walked in,' she said. 'Put him on, Ruth.'

I sat up.

'I'm over at Burnham-on-Sea, Ray,' said Angela. 'Have you found any similar cases?' She's listening, nodding. 'Yeah, like we talked about . . . You have?' She looked at me, her eyes wide. 'Where am I?'

'Tell him.'

'In the Estuary View guesthouse on the seafront. Can you come? Yes, now. It'll be worth your while, I guarantee it. You'll see when you get here. Good, just don't tell anyone.'

She hung up, looked at me and smiled. 'He's coming,' she said. 'Be about an hour and a half. He's just got to file his report from this morning.'

Chapter Twenty

The phone ringing woke me up.

'Oh, yes, thank you. Send him up.' Angela's voice.

It seems I'm about to meet the crime reporter from the *County Gazette*. A quick check in the mirror for blood soaking through the plaster on my forehead and I dropped into the armchair in the window. I don't want him finding me in bed, that's for sure, even if I do look like I've just crawled out of it.

He was tall, heavyset, likes his beer; about my age; wearing one of those waxed jackets with a corduroy collar that matches his trousers.

'Bloody hell,' he muttered. 'I've spent all morning at Blagdon Lake and I've just filed a report on the search for your body. They're out there now, dragging the lake.' He was glaring at Angela, rather than me, which seemed a bit harsh. It was hardly her fault. 'They've got divers in there and everything.'

'Have they got my car out yet?' I asked.

'Yes, they bloody well have, and you weren't in it.'

'Manual windows,' I said, with an apologetic smile.

'You changed your mind about suicide then?' he asked.

'It wasn't suicide,' I said, gesturing to my forehead. 'Somebody whacked me on the head, sat me in my car and pushed it into the water.' I thought suicide would be the assumption, though. Lazy.

'Who?'

'Not yet.'

'When?'

'When this is over I'll give you an exclusive.'

'It's got something to do with Sergeant Harper's death. I saw your performance at her inquest.' He took a handheld tape machine out of his bulging jacket pocket, pressed the record button, and placed it on the coffee table in front of me. 'You said the murder of Faith Bennett was connected.'

I leaned forward, switched it off, then took the batteries out. 'Not yet.'

Keenan sighed, sat down on the edge of the bed.

'Has there been any progress in the Faith Bennett investigation?' I asked.

'Not that they've told us,' he replied. 'There's only been the one press conference, the morning after her body was found.' Keenan frowned. 'D'you think her murder is connected to the others? Fiona Anderson and Alice Cobb?'

'I do, and somebody did this to me because of it.'

That's all I'm saying, for now; enough to keep him interested. He seems all right, but he's a journalist, first and foremost. And I learned a long time ago, there's no such thing as 'off the record', not with a crime reporter and certainly not when you're a police officer. We're fair game. Angela is different, of course. But then, first and foremost, she's Lizzie's sister.

'You said you'd found another case, Ray,' said Angela. She was standing with her back to the door, leaning on it.

'Easter, 1981,' he replied, sliding a notebook from his other pocket. 'A young woman was found dead in Clondara Terrace. It's off the Falls Road in Belfast. She was naked, multiple stab wounds. No one was ever prosecuted for it and there's very little detail available. I had a call from a journalist at the *Belfast Telegraph* and he said the locals have always thought British soldiers did it, but it's never been proven. Just "swept under the carpet", that was the phrase he used.'

Easter 1981 had a familiar ring to it. 'Wasn't that during the hunger strike riots?' I asked.

'That's it.' Keenan was flicking through the pages of his notebook. 'Bogside went up in Londonderry, Belfast too. Pretty much all weekend. Petrol bombs, shots were fired. The Anglian Regiment took the brunt of it in Londonderry and the Royal Green Jackets were on duty in Belfast.'

'Any pattern to the stab wounds?'

'I couldn't find any real detail on it at all. Newspaper reports at the time said a cross had been carved on her chest, but there's no mention of that in the official reports. My contact in Belfast couldn't find anything either, which is what made it stand out, to be honest.'

'How about a name?'

'Bernadette Ryan,' replied Keenan. 'There are still Ryans listed in the phonebook at an address in Clondara Terrace. According to my contact, it's believed two British soldiers became separated from their battalion during the rioting, took refuge in the house, and there she was. You don't need a vivid imagination to work out what happened after that.'

'Pretty much the same as what happened to Fiona Anderson, Alice Cobb, Lizzie, and Faith Bennett.'

'Five murders,' mumbled Keenan.

'Six,' I said. 'Martin Clarke was thrown off that bridge over the A303.'

'You'll never prove that.'

'Probably not.'

'Are you going to Belfast?' asked Keenan. 'I'll come with you, if you are.'

143

'An Englishman walking down the Falls Road.' Rubbing my stubble now. I'll need a shave before I go anywhere. And some sleep. 'You're a braver man than I am.'

'Yeah, maybe you're right.' Keenan puffed out his cheeks. 'Perhaps not.'

'So, what happens now?' asked Angela.

'I need some sleep,' I replied. 'A shower, a shave and a change of clothes. I'll worry about it then. In the meantime, whoever tried to kill me thinks I'm dead, and I'd be grateful if it stayed that way.'

'No one will hear it from me,' said Keenan.

'Or me.'

I smiled at Angela. A good kid. 'You'd better go back to work.'

'I rang in sick.'

I stood up, ushering them both to the door. 'You go. I really need some sleep.'

I'm standing in the bay window now, watching Angela running across the road to her Allegro. Keenan had parked in the car park right below my window and was already on his way.

I know. I lied. The shower and a shave bit was true, there's time before the taxi gets here. The fastest way to Belfast is by air and there'll be plenty of time to sleep on the plane.

It turned out there wasn't that long to sleep on the plane. I had longer on the train, getting to the airport, but didn't get much sleep then either. I had a bit of fun at the check-in, though.

'Passport,' said the woman at the desk.

'I don't need one,' I replied. 'It's an internal flight.'

'You need ID.'

'I've got my driving licence.'

I lied to Taylor; always have it on me. It's got the old address on it, but she doesn't need to know that. It's a bit crumpled too, and still feels slightly damp, but it did the trick.

Now I'm in a taxi on my way to the Regency Hotel. The taxi driver recommended it. I'm checking in to a hotel for two reasons. First, there are no flights home tonight, so I'll need somewhere to sleep, and second, someone might miss me if I disappear. It happens a lot in Northern Ireland.

'There's an RUC checkpoint on the way in, so I hope you've got your story straight,' said the taxi driver. His Irish accent is about as broad as they come, but he knows I'm English and is making an effort.

.'I'm visiting friends,' I said.

'Who's that then?' he asked. 'I might know 'em.'

'The Ryan family. They live on Clondara Terrace.'

'Are you sure about that?'

No, is the short answer to that question. Far from it. I'm watching the fields flashing by out of the window, lights in the distance just visible through the gloom. He's got the fans going, and the windscreen wipers are hard at it too.

I know how this works. And the risk I'm taking. An English ex-police officer knocking on a door in a Catholic part of town. A house where two British soldiers murdered the daughter. Hopefully, I'll have time to emphasise the *ex* bit of ex-police officer. Retired. Former.

'You do know that's a Catholic area?' The taxi driver is studying me in his rear view mirror, a look of concern on his face. If I didn't know better I'd think I was on my way to the gallows. 'Checkpoint coming up,' he said, before I had a chance to reply.

We're in a queue now, creeping forwards, officers from the Royal Ulster Constabulary scrutinising papers, searching cars. Did I say they were heavily armed? Well, they are.

'A couple of lads out joyriding tried to run one of these check-points a couple of months back,' offered the taxi driver. 'Just kids, they were. Shot them, so they did. Killed one. Shoot first, ask questions later, these bastards.'

'Just kids?'

'Aye.' He shakes his head. 'I wouldn't mention the Ryan family, if I were you. Tell them you're sightseeing, or something.'

I was ahead of him there. The RUC would've investigated the murder of Bernadette Ryan, been complicit in the decision to sweep it under the carpet, and the last thing they're going to want is someone like me raking it all up again. I've spent the last few days wishing I still had my warrant card, but I'm glad I haven't got it now.

A tap on the window. 'Get out of the car.'

'Better do as he says,' said the taxi driver.

There's a machine gun slung over the officer's shoulder and a pistol in a holster on his hip. He's wearing a flak jacket, although it's called body armour these days. 'Identification,' he said.

My driving licence. It's getting wet again, in the rain.

'State your business.'

'Sightseeing.'

A quizzical look, then he hands me back my driving licence. 'Wait here,' he said before disappearing into the guard post. It's concrete, with steel shutters over the windows and barbed wire. Lots of barbed wire. A telephone too. I can see the cable.

Two of them this time.

'You're a police officer.'

'Oh, for fuck's sake,' hissed the taxi driver, turning away.

'I was. I'm retired now, on medical grounds.'

'Retired?'

'Yes. I'm not here on official business,' I said. And it's true. I'm not. I'm here on unofficial business, which is entirely different.

'Sightseeing?' The sergeant is standing with his hand on his pistol. 'What sights?'

'I want to see where the *Titanic* was built.'

'The dockyards?'

'I'm a bit of a *Titanic* buff.' Actually, I'm not. I did see *A Night to Remember* once, so that'll have to do.

'You keep your wits about you, wandering about down there,' said the sergeant. 'They'll have the shirt off your back, without you even noticing it's gone.'

'Thank you. I'll do that,' I replied.

'On your way,' said the sergeant to the taxi driver. And we were, in double-quick time, accelerating into the night; putting on his seatbelt and changing up through the gears at the same time.

He's glancing at me in the rear view mirror again, a different look on his face this time. Seething. I can see that much even through his beard. He's got questions and I know they're coming. It's just a matter of where and when.

The lights of Belfast are up ahead now, that familiar orange glow you get when you're approaching a city at night: the lights of the houses on the outskirts; tower blocks climbing into the night sky. We slow for a hairpin bend, then turn sharp left off the main road.

Here we go.

He screeches to a halt in a lay-by on the nearside, pulls on his handbrake and turns in his seat. 'You never said you were a police officer.'

'You didn't ask.'

'Have you got any idea where you're asking me to take you? Who it is you're going to see?'

147

'The family of Bernadette Ryan. She was murdered in 19—'

'Everybody knows who Bernadette Ryan was, and who killed her. Look, if I take you down there, I'm responsible for you. As far as *they're* concerned, *I'm* responsible. So, I need to know why you're here.'

I can guess who *they* are.

'I'm not losing my fucking kneecaps for you; taking a feckin' gobshite police officer to their door. And a fucking Englishman at that. Jeez. That'll teach me to do a late airport run. Fuck.'

You get a feeling about someone. I do, anyway. Either I trust them or I don't, and I tend to make my mind up fairly quickly on that score. There are times, though, when I don't have a lot of choice, and this is one of those occasions. An extra risk I hadn't planned on taking, but needs must.

'I'm looking for the men who killed Bernadette,' I said. 'I'm not looking for anyone else in connection with anything else. Just Bernadette's killers. It's my belief that the same men killed my partner and three young women in Somerset. They nearly killed me too, which is why I'm being retired on medical grounds.'

'*Being*, so you're still police?'

'Technically.'

'And what the fucking hell d'you think Seamus Ryan's going to do when he gets his hands on you?'

'Her brother?'

'Aye.'

'I'm hoping he's going to tell me what he knows about her murder, then let me go and catch her killers.'

'Jesus, Mary and Joseph, it's the thing you dread, isn't it.' The taxi driver takes a deep breath, exhales long and slow.

He has got a name, but it's on the licence and I can't see it from here. He's got a name badge too, pinned on his pullover, but I can't see that either. Shame, really. If we're going to be buried in a shallow grave together, I'd like to have known his name. 'D'you know Seamus Ryan?' I asked.

'Everybody knows Seamus. And Seamus knows everybody,' he replied. 'He'll know you're in my fucking taxi by now.'

'Sorry.'

'You weren't to know.' I can hear him sucking his teeth, his mouth dry, probably. Mine is. 'All right. I'll take you there. Clondara Terrace,' he said. 'It's number three, just down from the Falls Road. The mother's decent enough. She'll tell you what you need to know, if she thinks you're trying to find the bastards who killed her daughter.' He's doing a three-point turn in the lane. 'Just let me do the talking.'

'Hotel first,' I said. 'I need to check in.'

Chapter Twenty-One

The Falls Road looks very different these days, although I'm seeing it from the back of a taxi at night. It's late, but not too late for a house call.

This is my first trip to Northern Ireland, so I've only ever seen it on the TV news, and then it's been reports of riots. Gangs of youths in paramilitary balaclavas throwing petrol bombs at soldiers and RUC officers. Cars on fire, rubber bullets; you can picture the scenes, I'm sure.

Then there are the bombings. The last big one had been the Brighton bomb in October.

The burnt-out cars have gone and there are people going about their business, dog walkers even. The streetlights are working, too, so I can see the murals on the gable end walls of the terraced side streets. Too many to mention, although one sticks in my mind: a figure wearing a black balaclava and combat jacket, pointing a gun at me. That's what it felt like, anyway.

You can imagine what I'm thinking, can't you? My life is in the hands of a taxi driver, and I don't even know the bloke's name.

'What's your name?' I asked.

'Fintan,' he replied. 'Fintan Ryan. Seamus is my cousin.'

'Small world,' I said.

'Belfast is a small place. And I've got twelve cousins.'

'Big families. I've got two kids and one grandson.' He doesn't need to know they don't speak to me anymore. I want him to know I've got a family, though. It might make them slightly less inclined to kill me.

'I don't know him that well, either, so don't go thinking I've got any influence over him. No one has.'

'Right.' I give an idle nod, not that he can see it. 'Does he live at Clondara Terrace?'

'God, no.'

'Did you know Bernadette?'

'Everybody knew Bernadette.'

Slowing down, indicating a right turn. The street signs look new; high up, out of reach.

Clondara Terrace.

He parks outside the second house on the left. 'You wait here,' he said.

There are a few kids about, a cat sitting on a windowsill opposite. It's just before ten and there are lights on in most of the houses. Net curtains are twitching, but all seems quiet. I'm staying alert, checking in the rear view mirror and the wing mirror for movement. Not that there's much I could do about it, anyway.

The rear doors open, sharply, and a figure jumps in next to me on the vacant passenger seat. Another on the nearside, pushing me into the middle. Jeans, black pullovers, balaclavas.

'What have we got here, then,' said the smaller one on my left.

It's a broad Irish accent, but young. Slightly built too, so I'm hoping it's a teenager. They're not armed, not that I can see anyway; certainly not brandishing anything.

There was a time I'd have used my elbows, but that's out of the question now.

'I'm with Fintan,' I said, glancing up at the house, hoping for any sign of movement inside.

'He's English,' said the other. 'Fucking English.'

The car is surrounded now, people banging on the roof. Kids, I think.

'What are you doing here?'

'Give us your money.'

Then it stops, just as quickly as it started; the sound of running, youths scattering in all directions.

'You two, get out.'

The voice is deep, Irish; the man large.

'I think he means you,' I said.

They do as they're told, slowly climbing out of the car, their heads bowed. Definitely kids, now I see them in the wing mirror standing next to an adult.

'Now, fuck off.'

I get it now. I was in the hotel long enough for Fintan to make the call, and there was a phone box on the corner. Covering his own arse.

Can't say I blame him.

No balaclavas this time, which I'm sensible enough to know is not a good sign. There's no harm in me seeing their faces if they're going to kill me anyway, is there?

There are three of them. I'm guessing it's Seamus who has jumped into the rear passenger seat next to me. Dressed in black, he's wearing a balaclava, but it's rolled up so it just looks like a woolly hat. Dark glasses and there's a big scar down his cheek, but the internal light's gone off again now the driver's door has closed. It looked like a burn, I think.

The two in the front are keeping their backs to me.

'An English peeler.' I can see his teeth, but I can't tell if it's a smile or a smirk. 'All alone in Belfast. What are we going to do with you?'

'I'm investigating the murder of your sister, Bernadette,' I said.

The movement was sharp, well-rehearsed, and now there's a gun barrel pressed to my left temple. I just have to hope he doesn't really want to make a mess in his cousin's taxi. I'm oddly calm, though, accepting of my fate. I'll either get out of this alive, or I won't. And I don't really mind either way, as you know.

I tell myself that, anyway.

'You've got some front, coming here,' said Seamus. 'Or a fucking death wish.'

'It's my belief that the same men have killed again.'

'We made a few phone calls, checked up on you. You're off sick, and you're supposed to be dead anyway; drowned yourself in a lake. Gives us a free pass, doesn't it, boys?'

Laughter all round, although I can't see the joke, myself.

There's a shaft of light illuminating the passenger compartment now and I can see the gun; a revolver of some sort. Then the rear passenger door is snatched open from the outside.

'Seamus Ryan, you let that man in this house, this minute.' A woman's voice, shrill. It's clearly an order and he obeys, albeit reluctantly. His mother, must be. 'Fintan says he's trying to find who killed our Bernadette. And leave that bloody gun in the car. I won't have guns in my house. Not now, not ever.'

'Yes, Ma.' Seamus turns to me. 'You, out.'

I'll speak when I'm spoken to, I think. Don't want to get carried away.

Literally.

The front doorstep is clean, recently painted that dark shade of red. It's frighteningly similar to Faith Bennett's farm cottage on the edge of South Petherton. Two-up, two-down; the bathroom on the ground floor in an extension beyond the kitchen. Wider, possibly; so, three-up maybe.

There's a large framed picture mounted on the wall over the fireplace: a teenage girl, flowing black hair, rosy cheeks and a big

153

smile. She's wearing what looks like a hand-knitted pullover, with flowers on it; a crucifix around her neck on a beaded chain. A single candle is burning on the mantelpiece beneath the picture. I say *picture*; I can't actually tell whether it's a painting or a photograph.

'That's our Bernadette,' said Fintan, my taxi driver. He's standing by the electric fire when I'm ushered into the living room.

'She was my daughter,' said Seamus's mother.

'What do I call you?' I asked.

'You don't.'

'My name's Mungo Willis,' I said. 'But everybody calls me Bob, after the cricketer.' Worth a try, but I'm not expecting it to break the ice this time. 'I've got two daughters—'

'Don't you tell me you know what I've been through. Don't you dare tell me that.' She's a small woman, her hair grey, piercing eyes fixed on me as she twists a rosary necklace around her fingers. 'I'm only grateful my husband wasn't here to see it.'

'Is he dead?'

'He is now,' she replied. 'He was in the Maze back then.' She kisses the tips of her fingers, reaches up and plants them on Bernadette's lips. 'She was my baby. The youngest.'

'You said the same men who killed Bernadette have killed again.' Seamus is standing in the doorway, his hands in his pockets. 'Where?'

'Somerset,' I replied. 'On the A303. Young women whose cars have broken down.'

'How many?'

'Four. It made national news, so you may have seen it?'

'Yeah, we saw that,' said Seamus. 'He's dead. They got him.'

'They didn't. An innocent man was framed. Murdered, which makes five.'

'How d'you know that?'

'Another young woman was killed last week.' It's going to be tricky, this. Getting the information I need, without giving too much away. Normally, I'd be the one asking the questions, but they're going to have a few of their own.

'Why did you try to kill yourself?' asked the mother.

'I didn't. They tried to kill me.'

'They know you're on to them, then?'

'They've changed their method,' I said. 'And she died before they were able to . . .' I let my voice tail off. It's too much detail for Bernadette's mother; she may know already, but she may not. 'Tell me what happened to Bernadette.'

'She was here on her own,' replied the mother. 'I'd gone to see my sister; Seamus and his brothers were out. There was a riot going on out there,' she said, gesturing in the direction of the Falls Road. 'About half a mile that way. Two soldiers—'

'Royal Green Jackets,' interrupted Seamus.

'—got separated from their company, ran this way and into the alley behind.'

'I'll tell him, Ma,' said Seamus, when tears began to trickle down his mother's cheeks.

She sits down in the armchair, gazing up at the picture of Bernadette.

'They came over the gate at the back and then broke in,' continued Seamus. 'One had been hit by a brick, apparently, and they were probably just looking for somewhere to hide, but instead they found Bernadette, here on her own.'

More detail could wait until Seamus's mother was out of earshot. 'Was there an investigation?'

'The RUC are a useless bunch of bastards,' muttered Seamus. 'You can be sure it would have been different if she'd been Protestant, mind. They'd have left no stone unturned then.' He was standing with his hand on his mother's shoulder now. 'As soon as they found out it was British soldiers, they dropped it. The Green Jackets were moved down to Derry and that was that. Bernadette was forgotten about.'

'Can I see where she was found?' I asked.

A dismissive wave of the hand from the mother.

'This way,' said Seamus.

'Do you want me to come?' asked Fintan.

'You stay where you are,' replied Seamus.

I follow him out into the hall.

'They broke the glass in the back door,' he said. 'There'd been a fight. We found a knife with blood on it, so she had a go, did Bernadette.' He shrugs. 'Wouldn't have taken much to overpower her, though. There were scuff marks on the wallpaper, so they'd carried her up the stairs. She'd have been kicking out for all she was worth.'

Seamus wiped away a tear then – I'm sure he did.

'She was a good kid. The best of us.' He's leaning on the banister now. 'I picked up a gun, like my da, but she thought the ballot box was the way to go. She'd have done it, so she would; gone all the way.' He steps to one side. 'Up you go,' he said. 'It's the back bedroom. Ma's left it exactly as it was.'

Seamus is behind me as I climb the stairs. Slowly, respectfully.

There's a flowery tile stuck on the door of the back bedroom: *Bernadette's Room*.

I turn the handle and push it open.

'We redecorated,' offered Seamus. 'There was blood all up the wallpaper. And Ma's changed the bedding. Obviously. There were a few posters, but apart from that . . .' His voice ran out of steam.

A single bed, a few teddy bears sitting on the pillows. A small fireplace with a painting of the Crucifixion on the wall above it. A wardrobe with mirrors on the doors. The curtains were open, a small yard out the back with a gate at the far end.

Faint bloodstains on the carpet.

'The gate was still locked, so they came over it,' said Seamus.

'She was on the bed?' I asked.

'Face down.'

'Who found her?'

'I did, thank God. It would've killed Ma to have seen her like that. Naked, blood everywhere. The bastards had raped her first.'

'The official report said there were forty-one stab wounds, but there's no mention of a pattern to them.'

'There was a pattern.'

'A cross?'

'How the hell would you know that?'

'The victims in Somerset had what looked like a Maltese cross cut into their chests while they were still alive.' I'm standing in the window now, overlooking the backyard, more houses on the other side of the alley that leads out to the Falls Road. I've got my back to Seamus, but I can see him in the reflection. He's fumbling in his coat pocket for something. 'The last victim died before they were able to finish it.'

'Hold out your hand.'

I turn around, my hand outstretched.

'I collect them,' said Seamus, dropping a military cap badge into my palm. 'We put a bounty on them. Got so many, they sent the bastards home in the end.'

The bronze cap badge is glinting under the ceiling light.

I see it now. Plain as day.

'That one's an officer's. Armagh, that came from.'

It's a Maltese cross inside a circular garland with a crown on top, battle honours listed on the four sides.

'They raped her, then cut their fucking regimental insignia into my sister's chest,' hissed Seamus. 'The Royal Green Jackets.'

Chapter Twenty-Two

'I know what those bastards did to her,' said the mother, when I walked back into the living room. 'We couldn't even have an open coffin at her funeral. And you know who these animals are?'

'Not yet,' I replied. 'I know they're still killing, but that's about it at the moment.' That's not entirely true, but I don't have any real evidence yet, do I?

'So, what happens now?' asked Fintan. 'I can take you back to the hotel. Then you'll need a lift to the airport in the morning.'

'Thank you,' I said.

'Is that it?' demanded Seamus. 'You've told us fuck all.'

'I've told you everything I know.'

'Just let him go, Seamus,' said the mother. 'He can't catch them from here, can he?'

There's a loud banging on the front door now, shouting out in the road too. 'Seamus. Open up!'

I don't like the sound of it, to be honest; just when I was beginning to think I was on my way too.

'I'll get it,' said Fintan.

Footsteps in the hall, heavy, at least three people. More, possibly.

I'm standing in the living room with my back to the door when it all goes black again. I'm still conscious this time though, breathing, and I can hear voices, so it must be a bag over my head. That'll be it.

'Sorry, Seamus,' said a gruff voice with a strong Irish accent. 'Orders.'

Two rear doors, so a Transit van, or a Bedford, possibly. I was thrown in the back, landed heavily on my right side; no chance to break my fall with my hands cuffed behind me. They're definitely handcuffs, I can feel the metal digging in to my wrists, and I've used them often enough myself.

There are people sitting either side of me on bench seats. I can feel their legs when I slide across the floor, the van taking a corner too fast. The occasional kick coming in.

Three voices I don't recognise. Seamus must be following. I hope he is.

There was a lot of shouting when I was bundled out of the Ryan house, mainly from Seamus. 'Don't you eejits do anything to him until I get there.'

A good sign, I thought. He clearly knows where I'm being taken as well.

I've given up trying to keep track of the twists and turns. I'm sure there were four lefts and we went around the same roundabout at least twice before we turned off. I'm working on the basis that's another good sign. If they were intending to kill me they wouldn't be quite so careful to cover their tracks.

At least, that's what I'm telling myself. There must be a chance, surely?

'An English copper,' said the voice behind me. 'There must be easier ways to kill yourself.'

'Don't talk to him, Shane.' That was the driver.

'No names.'

'Hardly matters, does it?'

We're out into the countryside now. I can hear leaves and branches scraping down the side of the van from time to time. Narrow lanes then. We pull in to a passing place, a car going in the other direction; I can hear the engine revving as it squeezes past. I thought about shouting, but what would be the point?

'Did any of you know Bernadette?' I asked.

'We all did.' I think that was Shane; younger than the others.

'I'm trying to catch the men who killed her.'

'Everybody knows who killed her. The Royal bloody Green Jackets.'

'The same men have killed again,' I said. 'Four times. Five, if you include the poor sod they framed for the murders.'

'I said don't talk to him.' The driver again.

'D'you know who these men are?' asked Shane.

'I know one of them. I'm close to finding the other.' A slight embellishment, perhaps. I still haven't got any real evidence, but needs must in my current situation. My options are limited. I thought I might have got away without revealing too much, but they're going to need to know I'm close to finding Bernadette's killers. It's my only hope.

'Have you told Seamus?'

'I didn't get a chance.' It's disorientating, pleading for your life with a bag over your head. There's snot running down my face, sweat stinging my eyes and the gash on my forehead. Breathing is becoming more difficult too. I try to flick the bag, hoping to let some air in.

The van is accelerating hard, then it brakes sharply for a right turn on to a rutted track. I slide across the floor of the van into Shane's feet. No kick this time.

A farm track, possibly. There's a smell, isn't there? Grass is flicking the underside of the van too. In the middle of nowhere certainly. I'm guessing we've crossed the border and I'm now in the south, but that's just a guess. We've been going about an hour, feels like, although I've lost any sense of time. I find myself wondering how many other people are buried in shallow graves on this farmer's land. Maybe even a racehorse. What was his name again?

The van slows to a stop and the older man climbs out of the back, opening a gate. I can hear the base of it being dragged. We pull forward, then the driver gets out, leaving me alone with Shane.

'You'll get one chance and you'd better make it good,' he said, his voice hushed.

'Who are you?'

'I'm nobody.'

The engine is still running and it sounds like barn doors are being opened, possibly. Everything is muffled in this bloody bag. The driver climbs back in and the van lurches forward. Then the barn doors are closed again, behind the van now.

Engine off. I can feel hands taking a firm grip of my ankles, before I'm dragged out of the back of the van, landing on the earth floor of the barn with a thud. The windscreen wipers were going on the way here and the ground is dry, so I must be in the barn.

'They'll be here in about an hour,' said the older man. 'You stay with him, Shane. And don't let Seamus in, if he gets here before they do.'

'Who's *they*?' I asked, once the barn door had been closed from the outside and the footsteps had faded in to the distance.

'Command,' replied Shane. 'They'll make the decision.'

No need to ask what decision that is.

Chapter Twenty-Three

I can smell pigs.

I knew I was taking a risk coming here, but thought if I disappeared, it would be a shallow grave somewhere in remote countryside. That's the natural assumption, isn't it? I hadn't even considered the possibility of being chopped up and fed to pigs. The best I can say is that I won't know much about it either way, I suppose.

Fifty miles from Belfast perhaps? There'd been a stretch of main road in there too.

So, there you have it. I'm in the hands of the IRA, somewhere in the southern Irish countryside; my fate well and truly out of my hands. I'm trying to stay positive; philosophical, you might say. It's either that or burst into tears and beg for mercy – give me time, though.

There's someone banging on the barn door now.

'Fuck off, Seamus.'

'Let me in, Shane, you little shite.'

'Not until Liam gets here. Sorry. Orders.'

There is a command structure to the IRA, so Liam must be higher up the food chain than Seamus.

I had thought I'd been winning Seamus over, or at least he'd seemed to accept we have a common enemy. I'm not daft. That doesn't mean he's on my side, not by any means, but it's better than the alternative. Why else would he have bothered to show me Bernadette's room? And he hadn't immediately shut down Fintan when he'd suggested a taxi ride to the airport in the morning. Things had been looking up at that point.

I'm also a good deal closer to my quarry. There can't be that many former Royal Green Jackets serving in the police.

Brian Druce is one.

And I know that Taylor is ex-army.

Yes, I'm closer, although right at this moment I couldn't be further away.

There are cars outside now, at least two. Seems I've drawn quite a crowd.

'Shane, open up.' A young woman's voice this time.

A steel bar is sliding across, then a large barn door is dragged open. It's still raining outside, a cold blast of air reaching me on the floor. I'm trying to count the footsteps, but it's not easy on the soft mud floor.

There'll be at least four: the woman, whoever she is, Liam, Seamus and Shane. More, I think. There are two standing behind me now, so I sit up.

'He is who he says he is. We checked.' That's Seamus's voice; I recognise him.

'Detective Inspector Mungo Willis. Avon and Somerset Police.' Deeper, older. Must be Liam. 'Hardly worth a bullet.'

I couldn't agree more.

'Take off the bag and let's have a look at him,' said the woman.

The bag is whipped off my head, leaving me blinking furiously in the light, the bulb right above my head.

Yes, it's a barn. Bales of straw stacked off to my left; bags of feed against the wall on the right.

There are six of them and they're all wearing balaclavas, except Seamus, but then I already know what he looks like. There's one behind me, as it turns out, I'm guessing that's Shane.

'What are you doing here?' Liam's voice again, although I can't tell which one of the figures in front of me actually asked the question. My eyes haven't adjusted to the light yet.

'I'm investigating the murder of Bernadette Ryan,' I replied. 'And the murders of—'

'You're not investigating anything, you lying bastard. The case is closed.'

'Fuck this shite,' snarled the woman. She springs forward, leans over and presses the barrel of a gun to the side of my left knee. 'Tell us what you're doing here.'

Shit, shit, shit. Not that knee, please God, not that knee. Not the other one either, for that matter. Start talking, Bob. And make it good.

'The men who killed Bernadette have killed again. There are three victims with the same pattern of cuts on their chests. Fiona Anderson, Alice Cobb and Lizzie Harper.'

'She was a peeler.'

'She was my partner and she died trying to catch the killers.'

'What about this new murder?'

Questions coming at me from all directions now. 'Faith Bennett died before they could finish the cross, so they left her,' I replied. 'It seems the victim must be alive.'

'Like Bernadette was,' said Seamus. 'It's the regimental insignia, the fucking Royal Green Jackets.'

'Tell me about this bloke they framed.' Liam again.

'Martin Clarke. An innocent man. The coroner's asked that his death is looked at again and there are two detectives on it.' My eyes have adjusted to the light now, but it's still hard to tell who is speaking with these balaclavas they're wearing. I suppose that's the point. 'He was a van driver, selected because he fitted the profile and had no alibis, then thrown off a bridge into the path of a lorry on the thirteenth of October last year.'

'That was the day after the Brighton bombing,' said Seamus.

'The murder weapons were planted in his car?' asked Liam.

'They must've been.'

'So, you're getting close?' The woman this time. She's still pressing the gun barrel to the side of my knee, but not quite so hard now. I glance down and her finger's not on the trigger now either.

'He knows who one of them is.' Shane sounds unsure of himself, more comfortable being seen and not heard in this company, probably. 'And he's close to finding the other he said.'

'When did he say that?' demanded Liam.

'In the van, on the way here.'

'I'm still gathering evidence,' I said. 'That's why I'm here.'

'They tried to kill him,' said Seamus. 'And we need to let him go. Ma said so.'

Maybe Ma Ryan has more clout than I gave her credit for?

'And what happens when you catch them?' Liam asked.

'They'll be arrested and brought before a court,' I replied, as matter of fact as I could manage in the circumstances. I'm oddly calm again, but I've got a feeling they're going to let me go. I've always been an optimist, deep down. 'They're still out there, and they're still killing.' There was an awkward pause, as if Liam is deciding one way or the other, so I thought I ought to fill it.

'I say kill him,' said the woman. 'This is bullshit.'

A last chance to make my case, then. 'My partner, Lizzie. Seamus's sister, Bernadette. Kill me and they get away. Again.'

'You've got some balls, I'll give you that.' I can see a shaking head; must be Liam standing second from the right. 'You swan in here, bold as fucking brass . . .' He looked at Seamus, then the

165

woman. 'Take off the cuffs,' he said, gesturing to Shane standing behind me.

My arms are wrenched back before being released, and I take the opportunity to rub my left elbow. My wrists will have to wait.

The woman has stepped back, holding the gun by her side now. 'If anyone finds out we had a British bobby in here and let him go, we'll be a fucking laughing stock,' she said.

'I want Bernadette's killers, Liam,' said Seamus. 'Ma wants them.'

'Behind bars,' I said.

'We can get to them in prison, don't you worry.'

I can live with that, before you ask. My job is to bring them before a court. What happens to them after that is down to someone else.

'All right, Seamus,' said Liam. 'Let him go, but if this thing blows up in our faces, it's your head on the block, not mine.'

I'm back in the van now, bag on my head, but they haven't bothered with the cuffs this time, which is a relief. There's someone sitting to my left and another opposite me. Yes, I'm sitting down this time, on a bench seat.

We've been going for about an hour, in total silence, when I feel the van turning. It must be a good, wide road; it's a full one hundred and eighty degrees, so we're now facing back the way we came. Then it pulls in and stops.

'The checkpoint's a mile down the road,' said Seamus, slipping the bag off my head. 'You were snatched by the IRA, didn't see anyone, didn't tell them anything, then dumped here. All right?'

I nod.

'Say it.'

'Fine.'

'We'll soon find out if you tell them anything else.' He's leaning forwards, right in my face. 'If you're not on our side.'

'I'm not on your side,' I said. 'I'm on Bernadette's.'

'That's good enough. Now, get out.'

The back doors open from the outside and I'm bundled out into the darkness.

'Just make sure you get those bastards' is Seamus's parting shot, then the front seat passenger slams the rear doors, climbs back in and the van accelerates away.

God alone knows what time it is, although there's a faint glow in the east, so not long before dawn, possibly, although that could be the lights of Belfast. The back light on my watch isn't working and it's too dark to see the screen; dark grey numbers on a light grey background. Who on earth thought that was a good idea? No wonder they gave the bloody thing away.

It must have been gone eleven when I was taken from Clondara Terrace. An hour into the countryside, an hour there and another hour back, so three in the morning. Maybe a bit later.

At least the rain has stopped.

I'm walking as quickly as I can, limping now on my left leg, which is agony to be honest. And my elbow's not much better. There's an owl hooting somewhere, and I can't get rid of the feeling I'm being watched. A British police officer walking alone at night along the road towards Belfast. I must be fucking mad.

A car has appeared behind me, heading towards the same checkpoint, so I'm hiding in the undergrowth at the side of the road.

I'll get snatched by loyalist paramilitaries now, knowing my luck.

Dragging my leg, I can see the checkpoint ahead. It might be the same one I went through on my way in from the airport, but then again it might not, they all look the same I expect. Concrete blocks and barbed wire.

There's a light shining in my face now – a powerful searchlight – and I've got my right hand up, shielding my eyes.

'Hands where we can see them!' A strong Irish accent, but different somehow; sounds a bit like that politician, Ian Paisley.

I can't see much of what's going on at the checkpoint with the light in my eyes, but the car had gone before I approached. I'm guessing there are several rifles pointing at me, as well as the light.

'Who are you?'

'Detective Inspector Mungo Willis, Avon and Somerset Police,' I shouted, nice and clear, so there'd be no room for mistakes. 'Retired.'

Two figures appear in front of the light, walking towards me, machine guns at the ready.

'What the fuck are you doing here?'

'I was taken from the street outside my hotel by the Provisional IRA. They dumped me about a mile back there.'

A cursory search for concealed weapons. 'All right, you can put your arms down now, mate,' said the RUC officer. 'They dumped you, you said?'

'About a mile that way.'

'You lucky bastard. By rights, you should be dead now.'

Chapter Twenty-Four

Three different RUC officers, each one more senior than the last. I wouldn't want you to think lying is something that comes naturally to me. It doesn't, but I stuck to my story and was eventually given a lift to the airport.

'They must've thought I was a serving officer, and as soon as they realised I'm not, they let me go.'

The last one, a detective superintendent, was the trickiest. He clearly had an informant.

'A British police officer was seen in the Clondara Terrace area of Belfast.'

'It could've been me, I suppose. I've got no idea where they took me. There were some houses, then I was taken to a farm somewhere.'

'Does the name Bernadette Ryan mean anything to you?'

'No.'

Lucky for me they didn't check with Avon and Somerset Police, but then why would they? I'm not a serving officer, and I wasn't in Belfast on official police business; just sightseeing. If they had done, they'd have been told I'm missing, presumed dead, and I wouldn't have got away with that lie about Bernadette.

No, they didn't check. They couldn't have done. I'll soon find out, though. Sharp would think I faked my own death, or something equally stupid, and there'll be a welcoming committee waiting for me at arrivals – to arrest me for wasting police time, probably.

Twat.

I'll need a car. I wonder if Martin Clarke's father has had that brake light fixed on the back of the Capri? I could do with a weapon too. Seamus offered me a gun, although I don't think he'd thought that through properly. He dropped me at an RUC checkpoint for a start, then there was airport security.

I am firearms trained, and I did my national service too, so I know what to do with a gun, not that I've ever killed anyone. I'm not sure I could either, to be honest, although if it was in self-defence then . . . who knows? You do what you have to, I suppose.

Let's hope it doesn't come to that.

I've been thinking about my next move, and my natural instinct, after nearly thirty years in the police, is to do this properly. So, I'm going to see Detective Chief Superintendent Sharp and I'm going to tell him what I know.

Bernadette Ryan.

The Royal Green Jackets.

My attempted murder.

Everything.

Except the attempt to frame me for Alan's murder. I don't trust him with that.

What should happen then is that he reopens the investigation properly this time, rather than assigning two junior detectives to look at it again just to keep the coroner happy. That would leave me free to watch Somerset play Middlesex at the County Ground in the sure and certain knowledge that the police will arrest the right people this time and, in doing so, exonerate Martin Clarke.

It's the right thing to do, and it's got to be worth a try.

No, I'm not holding my breath.

◆ ◆ ◆

The look on the face of the desk sergeant at Taunton police station was a picture.

'You're supposed to be dead, Bob, mate.'

'Easy mistake to make,' I said, bright and breezy. 'Is Sharp in?'

'He's just going home.' The desk sergeant picked up the phone. 'I'll see if I can catch him.'

It had been midday before the RUC finished with me, then the lunchtime flight from Belfast to London, followed by two and a half hours on the train, Paddington to Taunton. It's gone seven now, so Sharp must've been working late.

I left my stuff at the hotel too, which is a shame. Well, I say *stuff*, it was a carrier bag with a toothbrush and some cheap plastic razors in it, the stuff Angela bought me. I could've done with using it, really.

The security door at the side of the reception desk swung open.

'What the hell are you doing here, Bob?' Sharp was wearing his usual grey pinstripe suit, his shirt open at the collar, tie slung over his shoulder. There was a whiff of whisky – if we ever start enforcing the drink driving rules properly, he's going to be in deep shit – his face redder than usual too. 'They're still dragging that bloody lake looking for you.'

'We need a chat,' I said.

I don't call him 'sir' anymore. I used to – used to have to – but then he's pushing me out, isn't he? He's using my health as an excuse, but he's behind it. I'm under no illusions about that. I'm not a serving officer at the moment, either. The other reason is he's a twat. It's as simple as that.

He turned to the desk sergeant. 'Call off the search at Blagdon Lake,' he said.

171

'Yes, sir.'

'Do we have to do this now, Bob?'

'We do.'

He dropped his briefcase on a vacant chair. 'What is it?'

This'll tell you the sort of bloke Sharp is. There are three members of the public sitting in the reception area – an elderly couple and a young woman. I don't know why they're here, but the fact is they're here. Not unreasonably so, either; reception is open until nine.

'D'you want to do this here?' I asked, nice and calm. 'In public.'

'Oh, for fuck's sake,' whispered Sharp, over a sigh. He waved his hand at the desk sergeant, who opened the security door.

We're in an interview room now. A table, two chairs either side, blank walls.

'I should have you arrested for wasting police time,' he said.

I slammed the door. 'That's pretty much what I'd expect from you,' I said. 'I'm hit on the head, knocked unconscious, sat in my car and pushed into a reservoir, and your response is to arrest me for wasting police time.'

'Who?'

'You and I both know who,' I replied.

'Did you *see* him?'

'He's too clever for that.'

'You'll need to make a statement,' he said. 'I'll get Field and Webster to look into it tomorrow. They'll be in touch.' He was still holding his briefcase, edging towards the door. 'Is that it?'

'No, it bloody well isn't it.' I was standing between him and the door, and there was no way he was getting out until I'd had my say. 'Easter 1981, during the hunger strike riots in Belfast, a nineteen-year-old girl was murdered in a house on Clondara Terrace by two British soldiers.'

'We looked for similar cases, Bob. We've been through all this.' Sharp put his briefcase down and folded his arms.

'This one didn't show up because her injuries were never included in the official report.'

'You're saying there was a cover-up?'

'That's exactly what I'm saying. The murder was committed by British soldiers and they covered it up.'

'Who's *they*?'

'The British military establishment and the RUC. Her injuries were identical to Fiona Anderson and Alice Cobb's. Lizzie's too. I've been to Ireland, spoken to the family. The official report makes no mention of a pattern, but it was there, cut into her chest.'

'The Maltese cross?'

'It's not a cross, it's the regimental insignia of the Royal Green Jackets.'

'Bollocks.'

I had my hand in my jacket pocket and my fingers closed around the cap badge. That's right, Seamus gave it to me. My trump card; supposed to be, anyway. I took my hand out, sent the badge spinning towards Sharp.

He caught it, staring at it in the palm of his hand.

'The Green Jackets were taking a pasting during the rioting; petrol bombs, bricks. Two of them got separated, ran down a side alley off the Falls Road and jumped over the wall into the back of Bernadette Ryan's house. They raped her first.'

'I get it, Bob.' Sharp was breathing deeply now. 'There was no pattern to the stab wounds on Faith Bennett's chest, was there?'

'She died before they could . . .' I replied, not feeling the need to finish that particular sentence. 'The victim has to be alive.'

'Well, thank you, Bob. I'll certainly pass this information on to the team investigating Faith's murder and they can have a look at it.' He held the cap badge up. 'Can I keep this?' he asked.

'No, you can't.'

'Oh, right, fine,' he said, handing it back to me.

'What about the other murders?'

'Was Martin Clarke in the Royal Green Jackets?'

'He was never in the army,' I replied.

'Hardly relevant then, is it?' Sharp picked up his briefcase. 'Look, Bob, there's no doubt about this. If Martin Clarke had gone to trial, he would have been convicted of the murders of Fiona Anderson, Alice Cobb and Lizzie Harper. We've got counsel's opinion.'

'All right,' I said. 'Look at it another way. Let's assume he was convicted, rather than murdered, and he's sitting in jail serving three life sentences. Armed with this new information, he'd appeal those convictions and they'd be overturned. He'd walk free from the Court of Appeal and you bloody well know it. Get counsel's opinion on that.'

'I'm not having this conversation, Bob,' said Sharp, stepping forwards. 'Not now, and not with you. If you'll kindly step aside, there are places I need to be.'

'D'you know, what I can't work out is whether you're part of some big conspiracy to cover this whole thing up or whether it's just about you not looking like an idiot.'

'Fuck off, Bob.'

'It's easy to see how it gets out of hand. The military cover up one murder, quietly sweep it under the carpet – easy to see why too; political expediency, we'll call it – then the buggers kill again when they're in civvy street, and the cover-up goes on, otherwise it'll come out about the first cover-up. Now they're covering up the fucking cover-ups.' I glared at Sharp. 'I hope for your sake you're not part of this.'

'Be very careful, mate.'

'Or what? You'll kick me out of the police?'

♦ ♦ ♦

So, there you have it. I tried. Got a bit carried away, possibly, but I'm well past giving a shit about that.

What I have done, though, is let Taylor know I'm still alive. He may not know it just yet but he will do, soon enough. Probably won't bother to make it look like suicide next time he comes for me, either.

I'm in a taxi now, on my way over to Ilminster. I rang Martin Clarke's father and I can borrow the Capri. He's had the brake light fixed too.

Next thing will be to find a B&B somewhere off the beaten track and get some sleep.

Chapter Twenty-Five

I found somewhere the other side of Chard in the end, a farmhouse B&B near Forde Abbey; middle of bloody nowhere, really, but I slept soundly. I tried their breakfast, which wasn't bad, either. Not up to an All Day Breakfast, but sitting in a Little Chef is going to have to wait until this is over now, sadly.

A quick phone call to Yeovil police station and I found out what I needed to know. I didn't even have to give my name, which was a bonus.

'Can you put me through to Police Sergeant Druce, please?'

'He's on lates this week.'

'Fine. I'll try again later in that case.'

Lates means he'll be at home this morning, and his car was in the drive when I parked across it just after nine. I dropped him off once, after some piss-up or other, and it's a nice little double-fronted bungalow on the edge of Martock. I couldn't remember the house number, but he was in the garden pruning the roses.

I'm taking a bit of a flyer here, but I get feelings about people – I may have mentioned that before – and I don't think Druce is involved in this. A company sergeant major with three tours of Northern Ireland under his belt before he joined the police, I remember that much. I can't remember which regiment, though, so let's see.

If I'm wrong, then it was probably Druce who helped Taylor get me in my car and roll me into the water.

High stakes then.

He looked over when I shut the car door. 'You're supposed to be dead,' he said. He's taken off a gardening glove and his hand is outstretched. 'Glad to see you changed your mind.'

'About what, Brian?'

'Suicide.'

'It wasn't suicide, mate,' I said, gesturing to my forehead. 'Someone gave me a wallop, sat me in my car and—'

'Did you see them?'

I shook my head. 'It was dark. Didn't see a thing. I came to on the bottom of the lake. Thank God for manual windows,' I said, smiling.

'Come in and have a cup of tea. Sheila's here.'

'We'll talk out here, Brian, if it's all the same to you.'

'Talk about what?' He put his gloves on the gate post, balancing the secateurs on top of them.

'Where were you Easter 1981?' I asked.

'Belfast. Company Sergeant Major, B Company, First Battalion, Royal Green Jackets. Why?'

'What happened that weekend?'

'It was the hunger strike riots. All weekend it went on. Belfast and Derry. I think some of the Anglians got ambushed down Armagh way from memory too. It was a difficult time and we were ready for it.' He shrugged. 'Some of the hunger strikers were nearing the end and tensions were running high. It was always going to be a difficult weekend. I seem to remember the loyalists opened fire on a bookmaker's as well.'

'Does the name Bernadette Ryan mean anything to you?' I asked, just as the front door opened, a woman coming out with a watering can. She started watering a hanging basket.

Druce had reddened and was sucking his teeth, waiting for her to go back into the house, clearly.

'Who's this, Brian?' she asked.

'A colleague from work,' he replied. 'I'll be in in a minute.'

She got the message and ducked back inside the house, leaving the watering can on the doorstep.

'It was Easter Monday, the last day of the riots,' Druce said, when the front door closed. 'And we were out on the Falls Road in support of the RUC. Gangs of youths in balaclavas throwing petrol bombs and stones. They'd torched an RUC Land Rover the night before and it was still burning. Then suddenly their numbers exploded; there were hundreds of them, fuck knows where they came from. B Company was cut off at the western end, then there was gunfire – not from us, from them. We'd been issued with rubber bullets, and they weren't stopping a crowd like that.'

'Go on.'

'They rushed us. We got the order to retreat and suddenly we were running; they were running alongside us, lashing out, we were trying to hit back with batons. It was chaos. Two of the lads went down and the last time they were seen was scrambling into a ginnel behind a terrace of houses.'

'Who was it?'

'I don't know. Never did find out. We had a full complement the following morning and were told they'd made contact with an RUC patrol and been brought in. It was after that we heard a woman had been killed.'

'Are you seriously telling me a CSM wouldn't know which of his men were missing after a day like that?'

Druce snatched the secateurs off the gatepost. 'Don't you fucking dare, Bob. You've got no fucking idea what it was like.'

A fair point. I'd been spared that, mercifully.

'We were told a woman had been shot, and that's all we were told. It was nothing to do with the British Army; the RUC would deal with it. And you don't ask questions, Bob, you just don't.'

'What happened after that?' I asked.

'Next thing is we're being moved on, out to Armagh. We lost a few lads over the next couple of months; a sniper got one and there was a roadside bomb. Then we came home – early as it happens.'

'Was there ever an investigation into the woman's murder?'

'Not that I know of. I certainly never heard about it after that.' Druce was pruning the roses again, taking his anger out on them, the secateurs snapping shut. 'The RUC would've dealt with it.'

'Her name was Bernadette Ryan and she wasn't shot; she was raped and stabbed to death. Cut to pieces. The official report makes no specific mention of her injuries, but there were multiple stab wounds, almost identical to those inflicted on Fiona Anderson, Alice Cobb, DS Harper and now Faith Bennett.'

I watched the blood drain from Druce's face; told me he knew more than he was letting on, did that.

'How d'you know all this?' he asked.

'I've been to Belfast, spoken to her family.'

'They cut a cross into her chest?'

'It's not a cross, Brian. It's the regimental insignia of the Royal Green Jackets. Your regiment.'

'There's no way a soldier would've done that. Just no way.'

'They were having the shit kicked out of them by Catholic youths; they seek refuge in a house and find a young Catholic girl in there. You work it out.'

Druce's eyes had glazed over. He was miles away, remembering. I could see it in his face, plain as day. As if something was making sense at last.

'It's no fucking wonder you were told not to ask questions,' I said.

'The regiment comes first,' mumbled Druce. 'The reputation of the Royal Green Jackets is all that matters.'

'More than the lives of five young women?'

'It would've inflamed the situation,' he said. 'The riots were bad enough already, without that. I thought that's why they hushed it up. We were told it was a shooting and that she was a Provo.'

'Well it wasn't and she wasn't.'

We were being watched from the window now. I could see the net curtain twitching, although that might have been the small terrier sitting on the windowsill.

'Martin Clarke wasn't even in the army, let alone the Green Jackets,' I said.

'I never thought it was him.' Druce looked embarrassed, watching me out of the corner of his eyes.

'Why the fuck didn't you say something?'

'I'm just a traffic officer,' he replied. 'Who the hell would listen to me?'

'I would.'

'Yeah.'

'What about Sean Taylor?' I asked.

'He was one of us. A lance corporal.'

Chapter Twenty-Six

Druce knows more than he's letting on. If I was in any doubt about that before – and I wasn't – then it was confirmed by the speed at which he left his house once he thought I was safely out of the way. Actually, I'd parked in the pub car park at the end of his road and waited.

A very nice black BMW going far too fast in a residential area, but then he is pursuit trained, I suppose. He wasn't late for work, either. I should have followed him, really, but I can guess where he's going.

Besides, I'd have stood out like a sore thumb trying to keep up with him.

I need to get in touch with Angela. It's only fair. Field and Webster will be wanting a word with me too. Somerset's finest, tasked with investigating the attempt to murder me in Blagdon Lake. There'll be no fingerprints and I didn't see anything or anyone, so you can imagine how far that investigation will go. That's assuming they bother at all.

We'll have a bit of fun with the 'Can you think of anyone who might wish to kill you?' question, anyway.

I'm parked opposite the church in Hinton St George now. There's a fete starting in half an hour and I'm hoping Angela will turn up. Cutting edge journalism, and all that. The receptionist at the *Chard and Ilminster News* wouldn't tell me where she was, so I'm having to make an educated guess. They said they were sending someone to the fete, though, so I'm hoping it will be her.

She's a good kid.

I did leave a message for her – suitably cryptic, of course, just in case. Something about a famous England cricketer opening the fete.

Tapping on the passenger window.

'I thought I'd find you here,' said Angela, when I wound down the window; electric sadly, so you don't actually *wind*, you just press a button. Shame. 'I was expecting Ian Botham.'

'Sorry to disappoint.'

'I was joking.' She dropped into the passenger seat. 'How did you get on in Belfast?' She noticed my frown. 'That's where you went isn't it?'

'I had the barrel of a gun pressed to my temple, a bag over my head, I was kicked and punched in the back of a van. Usual sort of thing, really. I got out alive, so I mustn't grumble.'

'What about Bernadette Ryan?'

'She had the same pattern cut into her chest,' I replied. 'Hold out your hand.'

The Royal Green Jackets cap badge again.

She was staring at it in her palm, trying to keep her composure, stay professional; thinking of her sister, Lizzie, at the same time. 'Why was there no mention of that in the official report?'

'It was a cover-up. Belfast was already on fire with the hunger strike riots and you can imagine what would've happened if it turned out two British soldiers had murdered a Catholic woman.'

'But they did.'

'Yes, they did.'

'What regiment is this?'

'The Royal Green jackets.'

'Was Sean Taylor one of their soldiers?'

'He was.'

'So, what happens now?' she asked.

'We still haven't got any real evidence,' I replied. 'I certainly couldn't make an arrest based on what I've got. That's if I was still a serving officer.'

'There's a girl gone missing over at Chard,' said Angela. 'It might be connected, I suppose. Ray's over from Taunton covering the story.'

'What's her name?'

'Maxine Green.'

'I know a Maxine,' I said. 'She works at B & D Light Haulage in Ilminster, where Martin Clarke used to work.'

There are several cars parked outside the house on the edge of Chard, and I could see two detectives in the front window as we crept past. Some people will tell you they can smell a police officer a mile away. They can't. There's no smell, but there is a look and I could see it from the road.

My guess is two detectives and a family liaison officer. Hardly surprising they're taking it seriously, what with the murder of Faith Bennett only a few days ago and a few miles away.

I'll have to wait until the detectives have gone. Then I'll just have to get past the liaison officer, and the chances are I'll know them anyway.

We've parked about a hundred yards further along, outside a primary school.

'That's Ray's car, over there,' offered Angela, pointing. 'He wasn't sitting in it when we came past, though.'

'Probably in the pub.'

Angela was leaning over, craning her neck to see in the wing mirror. 'They're going, those two blokes we saw in the window.'

'You'll have to wait here,' I said, climbing out of the driver's seat.

'Really?'

'Yes, really.'

Steps up to the front door. If there's a liaison officer in there, then he or she will answer the door. Some I know, some I don't, so we'll see.

'Hello, Bob. What are you doing here?'

Sod it. Sue Bollard is a pain in the arse at the best of times.

'I thought you were off sick,' she said.

'I'm not here officially, Sue,' I replied. 'I just need to know if the missing girl is the same Maxine who works at B & D Light Haulage.'

A head appeared around the living room door. Face pale, eyes red, nose streaming. 'Yes, Max works there. Why? Who are you?'

'My name's Bob Willis,' I said. 'I met her the other day. Can I come in?'

'This is Detective Inspector Willis,' said Sue, poking her nose in. 'He's on sick leave at the moment, so you're under no obligation to speak to him, Janice. All right?'

'Are you looking for Max?' she asked, her eyes pleading with me. That's what it felt like, anyway.

'Yes, I am.'

'Let him in, Sue. The more the merrier, and if he's looking for Max, that's fine by me.'

The front door closed behind me and I followed Janice into her living room. There was a photograph of Maxine on the coffee table, an empty space on the mantelpiece. An ashtray, the smoke swirling as Janice walked past. My age, a bit younger, possibly. I'm guessing there's a sunbed in one of the spare rooms.

'When did you last see Maxine?' I asked. I thought it best to sound formal.

'She didn't come home from work last night.' Janice had sat down and was lighting a cigarette, the end bouncing in the flame as she spoke. 'I wasn't that worried. She's done it before. Girls of that age, you know. I thought she was stopping with a friend or something, but then she didn't turn up for work today. They rang and asked where she was.'

'Is her car outside?'

'She's got a little blue Fiesta and it's usually on the drive.' Janice was pulling hard on the cigarette now. 'I gave the number to the other officers.'

'You checked with her friends?'

'Rang everybody I can think of. Hospitals too. Then I rang your lot.'

'Does Maxine take drugs?'

'No. She doesn't even smoke. Hardly drinks.'

'Did she say anything to you about the death of Martin Clarke?' I asked.

'She was upset about it, we both were. He was a lovely lad, just the sort you'd hope your daughter would meet, you know. Then we're being told he was a sex predator killing young women and he died trying to resist arrest.' She curled her lip. 'That's not the Martin I knew, although I didn't know him well. Met just the once, in fact; that night when he came to pick up Max. Seemed like a lovely lad.'

'Did she say anything after it happened?'

'Not really. She had to copy his personnel file for the police, which she did. She gave it to Mr Jackson and that was the last she heard of it.' Janice was frowning at me now, a difficult question on the way. 'D'you think her disappearance is connected to . . .' She shook her head; couldn't bring herself to finish it.

185

My guess is she doesn't really want to know the answer anyway. Would you?

'Can I see her room?' I asked.

'Top of the stairs on the right.'

'Mrs Green looks like she could do with a cup of tea, Sue,' I said, anxious neither of them should follow me, glancing over my shoulder to check they weren't. 'Why don't you make her one.'

'That would be lovely, thanks.'

I got glared at by Sue, but I can live with that.

It was much the same as any young girl's bedroom these days, I expect. A single bed, wardrobe, stuff all over the floor. Different posters on the walls, of course. My daughters had Wings, Janis Joplin, Fleetwood Mac, stuff like that. These days it's Madonna, Prince and Bananarama. There's a cassette machine, one of those ones with the speakers either side, and a pile of cassettes on the windowsill.

I'm not sure what I'm looking for. I expect the detectives here earlier didn't know either, but they'll have had a good look all the same.

The duvet was scrunched up on the bed, so I unfurled that, laying it out flat. Nothing. Her underwear drawer was open, so I picked up a hairbrush and used that to look underneath the clothes. It seemed a bit creepy otherwise.

And it avoids leaving fingerprints.

There was nothing in any of the drawers you wouldn't expect to find. Same goes for the wardrobe.

I can hear footsteps on the stairs now, so time is running out. I haven't looked under the mattress yet, have I?

It hadn't been easy getting out of the house. Janice had been in floods of tears. She had me by the hand and wouldn't let go; kept saying she had a feeling about me and that I'd be the one to find Maxine. I tried to tell her that I'm off sick and don't have access to the same databases and searches that the police do, but she wasn't having any of it.

Then the call had come in about Maxine's car. It had been found in a lay-by on the A30 just west of Crewkerne, the keys thrown in the hedge adjacent to it. The family liaison officer, Sue, had taken the call and broke the news to Janice just as I was almost out of the door. I'm guessing Sue had wanted me there for moral support and I can't say I blame her, but it meant another ten minutes of hand holding and tears.

I hope that doesn't sound harsh. It's not meant to. I've just got places to go, people to see. Maxine to find.

'What's that?' asked Angela, when I dropped a file on to her lap through the open passenger window of the Capri a few minutes later.

'Martin Clarke's personnel file,' I replied, once I was safely sitting in the driver's seat. 'I managed to get it out of the house inside my jacket. It was under her mattress.'

'What's happened to her?'

'She didn't get home from work last night, apparently. And they've found her car dumped in a lay-by on the A30, so it's starting to sound ominous.'

'And what's she doing with this file?'

'No idea. She must have brought it home from work after I was there the other day. I'll need to have a good look at it, see what's so important about it. Problem is I didn't see the version copied for the police file, so I won't be able to tell if something's been left out. That all happened while I was in hospital.'

That said, Field and Webster should have access to it by now, so they might be of some use after all.

Angela opened the file. 'What am I looking for?' she asked.

'Not here,' I said, reaching across and closing it.

'Where then?'

'I'll drop you back to your car at Hinton St George. There'll still be some of that fete left for you to report on.'

'Sod that,' grumbled Angela. 'I can make it up, no problem. They're all the same, these bloody fetes.'

'There's a Little Chef on the A35 just the other side of Axminster,' I said. 'No bugger's going to be looking for me down there, are they?'

Chapter Twenty-Seven

There's not a lot in Martin's personnel file, to be honest. A work schedule; miles driven, deliveries made, that sort of thing. There's a copy of his CV from when he applied for the job, a doctor's note for a period of sick leave. Depression, apparently.

I've checked the dates of the murders and he was working nights on all of them, which is convenient. Out on his own in his van, no one to vouch for him. Long distance too – Manchester, Sheffield – giving him plenty of time. We knew that already, though – that he'd have no alibis for the murders. It's no good trying to pin a murder on someone who's got a cast iron alibi, is it?

The only other document is the police report into the accident he had a few weeks before he was killed, and that's pretty unremarkable too, apart from the identity of the police officer who attended the scene.

Taylor.

I'm left wondering what Maxine thought was so important about it that it was worth bringing home and hiding under her mattress. And possibly getting herself killed for. That's if she is dead, of course. There are still no reports of her body being found; Angela's rung the news desk.

There is an even bigger question that leaps out at me, but at the moment I'm more concerned by the car pulling in next to the

Capri. The car park is at the front of the restaurant and I saw them turning in, which begs the question of how the bloody hell they found me. We're not even sitting in the window, for heaven's sake.

Field and Webster.

The best I can say is that I've finished my All Day Breakfast; not up to the standard of Camel Hill, but it was all right.

'Did you tell your office where you were?' I asked.

Angela shook her head. 'No, why?'

'We've got company.'

'Mind if we join you?'

We were sitting at a table laid for four. Field slid on to the bench seat next to me, Webster next to Angela. And, no, they didn't wait for an invitation.

'You'll be Angela,' said Webster. 'Lizzie's sister.'

'She's a journalist,' I said.

I can't put my finger on it, but I'm feeling defensive for some reason. Field and Webster are supposed to be re-investigating Martin Clarke's death, which should mean they're on my side, or at least we're on the same side. It just doesn't feel like it somehow.

'How did you get on with Sean Taylor?' I asked.

'You know we can't talk about that, Bob,' replied Field. 'It's an ongoing police investigation and you're not a serving officer, are you?'

It was a rhetorical question; I decided to treat it as one anyway. 'I'm guessing you didn't ask him about the murder of Bernadette Ryan?'

'We didn't know about the murder of Bernadette Ryan at the time, but we'll be speaking to him again.'

'He was there, with the Royal Green Jackets. So was Brian Druce.'

'Sergeant Druce has been spoken to as well. The logs confirm he was on duty with Taylor on the nights in question, giving both an alibi, as you might imagine.'

'Conveniently,' I muttered. I do mutter sometimes. It used to drive Shirley mad.

'We'll be speaking to him again about the murder of Bernadette Ryan,' offered Webster. 'Now we know about it, and the insignia, thanks to you.'

'Tell us what happened at Blagdon Lake,' said Field.

'I was sitting in my car in the car park there. It was late. I was planning to get some sleep and got out for a pee. I hadn't seen a car arriving or anyone around; next thing I know I'm being hit across the forehead.'

'Have you had that looked at?' Webster was frowning at the plaster on my forehead.

'I had a shower last night and changed the dressing. It's fine.'

'What happened after that?' asked Field. He was making notes in a shiny new notebook.

'I regained consciousness and my car was in the water, so I waited for as long as I could, then wound down the window and swam clear.'

'And you saw no one?'

'No, but I've got a pretty good idea who did it.'

'Two coffees, please,' said Webster, when a waitress appeared at the table.

'Sean Taylor was attending the scene of a road traffic accident at the time, according to the accident report,' said Field. 'At the Sparkford roundabout.'

'Have you checked with the drivers involved?'

'Not yet.'

'Do so. Run the number plates if needs be.'

Field nodded, the realisation that the whole report could be a work of fiction slowly dawning on him. Must be new to police work.

'Check and double-check everything,' I said. 'Believe nothing and no one.' I must've sounded like Clouseau.

'We have done this before,' said Webster.

'Your car's gone off to Forensics, but I wouldn't hold out much hope.' Field moved his notebook to make way for his coffee. 'It did start though, after it had sat all night.'

'What about the search of Taylor's house?' I asked.

Angela was keeping quiet; listening intently. She'll make a good journalist.

'Nothing,' replied Field. 'I'm not sure what you were expecting?'

'Evidence that he's a serial killer would've been nice, but he's too smart for that.'

'There was nothing.' Webster took a sip of coffee. 'No murder weapons, no bloodied clothing. Nothing. And certainly nothing to suggest he murdered Martin Clarke. That's what we're supposed to be looking at, isn't it?'

'What did he say about that?' I asked, hoping they'd forget the 'not a serving officer' business.

Field and Webster were staring at each other, Field the first to raise his eyebrows.

'He gave a bit more information than was in his original witness statement,' said Webster. 'Although it was more of an opinion, to be technically correct. In his *opinion*, Clarke was attempting to jump on to the top of the lorry and misjudged the jump. Taylor didn't think he slipped or intended to kill himself. Apart from that he stuck to his witness statement. He'd pulled him over for a defective brake light, was in pursuit on foot, and you know the rest.'

I know what you're thinking. I should tell them about Taylor's attempt to frame me for Alan's murder. He's got form when it comes to planting murder weapons in cars, but there's something stopping me. It could easily blow up in my face and they'd only have my word that's what happened. It could equally look like I killed Alan and then tried to kill myself in the reservoir.

I suppose I don't trust them. I don't trust anyone, actually, but that's a different issue; the good doctor was supposed to have been getting to it in our next session.

I'd seen them coming and had time to hide Clarke's personnel file under the table. I ought to give them something and I've had a good look through it anyway. 'You've heard about the disappearance of Maxine Green?' I asked. 'She worked at B & D Light Haulage in Ilminster, with Martin Clarke. She'd even been out with him that night.'

'She's gone missing?' Field looked surprised.

'No one's told us,' snapped Webster.

'I found this under her mattress,' I said, producing the file from under the table.

Field snatched it from me and looked at the label. 'Why on earth would she have taken this?'

'Compare it to the copy of the personnel file given to police after Martin Clarke's death,' I said. 'Look for any differences. She clearly thought it was worth the risk stealing it, and that's the only reason I can think of.'

'You think her disappearance is connected to Clarke's death?' asked Webster.

'Anything else would be too much of a coincidence,' I replied.

'We need to get over to Chard,' said Field, standing up. 'See what the story is with this Maxine Green.'

'There's one other question you need to be asking,' I said. And this is the even bigger question that I still can't answer. 'How did Taylor know Martin Clarke had no alibis for the murders, unless he had access to that file?' I let that hang in the air for a second. 'He must've seen it, checked the dates.'

'That assumes Clarke wasn't the killer,' said Field.

'Obviously.'

'We'll be in touch, Bob.'

Webster was hanging back, taking longer than necessary to slide out of her seat, watching Field, making sure he was a safe distance away. 'We found this, Bob,' she whispered, placing a small key on the table in front of me. 'It doesn't fit anything in Taylor's house that we could find. It's a garage or a lock-up, something like that. We've checked the obvious places near where he lives but there's nothing.'

I picked up the key, closing my fingers around it.

'Sharp said we should forget it, but I can't,' continued Webster. Then she was gone.

A key. What the hell am I supposed to do with that?

Angela looked none the wiser. 'Looks like my dad's garage key. It could be a garage, couldn't it?'

'It could be any number of things,' I replied. 'A garage, a lock-up unit, self-storage.'

'What do we do now?'

'We think like police officers.'

'What's that supposed to mean?'

I sat back on the bench seat while a Jubilee Pancake was placed in front of me; a fork and spoon rolled up in a serviette. Like I said, you'll know if you've ever had one. 'They've checked the obvious places near where he lives, so that's Street out. He's not going to risk it in Yeovil either.'

'Why not Yeovil?'

'He's based at the police station.' I'm blowing on the cherry sauce now. You do have to watch out for that; like molten lava sometimes. 'But it's likely to be somewhere near the A303, isn't it.' A mouthful of pancake and ice cream. 'Near the A303, nice and quiet, remote. You get the picture.'

'On a farm even.'

'You're wasted on coffee mornings and fetes.'

'Don't be sarcastic. Where do we start, though?' She shrugged. 'We might as well throw a dart at a map.'

Not a bad idea, as it happens. I've done much the same in the past, although it had been a little bit more scientific perhaps; break the search area down into zones, work through them systematically. Easy when you've got a major investigation team behind you and can call on uniformed constables for the legwork; not so easy with two people, neither of them serving police officers.

There's the answer, of course, staring me in the face. Ask a serving police officer. I know a few, am owed a few favours.

'Why don't we just follow him?'

Another good idea, although that's the last resort. 'Firstly, he'd spot us a mile off, and secondly he might not go to the garage for weeks.'

'What d'you think's in there?' asked Angela.

'The car that hit me.' A deep breath. 'I dread to think what else.'

'Let's get going then. It's no good sitting here all day,' she said, sliding along the bench to the end.

'You need to get back to work,' I said.

'No way. I'm going with you.'

'And how do I explain to your father that I've got another one of his daughters killed?'

'You didn't get Lizzie killed.' Angela sighed. 'All right. What can I do?'

195

That's a relief. I'd been wondering how I was going to get rid of her. 'Speak to the crime reporter, Ray whatshisname, see if he's got any ideas; check for Taylors in Ilminster, see if any of them have got garages.' I'm making it up as I'm going along now, just to give her something to do, really. To keep her safely out of the way. 'Check with local storage firms, see if they've had a police officer visiting regularly. Local farmers, as you say; see if any of them rent out storage.'

Chapter Twenty-Eight

I dropped Angela back to her car at Hinton St George, then rang Yeovil police station from the phone box by the church.

'Can you put me through to Police Sergeant Druce, please?'

'Is that you, Bob, mate?'

I recognised the voice. Jim Bromidge; his turn for desk sergeant duty, obviously. 'Yes. It's me,' I replied.

'I thought you were . . . someone said you'd . . .'

'Well, I'm not and I haven't.'

'Pleased to hear it.'

'What about Brian?'

'He hasn't come in. He was due on duty at two, so God knows where he is.'

It didn't take me long to get over to Martock; far less time than it should have actually, thanks to Martin Clarke's three-litre Capri.

The blue Volvo hatchback that was in the drive has gone, but the black BMW is there, parked across it. I don't know where Druce went when he sped off earlier, but he's back now. Not gone in to work either. I'm guessing the Volvo is his wife's and she's gone out. Stands to reason.

I'm standing at the bottom of the garden path, looking up at the bungalow. It's one of those ones with a small window set into the middle of the roof, so they've done a loft conversion. There's a bucket of rose clippings on the front doorstep, a pair of secateurs on the top; I can see the handles sticking out. Druce left in a hurry, but then I remember that from the speed, the spinning wheels and the smell of burning rubber.

The front door is ajar. No sign of the dog and no barking when I rattle the gate, so maybe his wife took it with her. There's a doorbell, so I try that. I can hear it ringing inside the bungalow, loud and clear. I try a knock too.

No answer.

Terracotta tiles in the porch, boots and shoes in a jumble behind the front door, coats hanging on hooks. The handle of the inner door creaks loudly when I turn it, so if he's in there he'll know I'm coming in.

'Brian?'

Still no barking.

'Brian?' I tried again, louder this time.

There's a new carpet, hall table with a telephone on it; much the same as most houses I've been in. Dining room on the right, the door open. That makes the door on my left the living room.

I turn the handle, pushing it open slowly.

'Brian?'

'Come in, Bob.'

The television is in the far corner, a fireplace to my right, opposite the bay window. Druce is sitting in an armchair on the far side of the room, a whisky bottle on the low table in front of him, the glass next to it empty. He reaches behind him into an open drinks cabinet and takes out another glass.

'Drink, Bob?' he asked, placing the glass on the table and picking up the bottle. He begins pouring a large Scotch before I have a chance to answer. Then he empties the bottle into his own tumbler, filling it almost to the brim.

He picks up the spare glass and holds it out to me in his outstretched hand.

He's wearing full dress uniform. Green tunic with three stripes on each arm, green lanyard, medals, white belt. There's a cap on the arm of the sofa next to him, upside down, but I can see the Royal Green Jackets cap badge.

'Mrs Druce gone out?' I asked.

'Sheila's playing tennis.' A large swig of whisky. 'Did you serve in the army, Bob?' he asked.

'I did my national service,' I replied. 'Never went overseas. When I came out I joined the police.' A sip of Scotch – for appearances' sake, really, you understand.

'Man and boy, me,' Druce said. 'Twenty-six years.' Swirling the whisky around in his glass. 'I killed two during the troubles in Kenya; the Mau Mau rebellion, they called it. I was only a private then and my platoon was out on patrol; ambushed. When it was over I went and looked at the bodies. They looked like kids, really. Couldn't have been older than sixteen or seventeen, but they were shooting at me. What was I supposed to do?'

'Defend yourself.'

'Exactly.' Druce raises his glass in my direction, then takes another swig. 'I killed a Provo too; that was on my second tour. It was at a checkpoint outside Derry, a big fella with a beard. Got him right in the head and he went down like a sack of spuds. Mortar attack, that was, but I put a stop to it; got the Military Medal for that.' He looks down at the medals pinned to his tunic, holds one up between his index finger and thumb. 'This one.'

'Congratulations,' I said, raising my glass and taking another sip.

'I remember my father was so proud of that, his boy winning a gallantry medal.'

It feels like I'm humouring him and I'm starting to get a horrible feeling about what I've walked in on, to be honest. I've had a good look around the room, can't see any boxes or bottles of pills on the table or on the floor at his feet, though. No razor blades, no length of rope.

'You wanted to know about that night in Belfast,' he said, his speech becoming slurred now. 'Two lads from the Special Reconnaissance Unit brought them in just before dawn. They'd flagged down an RUC patrol; lost their weapons and all their kit, been running for miles.' He's still looking down at his medals, the Northern Ireland medal between his index finger and thumb this time – I recognise the ribbon; purple with dark green edging. 'I was told they'd killed a girl in a shooting,' he continued. 'That she'd been running towards them along a ginnel, raised her hand to throw something and they'd shot her. A girl, for fuck's sake, but it was dark and they didn't know that at the time. We knew all hell would break loose if it got out, though. So, at Lieutenant Jenner's direction, I falsified the records – the roll – to show they were present when the rest of the company had returned to base, and that was the last we heard about it. There was a bit of a stink, another night of riots, but that was it. When news of the murder got out, the British military denied any involvement in it and that was that.'

'What's the Special Reconnaissance Unit?' I asked. 'I've never heard of it.'

'No one has.' Another swig of Scotch. 'It's hush-hush, under-cover stuff. You don't want to know what they get up to. No one does. No one cares. We're at war, aren't we? And provided we keep it off the streets of dear old Blighty, no one gives a shit.'

'What about the police traffic logs?' I asked. 'Taylor's alibi.'

'I swear to God, I never knew what they'd done to that girl. If I had, I'd never have . . .' His voice tails off. 'The whole thing's on a knife edge, Jenner said. Think about the regiment. And I did. I went along with it.'

'The logs?'

'I can't bloody well remember, can I?'

I thought he might say that. What's more interesting is that he didn't say it wasn't Taylor. In his state that would have been his immediate response, surely?

'Logs can be changed,' he said. 'Just like a roll call.' Another swig. 'Taylor said he'd put us down as having been out on the road together a couple of times. I thought nothing of it, that he was seeing some lass on the side and didn't want his girlfriend to find out.'

'What about this key?' I've taken it out of my jacket pocket and am holding it up for him to see, not that he seems able to focus on it. 'It looks like a garage key, possibly, but we've checked where he lives and it fits nothing around there.'

'He's got an elderly grandmother over Ilminster way. He sometimes stays over there, I think.' Druce is beginning to sway from side to side, even in his armchair. 'Try there,' he said. He picks up the bottle and turns it upside down, grimacing when nothing came out.

I stand up. 'One last thing, Brian,' I said. 'You never mentioned the name of the soldier with Taylor that night in Belfast.'

'Didn't I?' He's standing up now, after a fashion, leaning against the arm of the chair behind him. He reaches over with his left hand, picks up his cap and places it firmly on his head.

'What about the missing girl, Maxine Green?' I asked.

'Sorry, mate, never heard of her. Look, Bob, it's been lovely chatting, but I need to be on my way.'

'What time does your wife get home?'

He snaps to attention, his heels clicking together, shoulders back. 'Company Sergeant Major Druce, B Company, First Battalion, Royal Green Jackets. Reporting for duty. Sir!'

It looks like he's saluting me, but there's a gun in his hand.

Chapter Twenty-Nine

'What is your emergency?'

How the fucking hell do I describe that?

'I'm at the home of Police Sergeant Brian Druce – 17 Havelock Place, Martock – and he's just shot himself in the head.'

'Is he still breathing?'

I did check for a pulse, before you ask. Your training takes over and I pressed my fingers to the side of his neck. Nothing. Not much chance, to be honest. Not with his brains all over the television. A Browning 9mm to the temple tends to have that effect. Is he still breathing? Fuck off.

'No,' I replied.

'What's your name?'

'Mungo Willis. I'm a detective inspector with Avon and Somerset Police.'

'Stay on the line, caller.'

I'm standing in the hall, by the table, the telephone to my ear, staring through the open living room door at yet another victim of this whole fucking mess. Taylor and whoever, leaving a trail of destruction behind them. Seven dead now, not including Maxine, wherever the hell she is.

Seven.

Just let that sink in for a moment.

And it all started with Bernadette Ryan. Brian Druce paid a high price for his part in the cover-up; bringing the regiment into disrepute as he saw it – the precious regiment.

He's lying on his side in front of the fire, the gun still in his right hand. Blood is soaking into the rug underneath what's left of his head. God alone knows where his cap went in the blast. I'm afraid I turned away; not embarrassed to admit it either.

His belt is still brilliant white and his tunic buttons are glinting in the sunlight streaming in through the bay window. I can't see his medals, though.

I can hear a car outside now. I hope to God it's not his wife coming home from tennis.

I lean over, peer through the inner door of the porch, which is standing open.

Yes, it is.

At least I can hear sirens in the distance now.

'His wife's here. I'm going to have to go and speak to her,' I said, placing the telephone handset on the table.

I don't need to spell it out, do I?

I'd closed the living room door and managed to get her into the kitchen for a cup of tea. She wanted to see him, of course she did, but took my advice, mercifully.

Would you want to see your loved one if they'd put a gun to their head and pulled the trigger?

I know, we all would, but take it from me, it's best avoided if you can.

'He wouldn't want you to see him like that' was the line that persuaded her. That and the promise of a cup of tea.

There were no tears, oddly enough. She hadn't been surprised, either.

'That bloody gun,' she said. 'I knew he'd kept it when he left the army, but he never would tell me where he'd hidden it. His little souvenir, he used to call it.'

I resisted the temptation to bombard her with questions. Druce told me pretty much everything I needed to know before he shot himself, everything he was prepared to tell me anyway. She seemed to want to talk, all the same.

'I should've seen it coming, really.' A shake of the head. 'He'd been depressed ever since that first girl was killed out on the A303. Never would say why. I begged him to tell me, get some help, but he wouldn't. He was never the same after he left the Green Jackets. None of them are. There's something about a life in the army.'

'Is there someone who can come and sit with you?' I asked.

'I'll ring my daughter,' she replied. 'She's only over at Honiton. I can go and stay with her for a few days.'

The bungalow was swarming with police officers and paramedics before we'd finished our tea, all of them making sure the living room door stayed shut. The road was closed outside too, but Sheila's daughter was allowed through the cordon.

That was when the tears start to flow.

'C'mon, Mum, let's pack a bag and get you out of here.'

Wise words.

'We'll need Luna's food.'

The dog, presumably.

'I'll get it,' said the daughter.

Then they were gone, an address and phone number left with a fresh-faced young constable I didn't recognise. 'We're going to need a statement from you as well, please, sir,' she said, opening her notebook.

'What's your name?' I asked.

'WPC Herbert, sir,' she replied.

I don't hold with that WPC nonsense. Lizzie had been a DS, not a WDS. The powers that be will get rid of it one day.

My statement didn't take long. He was in uniform, drinking heavily. I hadn't seen the gun. It must've been down beside his chair, hidden by the magazine rack and the coffee table. If I had, I'd have tried to talk him out of it, of course I would. He was in no fit state to drive, so no, I certainly wasn't going to let him leave. Then he suddenly stood up and . . . you know the rest.

'Did he leave a note?'

'Not that I could see,' I replied. 'I suppose I'm his suicide note.'

'Did he tell you why?'

'He told me he was deeply ashamed of his part in covering up the murder of Bernadette Ryan in Belfast in 1981 and giving false alibis for Police Constable Sean Taylor in connection with the murders of Fiona Anderson, Alice Cobb, DS Lizzie Harper and Martin Clarke. But it was about more than that for him; it was about bringing his regiment into disrepute.'

She was scribbling frantically in her notebook. 'Can you give me a minute, sir,' she said, reaching for her radio.

I was at the front door, on my way out as it happens, when she came running into the hall from the kitchen. 'CID are on their way, sir,' she said. 'Detective Chief Superintendent Sharp asked that you wait until he gets here. They'll need a detailed statement, and he wants a word with you, personally, he said.'

'He knows where I live.'

Actually, he knows where I used to live. There's no phone, though, and the post office is closed.

Tough shit, mate. You had your chance. And he probably just wants to tell me to keep my nose out of it; leave it to Field and Webster.

I'd parked about a hundred yards along Havelock Place and walked the last bit to Druce's house. I always do that, and I know you're wondering why.

I walked past the patrol car blocking the road, climbed in the Capri and drove away.

So, now you know.

Always park outside where a police cordon is likely to be set up. Force of habit, really.

I'll tell you another thing that occurred to me. Taylor and his trail of destruction. What about me and mine? There was poor Alan, whose only crime was being in the wrong place at the wrong time; killed by mistake or in an attempt to frame me. Mistaken identity was the more plausible, I think you'll agree. Taylor was trying to kill me and tried again at the lake.

Now there's Brian Druce. Would he have killed himself if I hadn't confronted him this morning? Maybe not today, I suppose, but it was coming. I suspect he knew that. On reflection, not my fault then.

Then there's Maxine, and Martin Clarke's personnel file under her mattress. My fault?

Buggered if I know.

I ought to check in with Angela, really, see how she's getting on. It had been a case of *don't call me, I'll call you*, mainly because she's got no means of contacting me at the moment. Convenient that. I've got a key, an idea of where Taylor's garage might be, and I don't want her getting in my way, or hurt.

It just got bloodier, this thing. I said it would.

And it's going to get worse, not better.

◆ ◆ ◆

There's a Gladys Taylor in the phone book as it turns out: Manstree Place, Ilminster.

I know it well. It's a block of council houses, with a large car parking area behind and two rows of garages. I've been there a couple of times before; domestic violence, a burglary. There was a murder too, some years ago, but that was a domestic as well; the wife was convicted of manslaughter and sentenced to time served. Walked out of court, she did, which was fitting.

I'm surprised I never drove Shirley to it, really, not that we should joke about these things. Gallows humour, sorry.

It's raining by the time I arrive at Ilminster. Lights are starting to come on in the houses and bungalows. I'm not that far from where Martin Clarke lived, drove past the end of his road to get here, as it happens. Is that relevant? I hear you ask.

No idea.

A terrace of bungalows faces the road, with handrails up the steps to each of the front doors. Neatly manicured lawns, white-picket fences and flower beds, window boxes too. I can see the top of a block of flats behind, and there's another terrace – houses this time – facing the lane that runs along the back. A nice view over fields, they've got.

I've left the Capri out on the main road, facing out of town. The road narrows into a country lane a couple of hundred yards further up and it will be the quickest way to get clear, if needs be. That's rule number two, always turn the horses for home.

Not that I've got a home at the moment.

I don't know what I'm going to find, is the short answer to your question. God willing, it will be Maxine, alive and well, although I'd settle for the car that hit me, murder weapons, blood-spattered clothing, trophies – we know serial killers often keep them: the victim's handbag, something like that. Basically, anything incriminating will do.

There are two lines of garages, all of them overlooked by windows at the back of the bungalows on one side and the houses on the other. It's a triangle of sorts, and impossible to believe that someone won't see me – or, more importantly, won't have seen Taylor coming and going, assuming I'm in the right place, of course.

I've started trying the key in the locks of the garage doors, working my way along one by one. Gladys Taylor lives at number 11, but there are no numbers on the garages.

'Can I help you?'

'Police,' I said, without looking up. 'Do you know which one belongs to number 11?'

'I'm number 15, so it'll be that one,' said the voice.

I turn to see a man pointing to a garage door further along.

'That's mine you're trying.'

'Sorry.'

He's hovering now, which might not be such a bad thing. An independent witness, and all that.

I bang on the door of number 11. 'Maxine?'

'Not that missing girl?'

'Stay back if you will, please, sir,' I said, turning to find the man right behind me.

'Of course. Sorry.'

'Has anyone been near this garage recently?' I asked.

'There's a bloke who comes from time to time. I think he's a relative of Gladys's, her grandson maybe. I know he keeps a car in there.'

Nothing for it. The key fits, so I turn it and lift the up-and-over door out of the way.

Light is streaming into the garage and I can see a car covered by a sheet. There's no foul smell, which I half expected.

'Maxine?'

No reply.

Old paint tins and gardening tools are gathering dust on a shelf on the left, a ladder lying across the rafters above the car. Packing crates against the wall on the right in the far corner, more against the back wall. There's a tin box too, under the small window at the back.

I hold my breath, pull the sheet off the bonnet of the car.

And there it is. A black VW Golf, the driver's side headlight smashed – my left knee; dents in the bonnet – my elbow. The windscreen has been shattered too – my head.

The good doctor would want to know how I *feel* about it, seeing it after all this time. Pain is the short answer. My left leg and elbow have started throbbing. My head too. Still, no time for that now.

Gloves on.

I roll the sheet back, disappointed there's no one in the back of the car. I had hoped Maxine might have been in there, asleep or drugged perhaps. I try the tin box next. It's locked, but I make short work of the lock with a screwdriver that was on the windowsill. Underwear, women's, bloodstained.

There's a toolbox in the boot of the car, so I've got that out on top of one of the packing cases now.

Nothing.

He planted the knife he used to kill Alan behind my spare wheel, so let's see, shall we? I lift the carpet in the boot and there's a towel, rolled up and wedged in behind the tyre.

I've seen enough.

'Can I use your phone, please, mate?'

Jim Bromidge would know what to do, and do it right, so I rang Yeovil police station, hoping he was still on desk duty.

'Is that you, Jim?'

'Where are you, Bob? What the hell's happened to Brian Druce?'

'Long story, mate,' I said. 'Look, I've found the car that hit me and it was a bloody Golf. It's in a garage at 11 Manstree Place, Ilminster. The property belongs to Sean Taylor's grandmother.'

'So, you were right all this time?'

'Don't sound so fucking surprised.'

'What else is in there?'

'A tin box with items that look like they belonged to the victims, weapons possibly hidden behind the spare wheel in the back. I haven't had a proper look, but it needs the full forensics. Obviously.'

'Bloody hell, Bob.'

'Where is he?'

'Taylor's gone over to Wiltshire to help with an operation they've got on over there. Quite a few of the lads have. Some peace convoy heading for a free festival at Stonehenge and there's an injunction in place to stop them; a big police presence, apparently.'

'Where exactly?'

'The hippies were in Savernake Forest, so they'll be coming down the A338 to join the A303. That's where the lads were asked to rendezvous.'

'How many?'

'A hundred and fifty from us, more from Hampshire. They're expecting about six hundred hippies and the police presence will be double that. You be careful if you're thinking of going, Bob. You don't want to get caught in the middle of that lot. You've done your bit. Just let DCS Sharp handle it from here.'

Chapter Thirty

Just let DCS Sharp handle it from here.

Yeah, right.

At least I know there'll be no traffic officers about today; too busy giving a few hippies a good kicking at Stonehenge. Any excuse. I know we used to enjoy a set-to with the mods and rockers on Weston seafront back in the sixties, but that was different. That was part of the game; what they were there for.

This is a peace convoy, for heaven's sake.

Hardly warrants full riot gear.

I'm heading east on the A303, foot flat on the floor in Martin's three-litre Capri. I know the road, where I can and can't overtake, where the stretches of dual carriageway are. I'm getting flashed by oncoming cars from time to time – drivers of a nervous disposition, obviously – but there's plenty in reserve and I can accelerate out of trouble easily enough.

I'll turn north at Amesbury, cut across country to join the A338 at Tidworth. Then I'll just have to find the convoy, which shouldn't be difficult.

There's a Little Chef at Amesbury too, but this is going to have to be done on an empty stomach, unfortunately.

I've seen the posters up and down the 303 for 'STONEHENGE '85', promising sex, drugs, rock and roll, anarchy, hilarity, permissiveness. I know, and the thought had crossed my mind. I don't think the good doctor would approve, though.

'DESPITE CERTAIN RUMOURS TO THE CONTRARY, STONEHENGE FREE FESTIVAL WILL BE TAKING PLACE AS USUAL THIS JUNE', the poster said.

I don't think so. Sorry. Someone's got an injunction to stop it and the police seem determined you're not going to reach Stonehenge at all.

It's got disaster written all over it.

And Sean Taylor's going to be right in the middle of it.

I know I said I turned away when I saw the gun in Brian Druce's hand, and I did. Just a fraction too late, though, and it's yet another vision etched on my mind. I keep seeing it, over and over, as if someone is stopping the video tape, rewinding and pressing play, again and again.

I can't stop watching it for some reason.

You have to understand the military for it to make sense. I was in for two years, my national service, but even then it's drummed into you. The regiment is everything; its reputation comes first. Nothing can be allowed to tarnish it. People have died for less, and Brian Druce has just added his name to a long list.

Some might say it's taking the easy way out; that he should have faced the music. A conviction for perverting the course of justice, loss of his job in the police, discretionary pension, all of it secondary to bringing the regiment into disrepute – that much was clear from the manner of his death. Nothing else mattered but that.

A high price to pay.

Winterbourne Stoke is coming up and I'll be able to see Stonehenge on the other side of this hill. There'll be police everywhere too, so I'd better slow down.

Two lanes off the roundabout, which will give me a chance to get past this caravan.

My plan? A good question.

I'm not sure I've got one, to be honest, other than confronting Taylor and getting him to tell me the name of his accomplice. You might well ask how I'm intending to do that, and I'm embarrassed to admit the answer involves violence. I'm not a violent man, by nature. It's not something that comes naturally to me – not my first response in any situation, frankly – but needs must. Too many people have died, and it has to stop.

I have to stop it.

Finding him will be the first challenge. He'll be part of a large police presence, some of them wearing riot gear, and I don't even have my warrant card to wave at any Wiltshire and Hampshire officers charging in my direction. I don't look like a hippy, but I'm not sure they'll be stopping to check.

I might know some of the Somerset officers, I suppose. They'll be deployed together, so look for familiar faces and Taylor won't be far away.

Kill him if I have to?

Only in self-defence.

◆　◆　◆

Going south on the A338. I manage to get as far as Shipton Bellinger before I hit the first roadblock.

'I'm visiting my elderly aunt.'

'Address, please, sir.'

'Manor Close, Shipton.' Don't ask, but I point in the general direction, for emphasis, and it seems to work.

'Go through.'

'Thank you.'

'You'll have to come back this way. There's a load of hippies down there and the A303 junction is blocked.'

I nod, grateful for the information. At least I know where the convoy is now.

I left the Capri in a residential area and I'm on foot now, cutting across a field towards a gate on the far side. The road is beyond that, but there's no sign of the convoy. Yet.

There's a bloke on a motorcycle, heading north; a nice old Norton. You can tell by the engine noise. I flag him down and he stops in front of me.

'Have you seen a convoy of buses and vans?'

'They're about half a mile down there,' he said. 'The police have stopped them getting on the A303 and there's a stand-off. I've never seen so many police.' He shook his head. 'Is there a phone box in Shipton, do you know?'

I'd passed one, as it happens. 'Yes, fork left just up there and it's outside the post office.'

'I'm going to ring some journalist friends of mine,' he said. 'I've got a bad feeling about this.'

'There's a roadblock beyond the village,' I said.

'I'll be back. I want to see what happens. They're a harmless bunch. I came across them last night up at Savernake Forest when I was out with my dog. There are just too many police and I'm not sure they know what they've got themselves into.'

Then he speeds off.

Walking along the grass verge now, there's a wooded area up ahead, trees overhanging the road, meeting in the middle, and I can see the back of a bus, an old horse lorry in front it. Stationary, it looks like; there's no smoke coming from the exhaust, so the engine can't be running.

I'm getting closer now and can make out brightly coloured flowers painted on the back of the bus, 'Peace and Love' in large letters, doves in flight and the CND logo. There's a banner too, painted on a sheet and draped in the rear window: 'STONEHENGE '85'.

I wonder if they've got room for one more?

The motorcyclist is back, sitting astride his bike, helmet balanced on the petrol tank, watching from a safe distance.

No such luxury for me, unfortunately.

I'm keeping tight to the side of the bus in the vain hope the police officers at the junction won't see me. There are large groups of them milling about on both sides of the road, truncheons at the ready.

The tree canopy above my head is thick, shafts of light streaming through what few gaps there are, reflecting off the windows of the bus, glinting on the riot shields a couple of hundred yards away.

I remember it well. The anticipation, the adrenaline rush when you get the order and wade in, hitting anything and everything in front of you with your truncheon; heads, arms, legs. I was a young man, you understand, and the mods and rockers would fight back. It was part of the game, a blood sport. That's how it felt, anyway.

This lot are very different.

I knock on the side of the bus at the back of the convoy and the young man sitting behind the steering wheel comes over and opens the door. He'd been rolling a cigarette and it was in his mouth, unlit.

'Room for one more?' I asked.

'Sorry, man, we've got kids on this bus. Try Zeke in the horse lorry.'

I'm standing on the bottom step, looking into the passenger compartment. The front row of seats is still there, but behind that they've all been ripped out. There's an old sofa, a kitchen area, beds.

It's a family home. Two toddlers are sitting on the floor, playing with hand-carved wooden animals, a pregnant woman on the sofa reading a book. I say *woman*, she can't be more than eighteen or nineteen years old at most. Just a kid, but then I'm getting old these days. Feeling it too.

An older woman – mid-twenties, possibly – walks to the front of the bus and tries to look over the horse lorry in front. 'We can't see a bloody thing from here,' she muttered. 'What's going on?'

'They've blocked the road with piles of gravel. Lorry loads of it,' replied the young man. 'Alan's negotiating with them, trying to get them to let us on to the A303.'

I step back out on to the grass verge. 'If the worst happens,' I said, 'keep the children out of the way and cover your heads.'

'We should leave now,' said the woman.

'It'll be fine,' replied the lad. He was lighting his cigarette. 'They're not going to *do* anything. Alan's negotiating with them and they can't arrest us all, can they?'

There's a bloke looking down at me from the passenger seat of the horse lorry. He'd been watching me in the wing mirror, creeping along the side of the lorry, trying to stay in the shadows.

I can see further ahead now, along a line of what must be over a hundred buses and vans, some of them towing caravans. Smoke is rising into the trees from the chimneys of some. I can hear voices now, down at the front of the convoy, shouting. Dogs barking. There's music too; someone is playing a guitar, a woman singing a song I don't recognise.

Laughter.

'The bloke on the bus said you might have room for one more, mate,' I said.

'Coming to the festival?' he asked, with a toothy grin, nicotine stains in his grey beard. He's wearing a sleeveless T-shirt under a black leather waistcoat and wouldn't look out of place on the back of a Harley-Davidson.

Takes all sorts, I suppose. 'Hoping to,' I replied.

'The side door is open. Hop in.'

I close the door behind me, shutting out the noise of the convoy ahead, although there's music inside the horse lorry. Sounds like Hendrix.

No horses, but then I hadn't expected any, although it's not been long judging by the smell. There's a seating area to my left, just behind the driver, a bed above the cab, a small kitchen area, a toilet in front of me, more sleeping bags laid out on the floor at the back. I count six, but there's only the two men in here. I'm guessing it's Zeke driving, and the biker.

'You've got a full house.'

'They're down the front, making sure the pigs behave themselves,' said the biker. 'It's supposed to be a peace convoy, ain't it.'

'You don't look like one of us,' said the driver.

'What does "one of us" look like?'

It starts slowly, one or two at first, before crowds of people begin running back along the grass verges on either side of the convoy, climbing into vans and buses as fast as they can, doors slamming behind them. Hendrix is quickly drowned out by the noise; a loud roar. It sounds like a jet taking off, but there's shattering glass in there too.

Then we see the police running down both sides of the convoy, hitting the vans and buses with their truncheons and riot shields, smashing windscreens and windows. It's like a wave coming towards us, breaking down the sides of the convoy; unstoppable.

'Get out! Everybody out! Give me the keys!'

The door at the side of the horse lorry is snatched open from the outside and three lads throw themselves up the steps, blood streaming down the forehead of one.

'Where's Jake?' one asked.

'He went down,' replied another, bolting the door. 'I didn't see him after that.'

The wave is coming towards us, the noise louder all the time. Shouting too, as the police try to drag people out through the smashed windows of the buses. Up ahead, one man is being dragged out of the driver's window of a van, another officer clubbing him with his truncheon, before someone inside pulls him back in.

Then it reaches us, the noise deafening on the side of the horse lorry. The windscreen shatters in several places from blows with truncheons.

I can hear shouts from the bus behind us: 'There are children on this bus! There are children on this bus!' A woman's voice, hysterical, the kids screaming now to add to the wall of noise.

Zeke is flailing at an officer trying to reach in through the open driver's window and drag him out. The biker in the passenger seat is doing much the same, but with more success. The officer had been trying to reach the keys, which were in the ignition in the middle of the dashboard.

'The convoy's moving up ahead,' I said. 'You need to follow.'

If only for the sake of the bus behind us, which is now surrounded by officers banging their truncheons on the side. Others are standing back, seemingly reluctant to get involved too directly, but none of them are wearing their ID numbers on their epaulettes.

It's an old trick.

'They're going into that beanfield on the left,' said the biker.

Buses and vans are turning off the road, driving straight through the hedge and into the large field on the nearside. Some bounce down a small embankment, before smashing through a wooden fence and setting off across the field, slewing from side to side on the crops.

'Go, go!' shouted the biker, leaning back as a truncheon smacked into the headrest behind him. He manages to grab hold of it, wrenching it from the officer's hand, snapping the leather strap in the process.

The engine starts first time and Zeke turns straight off the road, scattering the officers on the nearside. The banging is replaced by vegetation scraping down the outside of the cabin, the lorry taking a tree branch with it as it crashes through the fence and into a small woodland area of newly planted saplings, before emerging into the beanfield on the far side.

Now we're bouncing over the lines of beans, following the other vans and buses seeking refuge on the far side of the field.

I'm looking out of the back window of the horse lorry, trying to see if the bus behind us has followed.

But it hasn't.

Chapter Thirty-One

The police are lining up on the far side of the field now, blocking all of the exits. There's an area of woodland behind us, then a steep embankment down to the A303. We can hear the cars zipping past on the main road, the drivers oblivious to what's going on just a few yards away.

Someone is having a go at negotiating again and we're being told an ambulance is to be allowed through to treat several members of the convoy with head injuries.

I'm left wondering what happened to the family on the bus. I can see it, through what's left of the hedgerow, but there's no movement in or around it. Arrested, probably. Obstruction, but it would have to be a police officer in the execution of his duty, because it was Wiltshire police who obstructed the highway with their piles of gravel.

Someone has lent me a telescope they use for stargazing, and I've been scanning the police line for Taylor. I haven't seen him yet, but I've spotted several Somerset officers grouped together and there are others standing with them wearing riot helmets.

There's a gaggle of senior officers gathered out on the A338 too, near that last bus; and, if I'm not mistaken, the assistant chief constable is on the scene. I wouldn't want to be responsible for this shitshow, not that I've ever reached that level of seniority anyway. Few do.

Few are stupid enough to aspire to it.

I can see a TV crew too, the reporter filming a piece to camera, so maybe that bloke on the motorcycle does have some journalist friends.

I'm still not completely clear how this is going to end. I'm talking about my pursuit of Taylor. He's here. I know he is. I've just got to find him, and ideally before he finds me. I'm keeping out of the way, obviously, watching from the comparative safety of the horse lorry, one of the small windows in the side panel. I've got half an idea that if I can find him before the arrests start, and start they will, then I can make sure he's the one who has to arrest me.

See how he likes that.

This stand-off is going to end soon, and end badly. I like these people. They're optimists and they're convinced they can negotiate a way out of this mess. I've tried to tell them, without much success, and without revealing that I'm a police officer myself. I don't think that would go down too well.

As far as the top brass will be concerned, the police are here to enforce the injunction, and the four-mile exclusion zone around Stonehenge, even though we're seven miles away. A small technicality, easily overlooked. Then there's the issue of civil disobedience, multiple offences of obstruction, resisting arrest.

Yes, this is going to end badly. It's just a question of when. It's nearly seven o'clock now and sunset is at about nine-fifteen. They'll want to do it in daylight too.

The ambulance is loading up the head injuries. They're on stretchers, their necks in braces. They'll be leaving soon, and that will be when all hell breaks loose.

It's not going to be long now.

Some of the hippies have spotted the police lining up and are barricading themselves inside their vans and buses. Engines are starting up all around me, in the vain hope escape might be on the cards, I suppose.

Those two idiots throwing stones really aren't helping, shouts of 'we're a peace convoy' from their own side putting a stop to it quickly enough.

The police are forming into three groups and I can see the Somerset lot on their left flank. I'm making it sound like a battle, aren't I? That's because it's going to be a battle, make no mistake about it.

I'm guessing the Somerset officers will circle around the fence line on the eastern boundary of the field, get in amongst the vans and buses on the far side; another group will do the same from the right while the rest launch a frontal assault. They're the ones wearing riot gear and carrying shields.

Large diesel engines are revving away to my left and I can see four buses forming a square; trying to, anyway.

You couldn't make this up, you really couldn't.

The negotiations have stopped, a large man with a beard walking slowly back towards what's left of the peace convoy, his arms outstretched in bewilderment.

Suddenly the officers behind him are running, shouting, truncheons and batons raised above their heads. He realises too late, starts to run, but goes down from a blow to the head, an officer kneeling on him, dragging his arms behind his back and handcuffing him.

The shape of things to come. The hippies can see it now, not that there was much doubt, in my mind anyway.

They're running, climbing into and on to vehicles, trying to get away.

I'm watching the Somerset officers from the comparative safety of the horse lorry, and I was right. They're circling around, aiming for the vans and buses, truncheons at the ready.

And there he is.

Police Constable Sean Taylor, right at the back. I wonder if he knows I'm here? Word can't have reached Wiltshire yet, or he'd have been arrested for the murders. Why the fuck hasn't it? It's been hours since I made the call about his garage. What the hell are they waiting for?

The shouting and screaming is deafening, getting nearer. I'm watching a bus now, careering across the middle of the field, heading for the fence on the far side, although that'll only take them into the adjacent field. Officers are battering the windows with their batons as it goes past them, others trying to smash the windscreen with large stones. It slides to a stop and they're surrounding it now, kicking at the door.

Then they pile in, dragging the occupants out. The driver is dragged from behind the steering wheel and through the broken windscreen, then hit over the head with a truncheon.

Women and children are being led away in handcuffs. Yes, children.

There's a van on fire away to my right now, two young lads scrambling out of the back doors and into the arms of police officers. Not much sign of them being cautioned, read their rights. *They were resisting arrest, guv.* Actually, they weren't, but who's going to know?

Apart from me.

It'll never get to court, though. I can hear it now.

'Can you be sure the defendant was the officer who struck the victim?'

'Er, no, not really. None of the police were wearing their ID numbers and they were all in uniform, some wearing riot helmets.'

Case dismissed.

I know because I've been there myself, on Weston seafront. It's the universal get out of jail free card.

I can see a panic-stricken girl now, no more than a teenager really, tears and blood streaming down her face; she's running towards the horse lorry, carrying a baby, two officers in pursuit, truncheons at the ready.

This is it, Bob. Time to get your hands dirty.

I open the door of the lorry and help her up the steps. Then slam the door behind her, bolt it.

'Get up there,' I said, gesturing to the sleeping area above the cab. 'Pull the curtain across. If they find you, do not resist.'

She climbs up, then I hand her baby up to her.

'Thank you,' she mumbled.

I force a reassuring smile, before turning for the door, the officers now banging on the outside of the lorry with their truncheons.

I slide the bolt across, turn the handle and kick open the door, sending an officer flying backwards on to the ground.

'Detective Inspector Willis,' I shouted. 'Avon and Somerset Police, I'm here undercover. Now, back off!' I thought it was worth a try, and it stops them in their tracks, albeit fleetingly.

One of them lunges forwards, so I gave him a sharp kick in the head. It probably hurts me more than it hurt him, given that he was wearing a riot helmet, but it does the trick.

'I'm police,' I said. 'Now fuck off!'

Away to my left there's a line of hippies, lying face down on the bare earth, their hands cuffed behind them, but most of the officers have now encircled the buses that formed into a square. They're battering away at them with their batons, trying to force the doors. Several of the occupants are dragged out through the windows, beaten over the head, and then handcuffed before being dragged across to join the line on the ground, face down in the mud.

Several buses and vans are on fire, thick black smoke billowing into the evening air, and I can see officers on the far side of the field jostling the TV crew, arresting the cameraman.

I'm in amongst faces I recognise now – Somerset officers, and they recognise me.

'What are you doing here, Bob?'

'Undercover,' I replied.

He keeps running.

Some officers are standing back, appearing reluctant to join the melee. It's almost as if they know it's getting well and truly out of hand. And it is. It reminds me of those pictures you see on the telly, those bastards clubbing baby seals. Defenceless. I'm sure one or two of the younger men have fought back, but women and children?

When the dust settles there are going to be a lot of officers wondering what they fuck they've done. I've been there too, but that's for another time.

I'm watching a pregnant girl being dragged off one of the buses now. The officer seems to have spotted she's pregnant and is being careful, holding her by one wrist, coaxing her towards the line of hippies on the ground. That said, she's resisting. I can see that from here; twisting her hand and arm, trying to break free.

Then suddenly she's free and running towards me, towards the sanctuary of the horse lorry.

A second officer is running after her, lining up to bring her down with a truncheon to the head. Only one thing for it.

I used the telescope. Nice and weighty. Broke his arm. I felt the bone shatter, heard the crunch, then the screaming starts. He's on his knees now, holding his arm across his chest.

'Get in.' I'm helping the girl up the steps and into the horse lorry. 'Bolt the door. Hide above the cabin,' I whispered.

I'm listening to the bolt sliding across on the inside of the door and turn just as an officer slams into me.

Face down, my nose and mouth pressed into the mud, he wrenches my arms back and cuffs my hands behind me. Two sharp kicks into my rib cage, right side.

'Wanker.'

'I'm a police officer,' I said, turning my head away from the kicks that are raining in now.

'Yeah, right.'

'He broke my fucking arm.'

Two of them kicking me. Nice. At least my left side is protected by the horse lorry.

Then suddenly I'm being dragged to my feet.

'I'm arresting you on suspicion of obstructing a police officer in the execution of his duty and—'

'Duty?' I sneered. I'm good at sneering. You tend to do a lot of it in the police.

'What's your name?'

'Mungo Willis,' I replied. 'I'm a detective inspector with Avon and Somerset.'

The one with two arms available to him is rummaging in my coat pockets. 'Where's your warrant card?'

'I'm here undercover.'

'Convenient.'

'Not really. I'd rather be watching the cricket.'

'You broke my arm,' said the other, standing back. 'That's GBH, that is.'

'You were about to crush the skull of a pregnant girl. What if she'd miscarried? You'd be facing a manslaughter charge. *Constable.*' I'm standing with my back to the horse lorry, blocking the door, hoping they don't think to search it.

The shouting and much of the screaming seems to be subsiding now, hippies being led away across the field in handcuffs, dogs running loose, barking. Several officers are using extinguishers on the fires.

'What do we do with him, Dave?' asked the officer with the broken arm.

'Fucked if I know.'

'I'll take him,' said Taylor, appearing from behind the horse lorry. 'You need to get some medical attention for that arm.'

Chapter Thirty-Two

Taylor waits until the officers are a safe distance back up the bean-field, heading towards an ambulance parked out on the main road, and then leads me around the back of the horse lorry.

'What am I going to do with you, Bob?'

'Hardly matters now, does it.'

'What's that supposed to mean?'

'I found your garage, called it in,' I replied. 'There'll be Forensics crawling all over it now.' He slams his fist into the pit of my stomach and I drop to my knees, gasping for air. 'I've been to Belfast, know about Bernadette Ryan too.'

'What did Druce tell you?'

'Even your alibis have gone up in smoke. Your company sergeant major told me everything.' I'm still on my knees, leaning against the rear wheel of the lorry. 'Except the name of your accomplice.'

'Where's Druce?'

'Taunton police station, cooperating fully.' That's a lie, obviously, but he doesn't need to know that. 'At least we don't execute people in this country, so you can look forward to a long life behind bars; an ex-copper, a murderer and a rapist. I don't envy you that.'

'He came to see me, tried to persuade me to do the decent thing, for the sake of the regiment. I told him, fuck the bloody regiment.'

He's dragging me the short distance from the back of the horse lorry to the woodland behind it. There's no one in sight, the bean-field largely quiet now. Taylor chose his hiding place well.

'Skulking behind the lorry the whole time,' I said. 'You prefer your victims unconscious, I suppose. You fucking coward.' I can taste blood, but have no idea where it's coming from.

Then he throws me to the ground at the base of a large tree. I sit up, leaning back against the trunk. It's a small area, maybe two tennis courts, a mix of new saplings and larger trees, gloomy now the sun is going down.

'Why did you kill Alan?' I asked.

'It was supposed to be you,' he said. 'You interfering little prick.'

'Pulling me over and planting the knife in the boot of my car was a nice touch, if a bit clumsy.'

'I thought you must've found it.'

'And you must've forgotten I've got manual windows on my car,' I said. 'It was easy enough to wind down the window and swim clear.'

'No idea what you're talking about, Bob.' He reaches inside his police tunic and pulls out a knife, examining the blade, running his thumb along it, checking for blood.

If I can keep him talking long enough, someone might come along. Officers will be searching all the vehicles in the field before dark and they'll find the girls hiding in the horse lorry. There might even be some hippies hiding in here. 'Tell me what happened to Bernadette Ryan,' I said.

'You'll know, if you really have been to Belfast.'

'Why carve your regimental insignia in her chest?' I asked. 'Was it revenge?'

'They were giving us a pasting,' he replied. 'The Royal Green Jackets for fuck's sake, and all we'd got was rubber bullets.'

'She was just an innocent kid.'

'Innocent? None of them are bloody innocent. We were looking for somewhere to hide and there she was. Came at us when we broke in, throwing stuff, spitting, so we thought, right, you bitch . . .' His voice softened, fleetingly. 'We were just looking for somewhere to hide.'

'Got a taste for it, though, didn't you?'

'It was . . . fun.'

'Fun? You sick fuck. Fiona Anderson, Alice Cobb, DS Harper.'

'We couldn't stop.' He shrugs. 'We knew by then someone would have to stop us. Never thought it would be a useless streak of piss like you.'

'Why Martin Clarke?'

'He was a driver, fitted the profile, and we knew he had no alibis. It was easy enough to plant the stuff in the boot of his car, then throw him off the bridge into the path of that lorry. Nice and tidy, as it turned out; no loose ends.'

'Apart from me.'

'Apart from you.' He's examining the knife again, takes a step towards me. 'But I can soon clear that up.'

'What about Faith Bennett?'

'Couldn't help ourselves.' He's looking at his reflection in the blade, turning it. 'Thought it had all gone quiet and we'd get away with it. Would've done too, if it hadn't been for you. Sharp was adamant there was no connection with the others. Amazing what a change of method can do. *Modus operandi*.'

'So, tell me what your plan is now,' I said. 'You're not getting away with it, not now, so why not just give yourself up?'

'I'm not going to prison,' he replied. 'No way. I'll run, or take the easy way out, as they like to call it. I don't know why, though. There's nothing *easy* about it from where I'm standing.'

'Run?'

'Got to kill you first, of course, but I'll be miles away before they find your body. Either that or you were resisting arrest, pulled a knife, we fought.'

'You'll have to take these off,' I said, moving my hands to one side to remind him I'm handcuffed.

'I'll take those off when you're dead, Bob,' said Taylor. 'Don't you worry your little head about it one bit.'

He's standing over me now, the knife clenched in his right hand. There are beads of sweat on his forehead, and a smug grin on his face. I try lifting my leg, to give him a good crack in the bollocks, but he sidesteps it, lashes out, his boot connecting with the side of my left knee. I try to hide my wince. Fail.

'Soon be over, Bob,' he said.

Then he stops, a look of surprise on his face. There's a trickle of blood running down the side of his nose and into the corner of his open mouth. I see it now. It's coming from a hole in the middle of his forehead. More blood is dripping off the end of his nose.

Taylor drops to his knees, then falls forwards into the brambles at the base of the tree next to me. I stare at him, lying on his side. Dead.

Movement in the trees behind me, soft footsteps in the undergrowth, and a figure appears next to me, dressed in black from head to toe; trousers, pullover and balaclava.

I know who it is. And so do you. There's only one person it can be.

He rolls Taylor on to his back with his left foot and stands over him, emptying his magazine into Taylor's chest. Eight bullets in total. It looks like a PPK, or something similar. Silenced, obviously.

'That's for my sister,' he said, the familiar Irish accent as strong as ever. 'Did he give you the name of the other one?'

'No.'

'Wait five minutes, then walk out of the wood slowly.'

I listen to the footsteps running down through the under-growth to the road, then the sound of a motorbike accelerating hard eastbound on the A303.

Chapter Thirty-Three

It must've been longer than five minutes in the end. There were several officers searching the vehicles, two of them leading away the girls I'd left hiding in the horse lorry. Nice and calm, mercifully, now the heat's gone out of the situation. Anyway, I didn't really fancy walking out of the wood right where Taylor's body was lying, his brains trickling out of the hole in his forehead.

I've spent a lifetime bringing people to justice before the courts, but I have to be honest, this feels like justice too. And it was him or me, don't forget. It demonstrates the power of a common enemy – the life of a British police officer in the employ of the Crown saved by a Provo.

One day I'll look back on this and laugh.

Come to think of it, maybe not.

I've spotted a group of Somerset officers standing by a smouldering van, so I'm heading towards them.

'What happened to you, Bob?' asked one, when he saw my handcuffs.

'Some berk from Wiltshire didn't realise I'm police.'

'We'll soon have those off you, mate.'

'That's him, there,' said the voice.

I turned to see a group of officers marching towards me, one with his arm in a sling.

'That's the twat who broke my arm.'

Now, I'm looking at the inside of a police van, arrested on suspicion of obstruction and grievous bodily harm. There are several of us in the back of the van, all of us under arrest for one thing or another.

A pregnant girl, another carrying a baby; all three of them unscathed, the baby fast asleep.

Getting checked in took a while; over five hundred arrests were made, people taken to stations all over Wiltshire, most for comparatively minor offences of obstruction and resisting arrest. They're being processed and released on bail as fast as the custody officers can get through them, but like I said, it's taking a while.

'They can't arrest all of us,' someone said.

Turns out they could.

I'm in a different category, it seems. And they must have found Sean Taylor's body by now.

Two officers filed in to the interview room at Andover police station and sat down in front of me, across the table. They did mention their names, but I'm afraid I wasn't listening. Lax of me, I know.

'State your name for the tape.'

'My name is Mungo Willis and I am a detective inspector with the Avon and Somerset constabulary.'

Raised eyebrows? I'm left wondering whether they really didn't know.

'Do you want a solicitor present?'

'No.'

'You've been arrested for grievous bodily harm. What can you tell us about that incident?'

'If you give me the name of the officer concerned then I will respond to the allegation he makes,' I replied.

'We can't do that at this stage.'

'In that case all I will say is this. He was not wearing his identity numbers. I looked. And that is gross misconduct where I come from. We'll see what a jury makes of that. We'll also see what a jury makes of the fact that he was about to club a heavily pregnant woman over the head with his truncheon. That might fill the press gallery as well, mightn't it?'

'Are you admitting the assault?'

'I am not making any such admission. I've said all I'm going to say about that allegation and any further questions will be answered "no comment".'

'All right, then, Bob. Do you mind if we call you that?'

That tells me they know who I am and why I was there. How else would they know my nickname? 'Not at all,' I said.

'What were you doing there in the first place? I mean, you were part of the peace convoy as I understand it.'

'I wasn't *part* of the peace convoy. I joined it when it was already stationary at the roadblock, my intention being to detain Police Constable Sean Taylor, who was part of the police operation.'

'Ah, yes, Sean Taylor.' It was the turn of the other one to have a go, the older one who'd been scowling at me throughout the formalities and early skirmishes. 'We found his body in a small area of woodland below the field. What can you tell me about that, Bob?'

'He's dead.'

'I suppose you think this is funny?'

'Not really. I'd much rather he'd been brought before a court.'

'I'm not sure you quite understand the seriousness of the situation, Bob.' The younger one now. 'I should tell you that, at the moment, you're a suspect in his murder.'

'Oh really,' I said. 'In that case perhaps you should tell me how I managed to shoot him in the head and seven times in the chest with my hands cuffed behind my back.'

'Well, we—'

'And what I did with the gun afterwards. That would be interesting to know as well.'

'Why don't you just tell us the whole story?'

'Sounds to me like you know it already, but for the benefit of the tape: Sean Taylor and an as yet unidentified accomplice are responsible for the murders of Fiona Anderson, Alice Cobb, Detective Sergeant Lizzie Harper, Martin Clarke and Faith Bennett. They were also responsible for the murder of Bernadette Ryan in Belfast during the Easter 1981 hunger strike riots. I found evidence of Taylor's involvement in a garage at Ilminster and it was my intention to confront him at the earliest opportunity. Which I did.'

'And what did he say?'

'He confessed to the murders, including those of Martin Clarke and Bernadette Ryan, and I will happily give a detailed statement to the officers investigating those murders.'

'The case is closed, I thought.'

'Not for much longer.'

'Did he identify his alleged accomplice?'

'He did not.'

'But you're sure there is an accomplice?'

'Two soldiers from the First Battalion of the Royal Green Jackets were involved in the murder of Bernadette Ryan and two were involved in the murder of DS Harper, one of them driving the vehicle I found in the garage into collision with me. So, yes, there's an accomplice and he's still out there.'

'Tell us about Taylor's death.'

'He was shot.'

'Who by?'

'I don't know.' They'll know about my trip to Northern Ireland, surely? If I had to guess, I'd say DCS Sharp was somewhere in the building, pulling the strings.

'The bullets will be going to ballistics, obviously, Bob, but would it be fair to say they might be traced back to Northern Ireland?'

'I wouldn't be surprised,' I replied. 'The bloke who shot him had an Irish accent.'

'What did he say?'

'The first shot came from behind me and he told me not to turn around.'

'Who did?'

'He didn't introduce himself, oddly enough.'

'Where were you?'

'I was on the ground at the base of the tree. Taylor was standing over me with a knife, about to kill me. I'm guessing it was his intention to stab me to death; he said he'd make it look like I pulled the knife and we fought over it, so . . .'

'We found the knife, guv,' said the younger to the older.

'You went to Northern Ireland, I think. Fairly recently?'

'I did. It was my intention to investigate the murder of Bernadette Ryan.'

'And did you?'

'I spoke to her mother.'

'What about her brother?'

'I've no idea who else I spoke to. I was snatched off the street outside my hotel and driven to a remote farmhouse; it seemed remote anyway – about an hour's drive from Belfast. I had a bag over my head, they didn't use names. Then I was dumped not far from an RUC checkpoint.'

'And they didn't take the bag off your head once?'

'They did, but they were wearing balaclavas when they did that. All I saw was the inside of a barn somewhere.'

'Were you followed back to England?'

'How on earth would I know that?'

'All right, Bob, you're going to be detained here for the time being while we make further enquiries. One last thing before we finish, would you be prepared to give a statement for use in the prosecution of the hippies for obstruction and other offences arising out of today's events?'

'No,' I replied, matter of fact. 'I'll be giving a statement for use in their defence.'

Chapter Thirty-Four

They've left me in the interview room, so I'm guessing someone else will be along shortly. Sharp, I expect, although he'll make me wait. He's the type, if you know what I mean.

I could do with a cup of tea.

The door opened slowly. Whoever it is doesn't seem entirely convinced they want to come in at all. I can hear voices outside in the corridor, whispering, then a hand appeared, followed by DCS Sharp.

'Tea, white with one,' I said. I sounded a bit like a defiant child in the headmaster's office, watching the cane being dusted off, but I'm past caring now. Just let me out on bail and I can get on with finishing this bloody thing.

He sat down opposite me, reached across and switched off the tape machine at the socket on the wall.

'Off the record, Bob,' he said, with a smile that looked almost sincere. Unfortunately, I know him better than that. 'Never had you down as the hippy type.'

'I was there for Taylor.'

'Of course you were.'

'Are they going to let me out of here, or what?' I asked.

'Do you ever get the feeling you're being taken for a mug, Bob?'

'Every day.'

'Me too.' Sharp let out a long, slow sigh. He was leaning back in his chair, his fingers interlocked behind his head. 'Are those the same clothes you were wearing in the lake?'

'I didn't get a chance to change.'

'You'd have fitted right in at Stonehenge.'

'I don't fit in anywhere, not anymore, not after what I've seen.'

'It was a shame about Brian Druce; a shame you had to see that.'

'I was talking about what happened to the peace convoy.'

'I gather the lads got a bit carried away,' said Sharp, with a shrug. 'But we need to stick together, as always, mate. It's the golden rule.'

'I don't do rules. Not anymore.'

'The Wiltshire lot are concerned about the publicity and I've been sent to have a quiet word in your ear.'

'A quiet word?' My arms are folded now. 'What do they want me to do, plead guilty to GBH and obstructing a police officer? Because he sure as hell wasn't acting in the execution of his duty.'

'You broke his arm, Bob.'

'Fuck him. He was about to break a pregnant woman's skull.'

'Calm yourself, mate, and the whole thing might go away.' Hands up in mock surrender. 'Just leave it to me. Don't say anything to anybody, keep your trap shut. All right?'

I was staring at him, breathing deeply through my nose.

'And for God's sake don't go talking to the press, or giving a statement to the hippies' defence solicitors; anything fucking stupid like that.' Sharp softened. 'I really don't want to see you losing your pension.'

I drew breath, but he silenced me with a wave of his hand.

'I know you don't give a shit, Bob, but you will, believe me, you will. You can't spend the rest of your life living in a Volvo, for fuck's sake, and you're pissing in the wind if you think Shirley's going to have you back.'

That thought hadn't crossed my mind, actually.

'We found the murder weapon, by the way. The knife Taylor used to kill Shirley's husband, Alan. It was in the garage and it's been confirmed by the pathologist. I'm guessing it was Druce who told you about that garage?'

Sharp was looking at me quizzically, but I'm miles away now. It's a dark night and I'm kneeling at the bottom of a dry stone wall on the top of the Mendips. Taylor must've followed me, watched me searching my car, found the knife where I'd hidden it under the stones and taken it back to his garage. That's the only possible explanation.

Or is it?

Sharp tried again. 'Who told you about the garage?'

'Brian Druce told me about Taylor's grandmother in Ilminster, which led me to the garage.'

'A good find. Forensics are still in there. The car's definitely been involved in a collision, just as you said, which brings me on to an apology, Bob.' Sharp cleared his throat. 'You were right and I was wrong. You tried to tell me, and I wouldn't listen. So, there you have it.'

That was enough to snap me back to the present. 'I bet that hurt,' I said, trying not to gloat.

'You have no idea.'

'What else is in there?'

'Trophies, clothing, weapons, lengths of rope. You name it.' Sharp shook his head. 'Taylor confessed as well, I'm told?'

'To all of the murders; starting with Bernadette Ryan. Faith Bennett too – the change of MO was deliberate to throw you off the scent.'

'Bloody well worked too, didn't it?' Sharp's face reddened. 'I just didn't . . . couldn't bring myself to believe it was the same . . . Why would he confess, though?'

'Why wouldn't he? I was on the ground with my hands cuffed behind my back and he's standing over me with a knife about to kill me.'

'You got lucky there. Who'd have thought it? A British police officer saved by a member of the IRA.'

'Have ballistics confirmed it?' I asked.

'You took a hell of a risk,' continued Sharp. 'Swanning about Northern Ireland like that. You might very well have just disappeared; been buried in a shallow grave somewhere.'

'They recognised we share a common enemy.'

It was Sharp's turn to stare into space, his eyes glazing over. 'It means you were right about Martin Clarke too, of course. Poor bloke.'

'You need to tell that to his father.'

'Yes, I will. I'll go and see him myself. You have my word.'

'It also means I'm right about an accomplice still being out there.'

'You're going to need to have a word with Field and Webster, give them a statement,' said Sharp, standing up. 'Then we can wrap this whole thing up.'

'Field and Webster?' I frowned. 'Surely you're putting a whole team on it now? Somebody who knows their arse from their elbow.'

'It's done, Bob. Taylor's confessed; it's over.'

'And the accomplice?'

'Give it up. Go home, get on with your life.' Sharp took a deep breath, grimaced. 'We're being used, mate. All of us, all the fucking time.'

◆ ◆ ◆

242

The Capri was still where I had left it in Shipton Bellinger, the old man in the bungalow scowling at me from his front garden when I had been dropped off by the taxi. Clearly touchy about people parking outside his house.

We'd come along the A303 from Andover, turning north on the A338, the junction open, the dregs of gravel still lying in the gutter and on the grass verge.

The beanfield looked much the same as it had done the day before. Smashed up buses and vans all over the place, hippies trying to salvage the last of their belongings under the watchful eyes of uniformed police officers, some of them dog handlers.

I could see a van on the far side of the field, down behind the horse lorry, so forensic work was still going on in the trees. Taylor's body would be long gone, of course, the pathologist having dug out the bullets.

Ballistics? Not yet. It usually takes a while, but the Wiltshire lot let me go without charge anyway, oddly enough. I'm not even on bail, which came as a pleasant surprise. Perhaps the officer I'd hit with the telescope had seen sense, or more likely, been persuaded to see sense.

I've left the Capri on the side of the road and am standing at the edge of the field now, the hedgerow and fence in front of me lying broken in the beans where a bus or van had crashed through it, several sets of tyre tracks leading off across the crops. I can't tell what type of beans they are yet, the crops are only a few inches high, what's left of them. Broad beans, possibly. Never liked them.

I know I bang on about the mods and rockers, but that was the game back then. It was what both sides had come for, and by *both sides* I mean us and them. It had been a good way of 'blooding' new officers, an initiation ritual of sorts. But this was different, very different, and I'm left feeling ashamed. I've hunted high and low for the right word, and that's the closest I can get.

Ashamed.

Someone had given the order that every single person in the convoy was to be arrested for obstruction. What the fuck did they think was going to happen? Look, I'm not daft, I know a few of them fought back, some of the younger ones threw stones, but women and children? Not in my day.

Maybe it's time I moved on?

The best that can be said is that no one died.

Apart from Taylor, and I won't be shedding any tears for him.

Eight deaths, if you include Brian Druce and Taylor himself. It could've been nine too, if I hadn't had manual windows on my old Volvo, or Seamus hadn't popped up when he did.

There's a television crew filming off to my right, being careful not to set foot in the field, someone interviewing two hippies who seem keen to have their say. No doubt they'll have their day in court too. Or days. Over five hundred arrests made, not including mine. We never came close to that with the mods and rockers, only ever arresting them if they pulled a weapon. Anything else was fair game.

The taxi driver had the radio on for the drive over here, and the senior police officer being interviewed on the local news had claimed the hippies were throwing petrol bombs. Well, all I can say is that the only fire I saw was started by the police, and as you know, I was there the whole time, watching from the comparative safety of the horse lorry.

Sharp made it clear that I'm to keep my mouth shut, though. We'll see.

It may sound feeble, but I'm certainly going to be careful while there's a grievous bodily harm charge hanging over me. Carries a possible life sentence does that.

An apology out of Sharp. I hadn't expected that. I wouldn't want you to think this is something that happens to me all the time – being proved right about everything all along. I'm not sure it's ever happened before, actually. Not that I can remember.

I can't even enjoy the moment, to be honest. Not knowing Taylor's accomplice is still out there.

That one of the men who killed Lizzie is still out there; who killed Bernadette Ryan.

That Seamus is still out there too.

Sharp told me to go home and get on with my life.

But I can't.

Chapter Thirty-Five

Turns out Angela saw me on the lunchtime TV news, in long shot being led away in handcuffs. The Battle of the Beanfield they're calling it, apparently. Made the national bulletin too.

After that she tracked me down to Andover police station, got the crime reporter to find out when I was being released, and was on her second Jubilee Pancake when I arrived at the Little Chef at Camel Hill just after six.

I know, but I haven't eaten in two days.

'Well?'

It took about ten minutes to tell her what had happened – no names, obviously. All of it apart from that; the girl smiling and crying at the same time when I told her one of the men who had killed her sister was dead. How he died. Everything except who killed him.

'Can I tell my parents?' she asked.

I nodded.

'Ray knew about the garage being found when I spoke to him earlier, but nothing else. There's a press conference tomorrow afternoon at three and he's said I can go with him.'

'None of this is for publication,' I said, firmly.

'I know.'

'I'm telling you because you're Lizzie's sister, not because you're a journalist.'

'I know.'

I leaned back when a plate of food was placed in front of me, a knife and fork neatly rolled up in a paper napkin. I don't need to tell you what I'm having, do I?

It seems odd sitting here somehow.

Most of the tables are occupied, all of them motorists and their passengers going somewhere or on their way back from somewhere. I'm going nowhere, apart from round in circles, perhaps. Actually, that's not true; I am making progress. Sean Taylor confessed. He's dead too, and that's progress in my book.

Two men have died right in front of me, and here I am about to tuck into an All Day Breakfast.

Best not to think about it too much.

'Lizzie would be proud of you,' offered Angela. 'She loved you, you know. She told me once, said if you'd been twenty years younger . . .' She let the thought hang in the air, but it was soon lost in a mischievous chuckle.

The thought had crossed my mind – I may have mentioned that – but I'd arrived at the same conclusion.

'And a bit less of a pillock.' She laughed, the tears all but gone now.

'There's still another one of them out there,' I said, through a mouthful of bacon and egg.

'What's the plan?'

'There isn't one.' And there isn't. There shouldn't need to be one either, if Sharp would get his act together. And what was all that crap about being taken for a mug? Being *used*. 'I do need to go and see Shirley,' I said. 'Before someone else does. She needs to know the man who killed Alan is dead.'

◆ ◆ ◆

It's gone eight when I arrive in Blagdon, and the shop is shut. Lights are on inside all the same, so maybe Shirley is still in there. I rang Joanne from the Little Chef and she's back from London. A real trooper is Shirl. *The people of Blagdon need their post office open, so I can't just sit here wallowing in self-pity.*

Sounds like just the sort of thing she'd say.

'Go and see her, Dad,' Joanne said, before she put the phone down on me. 'God knows why, but she needs you.'

I haven't been up to the flat since Alan's murder; haven't been back to Blagdon since that night I found myself in the lake – which reminds me, I really need to find out where my car is and sort out the insurance. I've had other things on my mind, though.

The window is full of posters advertising this fete or that coffee morning, Sunday services at the church, bring-and-buy sales. There's even a missing cat. I can see through the gaps and Shirley is in there, true to form. Cashing up at the end of a day's work.

It's then that I notice the flowers. Bunches of them lined up along the pavement, leaning against the wall, handwritten cards pinned to them, the ink starting to run. Some have been there longer than others, some were bigger than others, but the message was always the same.

I wonder if anyone will miss me when I go? Or maybe that's just me, wallowing in self-pity?

I've been so caught up in this thing, I haven't stopped to think, to draw breath even. All those sodding flowers have just rammed it home.

Sean Taylor confessed to killing Alan instead of me. I know that doesn't make Alan's death my fault. Or does it?

Bloody well feels like it, I can tell you that much.

I'm still staring at the flowers when the lights inside the shop go off. I can hear the jangling of keys, so I knock on the window.

'Sorry, we're closed.'

'It's me, Shirley.'

The door opens, arms thrown around me in one movement. Shirley hasn't done that for years, not since the miscarriage, sobbing into my shoulder.

'Let's go inside,' I said, gently manoeuvring her back inside the shop and closing the door behind us.

She's wearing black from head to toe, black trousers and roll-neck pullover. A crucifix is hanging around her neck on a gold chain; used to be her late mother's and it never left her side.

It looks like any small village shop, fridges with milk and cold drinks, tins of everything you could ever need, cigarettes behind the counter, an off-licence section, magazines and newspapers. There's the post office counter too, on the far side, but what really stands out is the framed photograph of Alan by the till. It was taken on their honeymoon in Corfu and I've seen it before. It used to live on the sideboard by his armchair, from memory.

He's relaxing on a sun lounger with a newspaper, raising a glass to Shirley behind the camera.

A far cry from our honeymoon. I can't even bring myself to tell you about that. One word then: Pontins.

'I thought you were dead as well,' said Shirley. 'Someone told me about your car in the lake.'

She's still holding on to me for dear life, but I manage to reach around and gesture to my forehead. Actually, it's a lot better. The police surgeon looked at it when I was arrested and taken to Andover, changed the dressing and assured me it was healing well.

'I swam clear, then went to Ireland,' I said. 'Look, Shirl, has someone been in touch with you about Alan?'

'We've got a liaison officer but I've not heard from her for days.' She frowns. 'Why, do you know something?'

'Alan was murdered by Police Constable Sean Taylor. He confessed to the murder and said he was trying to kill me.'

'Mistaken identity?'

'Alan was in the wrong place at the wrong time.'

'Where's Taylor now?'

'Dead. He was killed last night by a member of the Provisional IRA. A single shot to the head, followed by seven shots to the chest.'

'And you saw him die?'

'Yes.'

'Good.'

It takes about ten minutes to tell Shirley the whole story. Well, *almost* the whole story. No names, obviously, and still no mention to anyone of the knife that Taylor had planted in the boot of my car, the same knife that mysteriously found its way from the bottom of the dry stone wall where I'd hidden it back to Taylor's garage on the edge of Ilminster.

Shirley had switched the lights on and made a coffee by the time I finished. Now we're standing either side of the shop counter, watching the steam rising from our mugs, neither of us entirely sure what to say for the best.

'How have you been?' I asked, to break the silence more than anything. Two years ago her reply would've been: *How the bloody hell d'you think I've been?*

'Not great. One minute my life's stretching out in front of me – growing old with Alan, watching the grandchildren growing up – and the next it's all ripped away in an instant.'

'I'm sorry, Shirley.'

'It's not your fault.' She's stopped looking at me and is staring at the photograph of Alan now, a small pot next to it; a collection for the lifeboats, Alan's favourite charity.

'Sure as hell feels like it,' I said.

'You weren't to know, and you had to go after those bastards killing those girls.' She takes a bar of chocolate off the counter, rips it open. 'It's as much my fault as anyone's, if you think about it. I was the one who persuaded him to let you have the flat upstairs.'

I pick up the photograph, look at it closely. 'He was a good man.'

'Never had a bad word to say about anyone, even you.' Shirley gives a sad smile. 'That was the last day of our honeymoon. Never missed his copy of *The Times*, did Alan. His day wasn't complete without a coffee and a read of the newspaper. He was furious, though, because it was a day late out there. I said to him, it's got to be flown out here, get over it.'

'Looks a bit better than our honeymoon,' I said.

'It was different. We were young, we didn't have two ha'pennies to rub together, but we still had fun.'

'Yeah, we did.'

'Don't ever think I wasn't happy.' She reaches across the counter and takes my hand. 'We're different people now. It happens, but I still love you and I always will. We just can't live together, that's all.'

'I know.'

'Look, Joanne's coming down next weekend. Come and have some dinner with us. She'd like that.'

'I doubt it.'

'Well, I would, so she'll just have to get used to it, won't she?'

'I should let you get home,' I said.

'Are you sleeping upstairs?'

'Probably.'

'I've had the door fixed, and the hall carpet's been ripped out. I've got someone coming next week to replace it.'

'Thank you.' I hand Alan's photograph to her and turn for the door.

'Finish this thing,' she said. 'For all our sakes.'

251

◆ ◆ ◆

I can see the new wood in the door frame adjacent to the lock. It just needs a lick of paint now and you'd never know what had happened. Same in the hall, really. The carpet and the underlay have gone, leaving bare floorboards and gripper rods along the skirting boards.

I'm sure I can see a bloodstain on the wall, and there'll be more, of course there will, even if they're microscopic. No real need for detailed forensics, though, not with the murder weapon and a confession.

Shirley's even done the washing up, something that slams into me when I glance into the kitchen. What was I thinking of, letting her go? Driving her away, actually, if I'm honest. And I rarely am, even with myself, let alone you.

The door to my incident room is still open, so everyone will have had a good look; workmen, everyone. I'm not sure how much use it will be now, because things have moved on. More people have died.

There was a cheap can of lager in the fridge and now I'm sitting in my deckchair, staring at the wall. It was the revelation about Bernadette Ryan and the Royal Green Jackets that changed everything. There's no mention of that anywhere, and how could there be? I knew nothing about it at the time.

You'd think it would be easy from here as well. Just look for former Green Jackets, check alibis, and tick them off one by one. Hopefully, Field and Webster are doing that very thing. I'll ask if I see them tomorrow.

People change names, though. Change identities. It's not as easy as you might think to find someone if they don't want to be found; have gone to some lengths not to be found.

There's still been no news about Taylor's death, so perhaps his accomplice doesn't know yet.

Still no sign of Maxine, either.

The fucking press conference tomorrow at three. Taylor's accomplice will bloody well find out after that, won't he? Taylor's death will be plastered all over the evening news. They'll dress it up as an IRA cell operating on the mainland I expect, but the effect will be the same. And it means I've got until tomorrow afternoon to sort this mess out once and for all.

My head feels like someone's got it clamped in a vice. My ears are ringing, for some reason, and I'm struggling to keep my thoughts from jumbling. The good doctor gave me pills for that when I first came out of hospital, but they made me feel worse. Catatonic, almost.

I've never been blessed with great clarity of thought. I'm no Sherlock Holmes. Things go round and round in my head and rarely come out in any sensible order.

The lager's gone, so I'm on my way down to the lake now. Not long after dusk and there are anglers packing up in the car park after a day's fishing. Maybe when this is over I'll go fishing; Shirley said Alan wanted his ashes scattered on the lake.

I've got several questions that I can't answer, but I can't work out at this stage whether they're of any significance or not. I could do with a good night's sleep, but that's not going to happen. So, instead, I'm standing on the end of the jetty, looking down at the reflection of the moon on the surface of the water.

Here goes then, in no particular order, as I say. Firstly, how did Taylor know that Martin Clarke had no alibis for the murders *before* he pulled him over on the 303? *We knew he had no alibis*, those were his exact words, before Seamus put him out of our misery. And mine in particular.

Maxine got herself in deep trouble trying to get Martin's personnel file out of the office too. Actually, that's another question, isn't it? Where the fuck is Maxine?

Secondly, why did the good doctor turn up just before someone tried to make it look like I'd killed myself, telling me she was worried I might be suicidal? That's easily dealt with, that one, and I'll be heading to her office in Exeter first thing in the morning. I haven't got an appointment, but she's bloody well going to see me.

Then I've still got the moving knife, the one that was used to kill poor Alan. How did it get from the base of that dry stone wall into Taylor's garage? Taylor followed me and retrieved it is the easy answer, but I was careful, bloody careful.

Maybe I'll take a detour over the Mendips, check that dry stone wall?

Something doesn't add up, but I'm fucked if I know what it is. Something doesn't make sense about that night I found myself on the bottom of the lake, either. Ask yourself this, if you were going to kill someone and make it look like suicide, would you do it like that?

No?

Me neither.

Chapter Thirty-Six

Writing things down often helps, I find. It was an idea that came to me while I was standing on the end of the jetty, staring at the reflection of the moon on the water, thinking about the last time I'd seen it . . . from underneath. It made for a late night, but then it was always going to be, wasn't it?

What I'm left with, though, is a detailed witness statement, setting out exactly what's happened from start to finish. All of it, *from the top*, as they say. God knows how many times I used that exact phrase when taking a statement from a witness or a victim.

I've done it hundreds of times over the years, thousands even, usually from the point of view of the investigating officer. This time, I'm investigating officer, albeit unofficial, victim and witness. And, no, I didn't hold back with what I saw at the Battle of the Beanfield.

Anyway, it'll save time when I finally catch up with Field and Webster, save me going over it all again. I remembered to pop into the post office and make a few copies, one left with Shirley in a sealed envelope for safekeeping. If anything happens to me, it's to go to Ray Keenan at the *County Gazette*. Not a scenario I'm planning on, you understand, but it's best to be prepared. Shame I wouldn't be around to see the shit hitting the fan, all the same.

Shirley knows the score and won't read it. I hope she doesn't anyway, because this time I've included everything, and I mean *everything*. Names, of course, and the wandering knife; not sure what she'd make of that, to be honest. I'm still not sure what I make of it, come to think of it.

Time will tell.

And, yes, I checked the dry stone wall on the way here. The knife has gone.

It's just before ten and I've left the Capri on Southernhay in Exeter.

I've rung the bell next to the large front door of the good doctor's consulting rooms. It's had a coat of paint – black high gloss – and it glistened in the morning sun. Someone's polished the brass too.

'Detective Inspector Willis to see Dr Mellanby,' I said, when I heard the intercom crackling.

The lock buzzed, so I put my shoulder to the door and marched in.

'Do you have an appointment?' asked the receptionist.

'No,' I replied.

'She's got a clinic this morning, I'm afraid.'

The waiting room was empty, apart from one person reading a magazine; something glossy and overpriced.

The good doctor's office was first on the right at the top of the first flight of stairs, so I turned back out into the hall and was halfway up before the receptionist had a chance to react. It turned out to be a fairly feeble shout of 'you can't go up there', and I was through the doctor's door before she'd finished the sentence anyway.

The slider thingy on the outside said *Engaged*, but I ignored it, of course I did.

'I'm with somebody at the moment, Bob,' she said.

A solicitor or an accountant, possibly. You know the sort. Sharp suit, silk tie, clean shaven, polished black shoes. Not the sort of person you'd expect to see in a consultant psychologist's office.

We make judgements all the time, don't we? About people we don't know. And there was a time I'd have said I didn't look like the sort of person you'd expect to see in a consultant psychologist's office.

The receptionist appeared behind me. 'I'm sorry, Caroline,' she said.

'Is this important, Bob? I am rather busy.'

'You turn up out of the blue, telling me you're worried I'm suicidal,' I replied, firmly. 'And three hours later someone tries to kill me and make it look like suicide. So, yes, I'd say it's important.'

'I'll go,' said the client, standing up from the green leather armchair. 'We'd almost finished anyway, hadn't we?'

'I'm sorry, Malcolm,' said Caroline.

'It's fine.'

'Tracey, tell my next client I'm going to be fifteen minutes, offer her a cup of tea or something.' She waited until the door closed. 'Sit down, Bob,' she said.

'I'd prefer to stand.'

'I appreciate you're upset, but you can't just barge in here when I'm with a client.' She took a deep breath. 'I had a call. She said her name was Shirley and I thought it was your ex-wife. She seemed genuinely concerned for your welfare. And, while we're on the subject, jumping in my car and going to find a client in that situation is not something I'd usually do, but for you, Bob, I made an exception.'

I'm not sure what I'd expected her to say, really, but it sounded plausible enough.

'I take it it wasn't Shirley who rang me?'

'No.'

'The other point worth making is that when I did catch up with you, you clearly weren't suicidal.' Caroline gestured to the armchair. 'Why don't you sit down and tell me what's happened?'

Five of the fifteen minutes, it took. No names, and no wandering knife.

'So, you were right all along.' Caroline shook her head. 'And you've even found the car that hit you.'

'In a garage over at Ilminster.'

'How did you feel when you found it?'

There we go again; they always want to know how you *feel* about everything, psychologists. 'Does it matter?' I asked.

'Only to your mental wellbeing.'

'I felt vindicated, relieved.'

'How about when Taylor was killed right in front of you?'

'Given that he was standing over me with a knife, about to stab me to death, I think it's fair to say I felt relieved again.'

'I saw reports of the peace convoy on the television news. I'm afraid it left me feeling sick to my stomach.'

'Just be grateful you weren't there.'

'When I suggested laying a few ghosts to rest, I meant making your peace with Lizzie's parents.'

'I did that. Actually, I had to do that, before I could do the rest of it.'

'I'm proud of you, Bob,' said Caroline, smiling. 'You took responsibility and now look at you. But, there is no conspiracy, you do know that?'

I waited.

'You came here thinking I was part of it, didn't you? That I'd somehow set you up; I was in on it, helping to make your murder look like suicide. I'm right, aren't I?'

'I had to ask the question,' I replied. 'For my own peace of mind.'

'Are you satisfied by my answer?'

'I am.'

'You know, after this, I don't think you and I will need to see each other again. Not professionally anyway. Our paths may cross at the cricket, of course, but that's different.'

'At the cricket?'

'I really enjoyed it.'

She's wrong, of course. Where there's a cover-up, there's a conspiracy; stands to reason. Bernadette Ryan was murdered during the hunger strike riots of Easter 1981 and the British Army covered it up. The only question is whether they're still trying to cover it up.

Or covering up the cover-up? That's more likely. That's why Druce took his own life.

And whether the good doctor is part of the conspiracy?

I told her I was satisfied with her answer, but the reality is I just don't know.

I'm heading east now – Ilminster bound – on the A30. Back to familiar country; home ground. I need to see Field and Webster, give them a copy of my witness statement and, more importantly, see if they're any closer to finding Taylor's accomplice.

And Maxine.

I wonder if the coroner knows Sharp has assigned two junior detectives to look again at Martin Clarke's death – or murder, as we now know it was? I wonder what he'd think if he did know?

I still can't quite fathom Sharp's attitude, to be honest. The garage alone should've been enough to warrant a major investigation team being assigned to the murders, then there's Taylor's confession. Maybe Sharp thinks I'm an unreliable witness? It's no secret I've had a breakdown, no real secret I've been seeing the good doctor, but the garage corroborates everything Taylor said. That and what Druce told me before he shot himself.

I expect it's more about Sharp not wanting to look like a twat for getting it wrong in the first place.

I haven't told you about Ilminster police station, have I? Twenty-one years I was based there. A drab little station; that hamstone-coloured brick, with small windows. Dark and dingy inside. There's only one pub within walking distance, and that's a dump too.

I won't miss it.

Field and Webster are in the car park as luck would have it, standing at the boot of their car when I turn in.

'You've been busy,' said Field, when I wound down the window of the Capri.

'My witness statement,' I said, handing several folded pieces of papers to Webster, watching her fold them again and stuff them in the inside pocket of her jacket. 'It covers everything, right up to date.'

'Thank you,' she said.

'I'm guessing you're working your way through former British soldiers living in Somerset?'

'What for?'

'Taylor's accomplice. Two soldiers killed Bernadette Ryan.'

'We're not at liberty to talk about the details of our investigation, Bob, you should know that,' said Field. 'You're not a serving officer.'

'Without me you'd have nothing. You'd be pissing in the wind.'

'We still can't talk to you about it.'

'Has Sharp put a team on it?'

'There's a press conference this afternoon at three, so try watching the six o'clock news.'

I've switched off the engine and am tempted to get out of my car, not that it would do any good. Banging my head against a brick wall, that's all I'm doing here. Wasting my bloody time. 'There's a lot of useful stuff in my statement,' I said. 'I suggest you read it and act on it.'

'We will,' said Webster, tapping her breast pocket.

The station looks quiet, the lights off in most of the rooms at the back, only one patrol car in the car park. Everyone will be out and about, I expect, and it seems hardly worth going in. I might find someone on the front desk, a couple of others in the kitchen, but that'll be it.

It makes me wonder how far this conspiracy really does go. And whether the police are involved. That said, knowing Sharp, if he is involved, he'll be more concerned about covering up his own fuck-up than anything else.

Chapter Thirty-Seven

It's coming up to midday now, so I've got three hours left until the press conference, six until the early evening news. He might know already, of course, if he's a police officer. Don't think I haven't thought of that. News travels fast in the police. In fact, I'm surprised Taylor's death hasn't been leaked to the newspapers long before now.

I joined CID in 1965, as bagman for a detective chief inspector who was retiring that year anyway. The old school type. He'd jumped into Arnhem and been one of the few who got back across the river, took part in the Rhine crossing in 1945. Bob Baxter his name was, and he really was called Bob. He gave me lots of advice, but two pieces have always stuck in my mind.

First, never let a woman see you naked apart from a pair of socks. Never have, never will. He'd had a few beers when he said that, mind you. And, second, there are times when you have to jump in with both feet and make something happen.

So, here goes.

The yard at B & D Light Haulage is empty again, apart from a large, articulated rig in the far corner and a couple of vans. The front door of the office is standing open, but there'll be no Maxine sitting at the reception desk. Odd that there's still been no news about Maxine. I half expected her body to turn up somewhere;

thought it would, hoped it wouldn't. Not much evidence of a major police operation to find her, either, which I can't quite reconcile. They'll be making the standard missing person, proof of life enquiries, of course they will, but it warrants far more than that, surely?

There are two cars in the car park. I've seen the silver Mercedes before, parked in exactly the same spot the last time I was here, the time Bruce Jackson turfed me out. A big lad; *no warrant card, no answers*, he said. Shouted, I should say.

The other is a BMW, so I'm guessing that'll be Derek – the 'D' of B & D Haulage. Derek Turnbull. I've not met him before, so it'll be interesting, if nothing else.

Jackson is sitting with his back to the window on the left, on the phone by the looks of things.

I'm standing at the top of the metal steps now, looking in to the prefabricated office. The door on the left is closed, but I can hear Jackson's voice, a low mumble through the soundproofed partition. Some words are making it through, all of them expletives.

The door on the right is open, presumably so the occupant can keep an eye on the front door, given that the reception desk is empty.

'Yes, mate. Can I help you?' He's a smaller man than Jackson, grey trousers, white shirt and braces. Younger than me by a good ten years, which makes him the same age as Taylor, give or take. A couple of days of stubble, but then it's supposed to be fashionable these days. At least, it is if you've been watching *Miami Vice*.

'I was looking for Maxine.'

Police work is all about lies; telling them as well as knowing when you're being told them.

'Who are you?'

'My name's Bob Clarke,' I replied. 'I'm Martin Clarke's uncle.'

'I see you're driving his car.'

'My brother lent it to me. He doesn't drive, so . . .'

'What d'you want with Maxine?'

'I just wanted to ask her some questions. She was out with Martin the night he was killed.'

'I thought it was an accident.'

'You thought wrong.'

Just a little nudge, to see if he gets defensive. I'm clutching at straws now. It's a good job I'm not here in an official capacity; it means I can lie through my teeth. It's strangely liberating, to be honest.

'Maxine's missing, I'm afraid; hasn't been in for a couple of days. Her mother's reported it to the police, but they don't seem to be taking it very seriously yet. I think they're treating it as a missing person case, working on the basis that she's run away.'

'Oh,' I said, looking surprised. 'That's a shame. I met her at Martin's inquest and she didn't seem the type to run away. Have the police spoken to you?'

'They came here when she first went missing and I told them the same. Not the type, if you ask me.'

I've taken a few steps into the office now and am looking at the certificates on the wall, pretending to be interested. 'I've met Bruce Jackson before, so I'm guessing you'll be Derek Turnbull?'

'That's me.'

'Ex-military?' You can tell. The haircuts become a habit, then there's the bearing.

'Royal Corps of Transport,' he replied. 'Fifteen years. This seemed like the obvious career choice after that. How about you?'

'Royal Green Jackets.' I'm watching him in the reflection of their employer's liability insurance certificate; no reaction.

'What was it you wanted to ask Maxine? Maybe I can help?' He's leaning against her desk now, arms folded. 'I knew Martin quite well, I interviewed him, took him on.'

'It was more about that evening, really. How he seemed, that sort of thing.'

'Can't help you there, I'm afraid. Wasn't here.'

Both feet, Bob Baxter said. There's a small red sofa against the far wall, and I'm sitting down now, making it clear I'm not going anywhere. 'I'm working on the basis that Martin was framed; murdered because he fitted the profile of the killer the police were looking for. The murder weapons were planted in the boot of his car, but what I'm wondering is how his killers knew he had no alibis for the murders?'

'Maybe they got lucky?'

'No, they knew. I'm talking about the murders of Fiona Anderson and Alice Cobb out on the 303. Two murders, months apart, and both nights Martin was working on his own, out and about in his van with no one to account for his whereabouts. Convenient, wouldn't you say?'

'Are you suggesting someone had access to his log, to his work records?'

'That's exactly what I'm suggesting.'

'I gave a copy of his personnel file to the police afterwards, but no one had access to it before. We keep the files under lock and key for obvious reasons; they're confidential.'

'Where were you at Easter 1981?'

He shakes his head. 'Northern Ireland. I did two tours; '78 and '81. Why?'

'Does the name Sean Taylor mean anything to you?' A bit obvious, perhaps, but I'm running out of time.

'No.' There was a spark of recognition, I'm sure there was; that flicker of doubt before he opted for *no*. 'Who is he?'

'The police officer who arrested Martin, planted the murder weapons, and I believe killed him; threw him off the bridge into the path of a lorry.' Actually, Taylor confessed, of course he did, but I can't tell Turnbull that, can I?

'Look, I don't know him. Martin was a good lad—'

'What did you think when you found out he was suspected of being the 303 Ripper?' I hate that phrase. It popped up a couple of times in the tabloids at the time.

'No way, couldn't have been him. We've got lads here who I could believe might do it – several of them – but not him.'

'What about your business partner, Mr Jackson, is he ex-military?'

'Yes, he is. Tanks, I think. Why?' Getting indignant now. 'You're not suggesting one of us—' He's interrupted by the sound of a phone being slammed down in the small office on the left. 'You can ask him yourself, if you like.'

Bollocks.

'Bruce, this is Martin's uncle,' said Turnbull, when Jackson emerges from the office.

I'm already on my feet, edging towards the door.

'No, it bloody well isn't. He was here the other day asking questions and I told him to sling his hook. He's a police officer, off sick; I told you before, no warrant card, no questions. Is that clear?'

'Yes,' I replied.

'Good. Now fuck off.'

'He said he was Martin's uncle . . .' Turnbull's voice tails off.

'We've had the proper police here, mate, all right?' continued Jackson. 'The day before yesterday, looking for Maxine, and I answered all their questions, showed them the diary, call records. Everything.' He's beaten me to the door and is blocking my exit. 'What the fuck is it you want to know anyway?'

'He wants to know how Martin's killers knew he had no alibis,' offered Turnbull. 'Seems to think they had access to his personnel file, his driving logs.'

'I thought he was making a run for it and fell?' asked Jackson, his brow furrowing.

'He was murdered,' I said.

Jackson walks over to the filing cabinet, unlocks it and opens the top drawer. 'His file's here,' he said, holding it up. 'Under lock and key.'

Yes, I know what you're thinking. I'm wondering the same thing. I'd found that file under Maxine's bed and handed it to Field and Webster only forty-eight hours ago, so how the fuck did it get back in that filing cabinet drawer?

Now I've got a wandering file to go with a moving knife.

What the episode did do, though, was to move Jackson out of the way, and I'm now on the top step, my hand in my pocket fumbling for my car keys just in case a quick getaway is called for.

I'm close now, I can feel it. Actually, I'm tempted to drop the bombshell and let them know Taylor's dead, see which one runs for it, but the police officer in me needs evidence. And there are still too many questions.

'Satisfied?' demanded Jackson.

'Yes,' I replied. 'Thank you.'

Jackson leans out of the Portakabin, takes hold of the door handle and slams it shut, muttering 'wanker' as he did so.

Two vans are turning into the car park as I walk across the gravel back to the Capri, now covered in a fine layer of yellow dust. I'll need to give it a clean before I hand it back to Martin's father, that's for sure.

I'm walking slowly, well aware I'm being watched from the office window. If I had to guess, I'd say both of them, but I'm resisting the temptation to turn around and check.

The two van drivers have parked their vehicles and are walking across to the office, pieces of paper in their hands fluttering in the breeze; a ritual Martin would've done umpteen times – getting his worksheet signed off.

The articulated lorry is still there, in the far corner. It's got a huge flatbed trailer attached, the canvas sides rolled back and tied. Make it obvious it's empty and you're less likely to be broken into, that's the thinking. What it does mean is that I can't see any logo on the side, but there's writing on the driver's door; stencilled and too small to see from here.

Trying not to make it look obvious, I reverse the wrong way out of my parking space and do a loop of the yard rather than turn around. Perfectly reasonable, you might think, but it takes me right past the articulated lorry.

Interesting. And far too much of a coincidence.

Terry Greenslade said he parked his lorry at a yard over at Ilminster and it turns out to be this one. What are the chances of that?

I can feel another visit to Stocklinch coming on, to the registered office of Greenslades Transport.

Chapter Thirty-Eight

We make judgements about cars, and the people they belong to as well, don't we? Last time I was here, there were two parked in the drive; his and hers. Now there's just the one, a big Rover. The Mini Metro has gone, so you know what I'm thinking.

I could be wrong, of course. The Rover could be hers and he uses the Metro to get to and from his lorry. That said, things become clichés for a reason, don't they? Stereotypes and all that.

Actually, I can see him in the garden at the back of the bungalow, which helps.

It's a funny little place, clad in hamstone, expanding foam still visible around the windows. If I had to guess, I'd say he built it himself. And not very well, now I take a closer look. There's already a crack above the bay window and scaffolding up to the chimney. That wasn't there last time I came, so perhaps they've had water coming in.

The roof seems to bow in the middle too, which can't be a good sign. Even I know that.

He hasn't seen me and is still digging. Looks like a raised bed at the bottom of the garden, but he's got more important things to be worrying about, to be honest. And that's before I get started on him.

It's the last bungalow in the lane and quite secluded. Eerily so, if you ask me. I hadn't noticed it before, but it backs on to woodland. Pine trees, dark.

There's no point ringing the bell. He hasn't heard my car and I doubt he'd hear the front doorbell going either, so I'm picking my way around the side of the bungalow, dodging the cardboard boxes, bits of sawn-off timber, roof tiles and the scaffolding.

'You again,' said Terry Greenslade, looking up, leaning on his shovel.

'Me again, sorry,' I replied. 'I've got a few more questions for you, if that's all right?'

'Well, it isn't really. I'm supposed to be finishing this . . .'

That means *yes* in my book. 'Good,' I said. 'Shall we go inside?'

'If we must.'

He still hasn't asked to see my warrant card, which is a bonus. I follow him into the kitchen and watch him sit down at the small table against the wall, a chair either side of it, piles of newspapers and unopened post.

'Let me switch this off,' he said, picking up a small radio. 'She's always got it tuned to Radio 1 and it drives me round the bend.'

'Is your wife out?' I asked.

'Gone over to Exmouth to see her sister.'

I'm still standing up, near the open back door, just in case. I'm not a big man, as you know, and I can't afford to get in a fight, not with my elbow and knee. 'I've been thinking about that night, obviously, and I can't understand why the officer issued you with a Producer and let you go. It was a fatal accident, wasn't it?'

Greenslade shrugs.

'Normal procedure would've been to have kept you at the scene until the accident investigators arrived. Not only that, but you should've gone straight to the station and given your statement as soon as *reasonably practicable*.'

'I don't know, sorry. I waited in my cab, just as he told me, then he appeared at the driver's side, handed me the notice and told me I could go. What can I say? You'd need to ask him.'

'I would, if he wasn't dead.' Time to get that out in the open, I think; see if anything happens. Besides, I've lost track of the time, but it can't be long until the press conference. Then it'll be plastered all over the news.

'Dead?' Greenslade looks ashen, and it hasn't taken long. 'What happened to him?'

'He was murdered by the IRA.'

'Fucking hell.' Eyes darting now. He'll start sweating next, you watch.

'Shot eight times at point blank range,' I said, casually. 'I saw it happen.'

And there it is, a little bead of sweat on his temple. Gone, now he's burying his face in his hands.

'Were you in the army?'

It's a question I know the answer to; I saw the photographs in the hall the last time I was here. They must be of him, pictures of a son would be in colour these days, not black and white.

'Eighteen years.'

Time to take a bit of a flyer, see what happens, but I've got half an idea. 'Royal Green Jackets?' I asked.

'First Battalion.' Greenslade's back straightens.

'Tours of Northern Ireland?'

'Three. '69, '71 to '72, and '74.' He's breathing deeply now.

'Tell me again what happened the night Martin Clarke fell from the bridge.'

'I was on an overnighter – Bodmin to Tilbury and back – and I was eastbound on the A303. A bit tired before I got going, which isn't ideal, I know. I'd got back from holiday that morning, slept on the plane, but it's never the same, is it?'

I try an understanding smile.

'I'd got away from Bodmin about nine, so it must've been about eleven-thirty at night. I'm always on the lookout for people on

271

bridges over the motorways and such, heard too many horror stories from other drivers; jumpers, you know how it is.' He grimaces. 'Selfish bastards. Never a fucking thought for the poor lorry driver.'

'Train drivers, the same.'

'Yes, them too. They get it more than we do.' He's found a packet of cigarettes in a small drawer in the kitchen table and is lighting one, the end bouncing around in the flame as he speaks. And trembles.

'Go on,' I said.

'So, I'm coming along the dual carriageway, towards the bridge, and I see movement. It looks like a figure climbing over the railings. I'm sure I saw a leg coming over, like he was stepping over them.'

I shake my head.

'What?' he demands, frowning at me.

'Those are exactly the same words you used last time I asked you; word for word. It's the same in your witness statement.'

'That's hardly surprising. I've been over and over it countless times in my head.'

'But the way you describe it never changes.'

'Should it?'

'Yes, it should.' Time for another flyer. 'Were you actually there at all, or was someone else driving your rig?'

'Of course I was there. I told you, I'd got back from holiday that morning and was doing an overnighter to Tilbury. I do it all the time, the roads are quieter.'

'The problem you've got is I know you're lying.' I lean back against the sink and fold my arms. 'The officer who issued you with the Producer was Sean Taylor.'

A flash of recognition from Greenslade.

'And before he was murdered by the IRA he told me what really happened – that he threw Martin Clarke off that bridge and into

272

the path of your lorry. That means you're either lying about what you saw or you weren't there at all. Now, which is it?'

'Look, you've got the wrong end of the stick, mate. I told you, I saw movement on the bridge, then he fell.'

'Tell me about your tours of Northern Ireland. You said '71 to '72, so I'm guessing you were there for Bloody Sunday?'

'That was Londonderry. The Paras. We were stationed in Belfast, but it went up all the same. Nothing like as bad, though. Not that time.' Greenslade is pulling hard on his cigarette, not that there is much left of it now. 'The worst was '74. We were further south, near the border, and came under mortar attack all the fucking time. Seemed like it anyway. We even lost our CO in a helicopter crash. The Provos claimed they shot him down, but they didn't. The pilot stalled it and down they went. Near Jonesborough, that was. Armagh.'

'Is there an association?'

'There's the Royal Green Jackets Association, yes. I'm secretary of the Somerset branch.'

'Is it active?'

'We meet regularly, always turn out for Remembrance Day services, that sort of thing; major anniversaries, stuff like that.'

'Many members?'

'Every former Green Jacket's a member, whether they want to be or not.'

'You'll know a Brian Druce then, in that case?'

'Yes, he's one of yours, isn't he? A copper. Nice bloke.'

'He's dead too.'

Lighting another cigarette. 'Not the fucking Provos again?'

'He shot himself,' I said. 'I think he thought he'd brought the regiment into disrepute; put on his dress uniform and put a 9mm Browning to his temple.'

'What had he done to bring the regiment into disrepute?' Eyes wide now.

The signs are all there. I'm sure you can see them too. Keep pushing and Greenslade is going to tell me everything.

'He covered up the murder of a Catholic woman in Belfast by two soldiers. It was during the hunger strike riots of Easter 1981. They raped her and they killed her. And Brian Druce covered it up.'

'What was her name?'

'Does it matter?'

Silence.

'From where I'm sitting, you're covering it up too,' I said. 'They've killed four more women. Fiona Anderson, Alice Cobb . . .' I'm watching him carefully as I reel off the names.

'They were killed by Martin Clarke, surely? Like I said before, I felt a bit better about it when I found out what he'd done.'

'He was framed. And the last one, Faith Bennett, was only murdered a few days ago. Sean Taylor was one and you know who the other is, don't you?'

'I'm sure I don't know what you're talking about.'

'Does the name Maxine Green mean anything to you?'

'She's the receptionist at the yard where I keep the rig.' He smiles. 'A nice lass.'

'She's missing.' Wipes the smile off his face, that does. 'And you never mentioned that you keep your lorry at the yard where Martin Clarke used to work; a detail that is conveniently missing from your witness statement.'

'No one asked me,' protested Greenslade. 'I answered the questions I was asked.'

'By Sean Taylor,' I replied. 'He was the officer who took your statement, wasn't he?'

No reply. Again.

I'm losing him. I can see it. He's retreating into denial. Next will come the demand that I leave. Then he'll make a phone call and pack a suitcase – two, if he remembers his wife.

Fuck it.

'I think you'd better leave,' he said. 'And I'll want my solicitor with me before I speak to you again.'

'All right, Terry, if that's the way you want it,' I said.

I'm in the hall now, taking the chance to look at the photos on the wall as I walk towards the front door. I can hear his footsteps behind me, and his breathing.

There's the picture of him on holiday in Corfu again, very much like the photograph Shirley had taken of Alan on their honeymoon: sitting on a sun lounger, reading the newspaper. Only Greenslade is sitting at a table in a taverna somewhere on the island, dark sunglasses, reading the *Guardian* – not his newspaper of choice, as he'd been at pains to point out last time.

Cabinet survives IRA hotel blast is the headline.

I remember that well. The Grand Hotel, Brighton, last October.

'Like I said, I'll want my solicitor present before I speak to you again.' Greenslade's parting shot, before he slams the front door of his bungalow behind me.

I'm sure the whole porch wobbled, although I'm loitering for another reason. The telephone is on the table in the hall and I want to know if he makes a call.

An old trick, but he's wise to it, a shout of 'piss off' coming from inside.

I'm halfway down the garden path when it hits me.

For fuck's sake.

Running now. There's a phone box in the village, outside the pub, and a call of my own I need to make.

Chapter Thirty-Nine

There are lines.

Some you cross, some you don't. Ever.

That's what I used to think anyway. And it's all about to change.

The only question then becomes whether the end justifies the means.

The best I can say is that I hope so.

I'm standing in the telephone box on the grass verge outside the church in the middle of Stocklinch. My call to Angela ended about five minutes ago and it took her less than that to find out what I needed to know.

I'm playing for time – time to think – watching the motorcyclist and pillion passenger out of the corner of my eye. They've pulled in behind the Capri and are just sitting there, waiting for me to come out. Dressed in black leathers, black full-face helmets with tinted visors, but I know who it is.

And so do you.

I turn away, pretending to be deep in conversation, buying a few more precious seconds.

I know Greenslade is lying. Know it and can prove it now too. So, here's what I'm going to do. I'm going to go back in, tell him what I know and give him a chance, *another* chance, to do the right thing. If he still doesn't, then I'm coming out.

What happens after that is anyone's guess, but I expect Seamus will go in, and you and I both know what that means, how that ends.

I can justify it on the basis that Seamus knows Greenslade is involved and will go in anyway. And I can't exactly stop him, can I? I'm under no illusions about that. There will come a point when we no longer share a common enemy, and then I'll just be a British police officer in the employ of the Crown – fair game. I've no illusions about that either.

For now, though, it's time for Terry Greenslade to face the music, but he sure as hell won't be dancing when Seamus has finished with him.

Best get it over with. I step out of the phone box, into the drizzle.

'Does he know?' Seamus asked, his voice coming from the pillion seat.

'He's not involved in the murders,' I replied. 'Let me talk to him first.'

'But he knows who killed my sister?'

'He does.'

'Fine.' Seamus taps the back of the rider's helmet, the motorcycle engine roaring into life. 'You've got five minutes. After that I'm coming in and we'll do it the old-fashioned way. The Irish way.'

There's no sign of Greenslade in the garden this time, but the rain might explain that. Still only one car in the drive too, which is a relief.

I ring the doorbell, wait. Knock on the open living room window.

'I thought I told you I've got nothing to say to you,' shouted Greenslade, through the closed front door of his bungalow.

'Bernadette Ryan was nineteen years old,' I said. 'A Catholic girl from Belfast. That's why the IRA are here, Terry, and they're coming for you. Tell me what I need to know and you might just live through this.'

'I don't know what you're talking about.' He's opened the door and is looking up and down the lane now, his eyes wide.

I push past him and into the hall, turning to watch him slam the door behind me.

'I really don't know,' he protested.

'Yes, you do,' I said. My voice is tight, a sick feeling rising in the pit of my stomach. I feel oddly nervous; for Greenslade, I think. He's got no idea what's coming. Or maybe he has?

He's standing in the hall, peering around the door frame to look out of the living room window, the high-pitched roar of a motorcycle engine in the lane outside. 'Who's that?' he demanded.

'They must've followed me,' I replied. 'Now really would be a good moment to stop the lying, Terry.'

'I'm not fucking lying.'

I pick up the framed photograph of him reading the newspaper in Corfu, hold it out in front of him. 'The Grand Hotel bomb went off in the early hours of the morning on Friday the twelfth of October, too late for the Friday editions of the national newspapers. This edition of the *Guardian* is from the following day, Saturday the thirteenth of October – I've just had someone check – which means it wouldn't have arrived in Corfu until the morning of Monday the fifteenth. There were no flights.'

Actually, I haven't checked that, but then he won't have done either.

'You can see what I'm wondering, can't you?' I continued. 'I'm wondering how you come to be sitting in a cosy little taverna reading this edition of the *Guardian* when you're supposed to have flown back to England on the Saturday morning and been behind the wheel of your rig when Martin Clarke was thrown under it.'

The blood is draining from Greenslade's face.

'You weren't driving it, were you?' I asked.

He's breathing deeply through his nose now, his head bowed.

'The clock is ticking, Terry.'

'I . . .' He was listening to the motorcycle engine revving outside. 'I . . .'

'Sean Taylor served you with a Producer, gave you time to get your statement straight, and then you rocked up at Ilminster police station when you got back from holiday and lied through your teeth.'

'Look, all I did was cover for them when they killed that nonce. Clarke killed those girls and they did us all a favour when they threw him under my lorry.'

'Clarke was innocent, Terry. They framed him. They killed the girls. Taylor confessed.'

'I don't believe you. And I can't . . .' He shakes his head. 'There's a code.'

'Is there.'

The motorcycle engine fell silent outside, that familiar whirr as it winds down. Then footsteps, boots on the tarmac.

'It's now or never, Terry. After this, I can't help you.'

He snatches the photograph from me, stares at it, then replaces it on the hall table.

'You're protecting a serial killer,' I said. 'He's murdered five women. You owe him nothing.'

Greenslade lets out a long, slow sigh, pushes open the living room door and sits down on the sofa, resigned to his fate.

'I've brought the regiment into disrepute, just like Brian Druce,' he said. 'If they're going to kill me anyway, they'd best get on with it. You and I both know it.'

A loud crash at the front door, the wooden frame splintering. The door swings open.

'You.' Seamus is pointing his gun at my head. 'Get out.'

He's taken his helmet off, which is not a good sign. You don't get to see Seamus's face and live. And, no, that's not a point that's been lost on me, either.

I'm standing outside the living room window now. I wouldn't want you to think I'm some sort of ghoul, but I need to hear what's being said, just in case Greenslade gives up the name of Taylor's accomplice. I really don't want Seamus getting there first, do I?

Both of them are in there and they've got Greenslade lying face down on the rug. I know what's coming. First it'll be the knees, then the elbows, assuming he's still alive by then. Maybe blood loss will put him out of his misery.

It's the same pistol and silencer combination I saw at the bean-field, Seamus standing over Greenslade this time, holding it in his right hand, making sure Greenslade can see it, that he knows what's about to happen.

'You murdering bastard, you're as bad as they are,' said Seamus, his sentence punctuated by several sharp kicks to the stomach and ribs.

Greenslade grimaces; vomits on the rug.

'Give us the fucking name,' said the motorcyclist. He's still wearing his helmet, but the voice sounds familiar. It could be Shane, the build is right. I can see it now he's off the bike.

'Martin Clarke killed the girls,' protested Greenslade. 'All I did was cover for them when they got rid of him.'

'Clarke wasn't a Royal Green Jacket, was he? Wasn't in Belfast in 1981, was he? Those bastards you're protecting killed my sister.

Taylor was one and you're going to tell me who the other is. Now.' Seamus is sitting on the sofa, adjacent to Greenslade's head, turning the gun in his hand, making sure Greenslade is watching. 'I'm going to count to ten,' he said.

Slowly, menacingly. 'One, two . . .'

Greenslade tries to get up, but the motorcyclist plants a boot in the middle of his back, slamming him down on to the rug.

'For fuck's sake, Terry,' I shouted, banging on the window. 'Give him up. You owe him nothing.'

I turn away when Seamus places the barrel to the inside of Greenslade's right knee; hear the muffled shot, before the screaming starts.

He's on his side when I summon up the courage to look back, trying to reach what's left of his knee with both hands. There's a gaping hole, blood and bone spattered on the inside of the glass.

Greenslade's gone quiet now, his mouth is open, but no sound is coming out; his face contorted in agony.

'Now for the left,' said Seamus.

I know. We can talk about my part in this later. My first task is to find the accomplice, then find Maxine. I'll worry about sleeping on the long, dark nights that follow, assuming I live through it.

Seamus is lining up the barrel of the gun with Greenslade's left knee now. 'Elbows next,' he said, leaning over him, grinning.

'All right, all right,' gasped Greenslade. 'I'll tell you.' He's on his back now, leaning forwards, both hands clamped over his right knee, the slightest movement in it met with another scream. Blood is oozing out from between his fingers.

'We're listening.'

The name doesn't come as much of a surprise. It was always going to be either the 'B' or the 'D' of B & D Light Haulage. Had to be, didn't it?

What comes as a surprise is the muffled gunshots as I run down the garden path, Seamus emptying his magazine into Greenslade's chest, probably, just as he had done with Sean Taylor. Actually, I suppose it didn't come as a surprise, if I'm honest. Greenslade had seen his face, after all.

It means there's no one to place me at the scene, either, which is convenient, if I'm being purely selfish about it.

◆ ◆ ◆

I'd parked the Capri turned for home and snatched the keys from the ignition on the motorbike as I ran past. It'll give me a bit of a head start, but not much. It doesn't take long to hot wire a motorcycle, if you know what you're doing.

I left the engine running when I stopped at the phone box; made an anonymous 999 call to report the murder – no names, you understand, but it would be nice to think emergency services might get there before his wife. No one should have to walk in on that.

And, yes, I remembered to hold the phone in the sleeve of my jacket.

Five minutes later I'm out on the A303, hammer down, wondering how far Seamus is behind me.

Wondering how long I've got.

Chapter Forty

They're both still here, which is a surprise. Maybe Greenslade didn't make the call after all? He had time, while I was ringing Angela from the phone box, so what stopped him, I wonder?

Perhaps he thought it was time Bruce Jackson faced the music too?

The yard is quiet; a few more vans and flatbed lorries have pulled in further along from the Mercedes and BMW, a sign that the working day is drawing to a close. Greenslade's rig is still there too, parked along the fence at the far end, the tarpaulins on the side of the trailer rolled back and tied in position.

The door of the Portakabin is closed, the blinds drawn, but there are lights on inside.

I've reversed the Capri in tight behind Jackson's Mercedes, blocking him in, and now I'm tiptoeing across the gravel, trying to get close to the office without being seen or heard. Hopefully he'll think it was another van arriving back after a day's work.

It also means my horses are turned for home, just in case.

Jackson's office is empty, so I continue around the side of the Portakabin and look in through Turnbull's office window. Empty too, but I can see his body slumped at the reception desk. He's sitting in Maxine's chair, his head tipped back, throat cut.

Fuck it.

What a mess.

I can see Jackson at the far end of the Portakabin too, sitting on the sofa. He's looking at the blood-soaked knife in his right hand. Then he wipes the blade on the edge of the cushion next to him.

I'm beginning to think I should have called this in, but actually there's no real need. It'll all be out in the open soon enough when Shirley posts my letter. And it hardly matters what happens to me, does it?

Jackson's going nowhere. Not now.

I've crept around to the front of the cabin and have my hand on the door handle, turning it slowly. Ideally, I want him sitting down when I walk in. It might give me half a chance.

'You took your time,' said Jackson, when I step into the reception area.

He's still sitting on the sofa and I've left the door open.

Turnbull's shirt is saturated, the blood forming a puddle on the floor at his feet. I can see it under the desk. What it tells me, though, is that Greenslade did make the call after all.

And that Jackson has decided not to run.

Unless he wants to kill me first.

'What did you have to kill him for?' I asked.

'He was asking too many questions.'

'Nice.'

'You really are a pain in the arse, Bob,' he said. 'Why couldn't you have just left things alone?'

'Left you to carry on killing innocent women, you mean?'

'We'd stopped.'

'Faith Bennett would disagree. If she had the chance.'

'That was Sean.' Jackson shakes his head. 'Never could control himself.'

'You weren't there, I suppose?'

'No, I was there,' said Jackson, with a smirk. 'Never could control myself either, not after the Irish girl. It's like a drug, Bob. Addictive.'

284

'Is it really?'

'You should try it.'

'I think I'll stick to cricket.'

He's turning the knife in his hand, cleaning the last of the blood off the blade on the arm of the sofa. It's a hunting knife, ivory handle. It would throw well, so I'll need to be on my guard.

'You've taken a bit of risk, marching in here, unarmed.'

'I called it in, so it's just a matter of time.'

Jackson takes a deep breath. Nods. 'Where's Terry Greenslade?' he asked.

'Dead.'

'The Provos?'

'Kneecapped him first; that's when he gave you up,' I replied. 'They're on their way here now. The only question is who gets here first, the police or the IRA?'

'Both at the same time should be interesting.' Jackson forces a half-hearted chuckle.

'I'm guessing it was you driving his rig when Taylor threw Martin Clarke off the bridge?'

'Thought we'd got away with it too.'

The knife is sharp, I can see that now he's stabbing the sofa cushion with it.

'Our only mistake was letting you live.'

'I'm sure it wasn't deliberate.'

'I should have backed up and gone over you a few times. Done the job properly. But Sean said accident investigators would've been able to tell. As it was, it looked like an accident, didn't it?'

'I knew.'

'Yeah, but nobody believed you, did they? Poor little psych-job copper, crying in the wind.'

'Turnbull told me you were in the Tank Corps. What was all that about?'

'A smokescreen, to put a bit of distance between me and my past.' He stands up, snaps to attention. 'Lance Corporal Bruce Jackson, First Battalion, Royal Green Jackets.'

'On the run in Belfast, in the middle of a riot.' I'm watching him closely and so far he's making no attempt to close the distance between us. He's still holding the knife by the handle too. If he switches to holding it by the tip of the blade, I'll know what's coming. At the moment, there's still a glass coffee table between us.

I can hear a siren, and so can he, but it's fading into the distance; racing out to Stocklinch, probably. No, what I'm listening for is the sound of a motorcycle, the high-pitched whine of a racing bike. Nothing yet.

'Your lot are being slower than usual,' said Jackson, grinning. 'I thought you said you'd called it in.'

'I did. You're finished. Done. It's over.'

'Not quite yet. I thought I might take you with me, Bob. What d'you think?'

'Don't care,' I said. 'My job is done.'

It is – and actually, now it comes to it, I don't care. There's still a survival instinct, though. There must be. I can feel myself edging towards the open door.

The movement was sharp. Jackson is off the sofa, leaps over the coffee table and kicks the door shut before I have a chance to react. Then his fist slams into my cheekbone, sending me reeling backwards on to the photocopier.

I can't say it hurt much and there's no blood in my mouth. For now.

I'm expecting more of the same, though, wondering when Seamus is going to arrive and whether it was such a good idea to pinch the motorcycle keys.

'Your left leg, wasn't it?'

Jackson smiles as he aims a kick at the side of my knee that sends me buckling to the floor. A searing pain is roaring up my leg. I can't imagine being kneecapped is much worse than this. And whatever happens to me, it can't be as bad as what Lizzie went through.

I've got him. He knows it and I know it. A kick to my stomach this time, but I can't help smiling through the pain.

He's standing over me now, a lopsided smile on his face, the knife in his right hand. 'How about I cut a regimental insignia into your chest, Bob?' he said. 'How about that, eh?'

There are lines. I know I've talked about them before, crossed a few too, but that is a step too far. 'You'll have to kill me first,' I said.

'That's no fun, is it? I like to look into the eyes when I make the cuts. It's a spiritual thing. I wouldn't expect you to understand.'

There's a small fire extinguisher on the floor, down the side of the photocopier. I'll get one chance and timing will be everything. Fuck it up and that will be that.

Still no motorbike. Too fucking clever by half, Bob, nicking those keys. I'd like to say I've been in worse scrapes, but truth is, I haven't. I keep telling myself I don't care. I wonder what the good doctor would make of that?

He's bending over me now. I'm not sure if he's going to stab me first, but I'm not hanging around to find out.

I reach out with my right hand, my fingers closing around the handle of the fire extinguisher. It's light – powder, probably, for electrical fires – and swing it at the side of Jackson's head.

He straightens up, steps backwards, reeling, his left hand pressed to the side of his skull.

It's no time to hang about, so I'm up and hobbling for the door, dragging my left leg. It takes my weight, just, not that I've got a lot of choice. It has to.

I snatch open the door and fall out of the Portakabin on to the gravel, my legs buckling underneath me at the top of the steps and sending me crashing down. I can hear footsteps behind me. Jackson is standing over me again, lashing out with his foot. I turn my head and look up at him, blood trickling down his left ear.

There is no pain now, oddly enough. I can feel the kicks landing and I'm struggling to breathe, but it doesn't hurt.

'Why couldn't you just leave well alone, Bob?' snarled Jackson, fumbling in his pocket for a set of keys.

I can smell burning now, and look back to the office to see flames flickering inside the Portakabin, a plume of smoke rising from the open door.

Jackson has gone, but where? I feel relief, tempered by the sure and certain knowledge he won't be leaving me alive, so what the fuck is he up to?

Then I hear it.

The engine of Terry Greenslade's articulated lorry rumbling into life.

So, that's the plan, is it? I'm to die under the wheels of that lorry, just like Martin Clarke.

I watch it turning towards me at the far end of the yard, the wheels of the trailer being dragged sideways through the gravel. It's a tight turn, but now he's lining up the cab right at me, accelerating hard.

If I move too early he'll be able to turn the rig on to me and keep turning no matter how far I get. I won't make it to the cars on the far side of the car park, so my best chance is going to be rolling out of the way at the last minute, then keep rolling to avoid the trailer wheels.

I'll never get up in time, and crawling won't be fast enough, not with my left leg and elbow slowing me down. So rolling it is.

Having a plan helps, as I watch the lorry accelerating towards me across the yard. I can see Jackson at the wheel, laughing.

Let's see who enjoys the last one.

It'll be the left wheels. If he tries the right, he won't make the turn at the gate. I can see him lining up.

Thirty yards.

Twenty.

Ten.

I'll go at five and hope for the best. Either it will work, or it won't. Now.

I've tucked my arms in ready to go and am rolling for all I'm worth towards the Capri. Eyes closed, naturally, but I feel tyres clipping my shoe as I roll clear.

Must keep rolling to avoid the trailer wheels.

Now, I'm wedged under the front of my car. I open my eyes and look back to see the rear end of the trailer clip the gate post as the lorry makes the turn on to the main road and accelerates towards the A303.

That's where this is going to end, is it?

There are tracks in the gravel where the lorry made a tight left turn. Not tight enough, as it turned out, and I'm still in the game.

Up and hobbling around the front of the Capri, my left knee is moving and I'll be able to use the clutch. Now we'll really see what Martin's three-litre engine is capable of. And I'd like to try to keep it in one piece, if I can, for his father's sake.

My wheels spin as I race out of the haulage yard, sending gravel flying into the side of Jackson's Mercedes; not that he'll be needing it where he's going – wherever that may be.

I could do with a police radio, really. I used to have one in the Volvo, before . . .

What's concerning me is how I'm going to stop an articulated lorry out on the dual carriageway, but I'll worry about that when I've caught up with him.

Chapter Forty-One

Changing gear is fine. I managed to protect my left elbow from most of the kicks raining in on me. And my left leg is riding the clutch. Bad driving, I know, but needs must. Perhaps I'll switch to an automatic after this?

After this?

We'll see.

I have to put my hand on my knee and push to get the clutch pedal down, but it's doable, and my leg seems to be freeing up, if anything. The pain is easing off anyway, apart from my ribs.

I'm dropping down through Ilminster in third gear, overtaking a line of cars waiting at a set of traffic lights, the engine screaming; flashing my lights and sounding the horn, so people can see and hear me coming.

What I wouldn't give for a siren. I used to have a magnetic one that I could put on the roof of my car, and a blue light for the dashboard.

There's no way Jackson will go over the Blackdowns and into Devon, not if he wants to get away. That leaves either the A358 and then the motorway at Taunton possibly, or the eastbound stretch of the A303. I hope he's gone that way. At least I know the road like the back of my hand.

Traffic is light, so it must be after rush hour, not that there's much of one in Ilminster; heavy traffic heading west, though. I've lost track of the days, but it might be Monday, I suppose. Shouldn't be any weekenders about.

I manage to squeeze through at the lights on the wrong side of the road, then accelerate hard towards the roundabout. I can see two articulated lorries up ahead, both indicating a right turn, but there's no sign of Jackson. No sign of him accelerating away to the west either, and I can't be that far behind him, surely?

He must've gone east.

He must've done.

I'm revving the engine as I approach the roundabout, more out of frustration than anything else. I've got to go one way or the other; get it wrong and it's all over. What's worrying me is that he'll kill himself, maybe take innocent bystanders with him in that bloody lorry, when he really needs to be taken alive and brought before a court.

Seamus might have something to say about that, though.

East it is. I turn the wheel to the right, accelerate past the bollards on the wrong side of the road and go the wrong way around the roundabout. A gap in the traffic opens up nicely and I go for it.

Now, I'm accelerating, my foot hard on the accelerator, pressing it to the floor.

You're wondering what I'm going to do when I catch up with him, and so am I. Perhaps I can get alongside and drag him out of the cab if we get stuck in traffic? There are several roundabouts, a couple of sets of roadworks too. I might even be able to get the bonnet of the Capri wedged under the wheels of his cab, although I wouldn't fancy explaining that to Martin's father. That said, he'd probably think it was a fair swap: the car for the man who killed his son.

Better still, I'll get the chance to run Jackson over. See how he likes it.

There's a line of lorries ahead, on the long climb up to the short stretch of dual carriageway at South Petherton. Four lorries crawling up the hill, another in the overtaking lane, going past them slowly, a queue of cars behind it.

That'll be Jackson. I can see the tarpaulin billowing at the sides of the trailer.

Change down, accelerate.

At least I've got him in sight now. There are sections where he disappears from view behind trees, but he's not going anywhere. Not now. And I'll be right behind him before we get to the end of the dual carriageway, if those caravans keep out of the way.

Then it's the run down to the Cartgate roundabout, the Ilchester stretch after that, and Lizzie's lay-by. Another roundabout at Podimore. Then Sparkford.

I'm on the dual carriageway, in a line of cars in the outside lane. You know the ones, they cross the hatched lines and accelerate as if their lives depend on getting past this lorry or that caravan up ahead.

Well, mine does.

There's a Porsche in front of me, but I'm keeping up with it. I'm thinking it will provide good cover, that Jackson might not notice me flying up the outside. I'll get in front of him before he knows what's happening. Then I stand a chance of stopping him at the next roundabout.

I'm level with him now, both sun visors down so he can't see my face.

He's coming across, squeezing me on to the central reservation. Fuck it.

I stamp on the brakes, the car snaking. The offside wheels are in the gravel on the central reservation, the huge wheels of the trailer looming large in the passenger window. The cars following me have spotted what's happening and braked, a gap opening up behind me.

What they don't know is that the driver of the lorry is doing it deliberately.

I can hear something scraping down the front wing of the Capri – the rear mudguard of the trailer, possibly – then I'm in the clear, back behind the lorry.

I have a look up the nearside, but he sees me coming and cuts back across. I'll never get past him like this. On the climb past Ilchester, possibly, but not here. He's carrying too much speed.

The roundabout it is then. He'll go one way and I'll go the other – the wrong way.

The traffic is slowing on the approach now. I'm still in the inside lane, behind Jackson. I don't want him to know what I'm doing until the last second. He'll have his wheel turned to the left and won't have a chance to respond.

Is there too much traffic coming round the roundabout westbound? Looks like it. I'll have to stay tight to the central island, maybe even put my wheels on the kerb.

He's almost stationary now, but I'm resisting the temptation to jump out and run around to the front of the lorry. Not that I can run very quickly anyway, but he's probably got the door locked. Either that or he'd kick it open in my face.

Waiting. I can feel my heart beating in my chest, hear it almost. I'll need to time it right, make sure he's committed to the A303 off the roundabout, before I take my chance.

Then he's accelerating on to the roundabout and I go for it, dive into the outside lane and accelerate towards the westbound traffic – the oncoming traffic.

There are only two cars coming towards me, both in the inside lane. No one coming right around the roundabout, not yet anyway. I'm making the turn around the island, my wheels tight to the kerb when I see a car in the outside lane westbound, waiting to come on to the roundabout. The driver is looking to his right, hasn't seen me, but then I've got no right to be there anyway, have I?

He looked at the last second, stamped on the brakes.

Jackson is turning left to continue on the dual carriageway, tucked into the inside lane as he makes his turn. Now's my chance. I race across the roundabout, accelerating past his cab before he has a chance to react. Not that he could; a sharp turn to the right and he'd jackknife the lorry.

Now I'm in front.

Ilchester next, and Lizzie's lay-by. His speed will drop on the long climb, so maybe I can box him in, force him to stop even? On the single-lane stretch before we get to the dual carriageway, he won't be able to get past me there, not with the constant stream of westbound traffic coming towards us.

I've slowed down now and the lorry is looming large behind me in my rear view mirror. I'm in third gear, the engine racing, but it means I should be able to accelerate out of trouble if I have to. Plenty of petrol too, so I can stay with him for as long as it takes, assuming he doesn't run me off the road.

His acceleration takes me by surprise, as does the shunt when he rams the back of the Capri.

I'm watching him in the mirror, pulling out to overtake, accelerating, then he slams into the rear wing of the Capri and suddenly I'm spinning, the car kicking into the air as it hits the kerb, before coming to rest on the grass verge, facing the wrong direction.

Now the lorry is accelerating, thick black smoke belching from the exhaust.

Maybe it was a bit optimistic, trying to stop a lorry with a car, but the engine is still running and I can keep him in sight at the very least.

A Land Rover spots me turning on the grass bank, flashes me, letting me out into the line of cars following Jackson's lorry. I've lost a couple of hubcaps and the rear lights are probably smashed again, but the car accelerates and brakes normally. What more do you want?

He's twenty or so cars ahead of me now, some positioning themselves to get past when the dual carriageway opens up.

Not me, not this time. I'm staying back.

I'll be watching what happens from a safe distance.

At the moment, I'm focusing on my wing mirror, a motorcycle flying up the outside of the line of cars; black leather clad motorcyclist and pillion passenger tucked into racing position.

Seamus has the means of stopping Jackson. And Jackson won't know about the motorbike. Can't know.

Cars are streaming past the lorry by the time I reach the hatched lines, some slower vehicles tucking in behind. Then the motorcycle flashes past my driver's window. No acknowledgement from Seamus, but he must've seen me.

I pull out into the outside lane, hoping I might distract Jackson. And see what happens. I want to see what happens. I make no apology for that.

The motorcycle must be going over ninety as it flies past the lorry. If Jackson tried to respond, he left it too late. There may have been a turn of the wheel to the offside, a feeble attempt to block it, but I can't really tell. Either way, the motorcycle is in front now, Seamus sitting up on the pillion seat as the bike slows.

Then he turns, the gun in his right hand, and empties the magazine into the cab of the lorry just as we go under the A37 bridge.

It happens in slow motion after that, the lorry continuing on for a time, before gradually veering left. It mounts the kerb, crashes through the fence and slides down the embankment, before coming to rest on its side in the field.

Most of the traffic is stopping now, the occasional car taking its chance in the outside lane. I've pulled in to Lizzie's lay-by and am watching the motorbike. It's parked on the edge of the road further up, about a hundred yards away, and Seamus is walking slowly back to the gap in the fence, scrambling down the bank. He's holding the gun in his right hand, an empty magazine dropping to the ground, quickly replaced as he reloads.

Now he's standing in front of the lorry, peering in through the windscreen, his head tipped to one side. He's still got his helmet on, so I can't be sure, but I suspect he's smiling as he empties another magazine into Jackson.

He's seen me, parked in the lay-by, I know he has, but he's too far away to shoot at me and passers-by are starting to get out of their cars now.

He looks at me, in my direction at least, gives a small nod, and then is gone, the motorcycle accelerating hard eastbound, just as it did after he killed Sean Taylor during the Battle of the Beanfield.

I'm tempted to go and check on Jackson, but find myself following the motorcycle.

Don't ask me why, because I don't know.

Chapter Forty-Two

The eastbound traffic stopped, so I was able to accelerate out of the lay-by at the far end and put my foot down on a clear dual carriageway. Several motorists got out of their cars and were standing in the road behind me; no one else daft enough to pursue an armed man, I suppose, although I could see two people in my passenger side wing mirror, scrambling down the bank to the lorry.

A nice idea, but there is no chance whatsoever that Seamus left Jackson alive.

None.

So, here I am, the have-a-go hero chasing after a killer. That's what they'll be thinking behind me, what they'll be telling the police. Some might have seen me tangling with the lorry before, possibly, but that would look to all intents and purposes like a routine collision and the lorry driver's fault. I can hear the witnesses now:

'He pulled across into the side of the Capri.'

'Couldn't have seen him.'

'The bloke in the car was bloody lucky.'

And I was.

I'm doing a shade over a ton now, on the run down to the Podimore roundabout. I'm guessing the motorcycle will head north from there, across country; more chance to get lost in the narrow lanes.

Yes, the motorcycle is out of sight, of course it is. Long gone, but I stopped following it before I reached Podimore, instead I've flicked the sun visors out of the way and am watching a Gazelle hovering high over the roundabout. Helicopters are a common sight around here, of course they are. Yeovilton can't be more than a few miles away, but that's a naval air station and this is an army helicopter. This one is circling, looking for something, and I'm guessing we're looking for the same thing.

If I'm right, the helicopter will be following Seamus, so I can just follow the helicopter.

It's turning north, just as I thought.

North-east now, so that'll be the A37. It's an old Roman road, long straights with a kink at Charlton Adam to slow everybody down. It's a popular spot with motorcyclists, and I can see why as I fly down the outside of a long line of cars. I'm up to ninety, on the wrong side of the road, but I'll tuck in behind that van up ahead. There's a nice gap to wait for the oncoming cars to pass, then go again.

I'm guessing Seamus will turn west at some point. It's just a question of where, and whether they're still in sight when they do; there'll be a fishing boat waiting for them, somewhere off the coast of mid-Wales, perhaps. Suitably remote.

I'm getting hooted at now, cutting it a bit fine with the minibus travelling towards me. I can see him flashing his lights, braking hard. I swerve back to the nearside, almost lose the back end, the nearside rear tyre kicking up gravel and dust.

Glance up; the helicopter is still there.

Accelerating again.

Charlton Adam, one mile.

The helicopter has moved off to the right of the main road and is turning south-east now. There's a right turn coming up, according to the road signs, so the motorcycle must have taken it. South-east will take him back to the A303. Crafty. Perhaps even a rendezvous with another getaway vehicle. A van even; ride the motorbike straight in and away.

It's a narrow lane, the Capri slewing from side to side as I make the turn at speed. I change down, then get that soft click when I step on the accelerator and the pedal hits the metal buffer on the floor.

Glancing up when I get the chance; the helicopter is hovering now, perhaps a mile or so further ahead.

Fork right at the farm entrance, a wide concrete plinth, wheels spinning on cow shit.

There's woodland up ahead. I can see the tops of the trees, the helicopter almost directly above it, and me now.

Oh, shit.

I step on the brakes, the car sliding on the dry mud and grit, clouds of it billowing into the air, settling on the bonnet and windscreen. Too slow with the clutch – my left leg again; the engine stalls. I slide to a halt sideways across the lane.

I guess it had to end this way, didn't it? Maybe it's why I had to follow Seamus?

The motorcycle is lying on its side, twenty yards away, two army Land Rovers beyond it, another twenty yards further on perhaps, blocking the lane. There are more behind me now, directed in from the north by the helicopter, probably. I certainly wasn't being followed, I know that much.

Seamus is lying on his back, his right hand still inside his leather jacket where he went for his gun. His left arm is moving, so he's alive.

Further on, the motorcyclist is lying in the road, helmet on, visor up. Detective Constable Field is standing over him, saying something, but I can't hear it from here.

Two shots to the chest.

DC Helen Webster has walked forwards from her position behind the Land Rovers and is standing over Seamus. She kicks away his left hand, uses the barrel of her pistol to open his visor, straightens up, says something.

Two shots to the chest.

I get out of the Capri slowly. Guns are trained on me from behind the Land Rovers front and back, the soldiers wearing balaclavas under their helmets, green rather than black.

'You weren't supposed to see that, Bob,' said Webster.

'Don't look so fucking surprised,' snapped Field. 'What did you think was going happen? How the fuck did you think this was going to end?'

'Who are you?' I asked, in as loud and clear a voice as I could muster. 'Because you sure as hell aren't police officers.'

'Special Reconnaissance Unit,' replied Webster. 'The army makes the mess, we clean it up.'

'You executed them.'

'We did, Bob.' Field this time.

'That's murder.'

'That's war. We're at war with these people.'

'It was you, wasn't it? All along, it was you.' I'm nodding to myself, and it's a rhetorical question, really, but Webster answers all the same.

'We made sure you were coming round before we rolled your car into the lake, and you did have manual windows. We even waited there until we saw you reach the bank. Thought it might keep you motivated.'

'Motivated?'

'You went to Ireland, didn't you?'

'We played you like a fucking guitar, mate.' Field sneers. 'Who d'you think fed you Bernadette Ryan? One call to the *Somerset County Gazette* was all it took.' He's kicking the motorcyclist's feet, looking for signs of life. 'I'm calling from the *Belfast Telegraph*,' he said, putting on a broad Irish accent. 'You're like one of those dolls; point it in the right direction, pull the string and off it goes.'

'You knew I'd go to Belfast, speak to her family. I could've been bloody well killed.'

'It was a risk we were prepared to take.' Field gives an apologetic shrug. 'We knew who was killing the girls – we'd been watching them for months – we just needed you to lead Seamus to them. Right on cue, he's over here, cleaning up the mess for us. We knew he wouldn't be able to help himself.'

'Covering up your cover-up.'

'And what d'you think's going to be the story?' Field is unscrewing a silencer from the barrel of his pistol. 'An IRA cell operating on the mainland, assassinating former Royal Green Jackets, intercepted by the SAS and killed after a short exchange of fire somewhere in rural Somerset. That's what it'll be, mate. We'll probably all get medals too.'

'What about Martin Clarke, and Alan?'

'Collateral damage. It happens.'

I'm watching Webster now. She's walked past me to the back of the Capri and is feeling under the offside wheel arch with her hand. 'We might as well have this back now,' she said, holding up a small black box in the palm of her gloved hand. 'I remembered to take it off your Volvo.'

That explains a lot: how they kept finding me in the Little Chef, even when I went off the beaten track; how they were waiting for me in the car park at Ilminster police station. 'The knife that Taylor used to kill Alan . . . it was wrapped in a towel.'

301

'We watched Taylor put it in the boot of your car. Watched you hide it at the bottom of the dry stone wall,' replied Webster. 'We put it in his garage where it belonged. The last thing we wanted was you getting arrested for that.'

'And the personnel file?'

'We put that back, didn't want Jackson missing it.'

'What about Maxine?' I asked. 'Where is she?'

'She's in a safe house, happy as Larry.' Field smiles. 'We told her it's for her own protection and she went along with it. Didn't give her a lot of choice, mind you. Focused your mind on B & D Light Haulage, though, didn't it? That, and the file.'

'She'll be released tomorrow,' offered Webster. 'Told to keep quiet. She's not the brightest spark, but she'll go along with it if she thinks she's in danger. She isn't, but we'll tell her she is.'

'Put the fear of God into her, we will,' said Field, grinning.

I take a deep breath, fold my arms and lean back against the side of the Capri.

'I know what you're thinking, Bob,' said Field. 'I can see it in your eyes. You're thinking of going to the press, blowing this whole thing wide open. But I wouldn't if I were you. You've done your country a great service, mate, don't fuck it up now.'

'A great service?'

'Justice, delivered the old-fashioned way maybe, but the bastards killing those girls are dead. What more d'you want? Greenslade too.' Field shakes his head. 'That was a hell of a spot. Even we didn't know he was lying about driving his lorry that night.'

Blood is starting to puddle up underneath Seamus's body. It's a strange feeling I have; conflicted, I suppose, as the good doctor would say.

Seamus was a member of the IRA and would've cheerfully murdered me given half a chance, and yet he saved my life twice. Once in Belfast – I'd never have got out of there alive if he hadn't

302

wanted to follow me back to Somerset – and then again when Sean Taylor was about to stab me to death. He did it because it suited him to do it, I know that. He needed me alive, to lead him to his sister's killers, but it's still . . . *conflicting*. That's the best word I can find for it.

I'm not going to shed a tear for him, though. I wouldn't want you to think that.

Four soldiers step out from behind the Land Rovers, pick up the bodies and load them unceremoniously into the back. Not even a stretcher, legs and arms dangling. Another picks up the motor-bike, wheeling it towards a ramp placed at the back of the long-wheelbase Land Rover.

'There'll be two more Provos stepping in to replace them before you can say "united Ireland",' said Webster, kicking gravel and dust over the puddles of blood in the road.

'So, what happens now?' I asked.

'Nothing, mate,' replied Field. 'Unless you really do want to go to the press and all that shit. Then, I'm afraid, you'll be another victim of the IRA cell, caught in the crossfire.' He's pointing Seamus's gun at my head now. 'You recognise this gun, I'm sure. It was used by a known member of the IRA to kill Sean Taylor, Terry Greenslade and Bruce Jackson. It's also been connected to the murder of an RUC officer in Derry, shot on his own doorstep. A wonderful thing, ballistics. It would be sad if it had to take the life of another police officer.'

'The other alternative,' said Webster, 'is that you forget what you've seen here and the case stays closed. Go home, watch the cricket.'

'And that GBH charge goes away,' said Field. 'When you broke that officer's arm with the telescope.'

'There are still the inquests.'

'A D-Notice will block all press coverage; in the national inter-est, you understand, Bob. The coroner might get a visit from a faceless suit from some government department or other as well. You get the picture. Just be very careful what you tell the families.'

I know I said I didn't care, but I do, now it comes to it. I was prepared to die trying to find Lizzie's killers, but I've done that. They're dead and I'm still standing, as the song goes.

'DCS Sharp will be going to see Martin Clarke's father tomor-row,' said Field. 'He'll be told his son is innocent and officially cleared of any suspicion in the murders of Fiona Anderson, Alice Cobb and your colleague, DS Harper. Is that good enough for you?'

'It is.'

'Go home then.'

'One last thing.' Webster stops at the passenger door of the Land Rover, turns. 'It was me, Bob. Sorry. I phoned Dr Mellanby, pretended to be your ex-wife, told the doctor I was worried you were suicidal. She seemed genuinely concerned; even asked if I knew where she could find you.'

Chapter Forty-Three

It's day two of a four day County Championship game against Hampshire. I missed the first few overs; came the long way round, via breakfast at Camel Hill. Tied a fresh bunch of flowers to the sapling in Lizzie's lay-by too.

They'll be the last, I think. Lizzie can rest in peace now, and I can sleep at night. Yes, there's still the guilt, there always will be, but I've made my peace with it, with her, and with her family.

I waited until after Sharp had been to see Martin Clarke's father, gave him back what was left of the Capri. I offered to pay for the damage, but he wouldn't hear of it. A man of few words. I told him the men responsible for the death of his son were dead. He'd seen the reports of the IRA cell on the BBC news, knew about the SAS ambush at Steart Wood. It's a real place, on the map and everything. Who knew?

He asked me if that had something to do with his son's death and I didn't deny it. Couldn't.

Sharp had told him there'd be a press release acknowledging Martin's innocence. And that was enough for him, apparently.

A nice bloke, Martin Clarke's father, destined for a lonely old age, his only son dead.

Makes you think, although it's best not to, I find. I may have mentioned that before.

I've got a new Volvo. Well, I say *new*, it's three years old, one previous owner, full service history. Same colour, but the estate version this time – more room to sleep in the back. Manual windows too. And Field, or whatever his name was – I didn't waste my breath asking – turned out to be as good as his word. I had a letter, and the GBH charge for breaking that constable's arm with the telescope has been quietly dropped. I'm not surprised, though. It was my day in court and they were hardly going to hand it to me on a plate, were they?

'I thought I might find you here,' said the good doctor, sitting down next to me in the stands.

I haven't spoken to Caroline since that day I stormed into her office, accusing her of all sorts. Embarrassment, I suspect.

'I owe you an apology,' I mumbled.

'Forget it,' she said, waving the suggestion away with the back of her hand. 'Did you find out who rang me?'

'I did.'

'Who was it?'

'Can't say, I'm afraid.'

'Like that, is it?'

'Coffee?' I asked, changing the subject, deflecting. I've had to do a lot of that lately, with Angela in particular.

'I've brought my own,' Caroline said. 'Got myself a season ticket too.'

'Really?'

'My husband is a cricket fan, so . . .' She was trying to make sense of the scoreboard.

'Caught the bug?'

'I wouldn't go that far,' she replied, smiling. 'How have you been?'

Oh, God, here we go. She'll be asking me how I *feel* about it all next.

'Fine,' I said. 'Catching up on lost sleep.'

'What about the men who killed Lizzie and Alan?'

'Dead.'

'Does Shirley know?'

Shirley is the only person I've told the whole story to, apart from you. She deserved that, at the very least. Even the bit about the wandering knife. Everything. I think you'll agree I owed it to her. Owed her more than that, to be honest, far more, but that was all I had to offer. She took it well, but that's Shirley for you. Even handed me back the letter unopened.

'She does,' I replied.

'How did she take it?'

'Stoically.' It took me a moment, but I found the right word in the end.

'So, what about you, Bob? What happens now?'

'Sharp came to see me,' I said. 'Asked me if I want to do some consultancy work. They're putting together a cold case unit, reviewing old files, unsolved stuff, you know.'

'It would keep you busy.' She was applauding something; a four, possibly. I can see a fielder trotting down to the boundary rope in front of us.

'I told him I'd think about it.'

'The money would be useful,' Caroline said.

'My full pension has been confirmed, but it would mean Shirley could start charging me rent for the flat, I suppose.'

'It would do you good, keep you busy.' She frowned. 'I see you haven't got your scorebook.'

'I don't need it anymore,' I said. 'There's nothing left to dwell on. It's all been dealt with. I can just relax and enjoy the cricket.'

'Instead of copying it all off the Ceefax,' said Caroline, laughing.

'You knew?'

'Of course I did.' Concern is etched on her face now; I can see it in her eyes too. Here it comes. 'And you're feeling good about it all?'

'I am,' I said, resisting the temptation to sigh.

'Avon and Somerset paid for ten sessions and there are some left, if you need to see me, Bob. Any time.'

◆ ◆ ◆

I know what you're thinking. You've got one last question.

You want to know whether I knew Seamus was there when Sean Taylor handcuffed me and marched me in to the trees behind the horse lorry intending to kill me.

Am I right?

It would be easy to deny it, of course it would, if I really didn't know he was there. Just a straightforward, and slightly outraged, 'No, I didn't know, how could I possibly have known that?' and you'd have to accept it, wouldn't you?

On the other hand, if I did know, then the easiest way out would be to change the subject, deftly move the conversation along. But that wouldn't be fair; you've asked me a straight question, and you deserve a straight answer. So, here goes.

One hundred and four for one, in reply to Hampshire's two hundred and fifty-six all out. Somerset have got Ian Botham and Viv Richards still to bat too, so it should be a good day's cricket.

You're welcome.

AUTHOR'S NOTE

I've had a lot of fun remembering what life was like in the 1980s, and from a purely selfish point of view, it's been something of a relief not to have to worry about DNA, CCTV, ANPR cameras, mobile phones, the internet. That said, it's been a sobering experience writing a historical crime novel set the year after I left school!

I can't remember the last time I went in a phone box. And who remembers running in to one, only to find it needed a phone card? Stopping at a Little Chef for an All Day Breakfast, followed by a Jubilee Pancake?

Happy days, viewed through rose-tinted spectacles, perhaps.

I have a soft spot for the A303. Always have. I spent my formative years moving between London and the West Country, on the road most weekends; westbound on Friday evening, then back to London on the Sunday evening. Always with a stop . . .

I can't say I know the road like the back of my hand anymore, but I did once. It has changed so much, and is still changing, a new set of roadworks greeting me on the rare occasions I venture out these days, another single-lane stretch being turned into dual carriageway. Mercifully, I managed to find an old road atlas from 1985 online. And a 1984 Ordnance Survey map of Ilchester that I had shipped from Florida.

I also have happy memories of watching Somerset at the County Ground in Taunton in the early 1980s, although cricketing aficionados will have spotted that I have taken a few liberties with the 1985 fixture list. Poetic licence, I prefer to call it.

There are lots of people to thank, as always. My wife, Shelley, without whom Bob would not have sprung to life on these pages. My dear friend, Rod, for his critique. Once again, David Hall and Clare Paul have been extraordinarily generous with their local knowledge. And last, but not least, my editorial team at Thomas & Mercer, Sammia Hamer and Ian Pindar.

I do hope you enjoyed Bob's first outing. It won't be his last!

Damien Boyd
Devon, UK
September 2024

ABOUT THE AUTHOR

Photo © 2013 Damien Boyd

Damien Boyd is a solicitor by training and draws on his extensive experience of criminal law, along with a spell in the Crown Prosecution Service, to write fast-paced crime thrillers featuring Detective Inspector Nick Dixon.

Follow the Author on Amazon

If you enjoyed this book, follow Damien Boyd on Amazon to be notified when the author releases a new book!

To do this, please follow these instructions:

Desktop:

1) Search for the author's name on Amazon or in the Amazon App.

2) Click on the author's name to arrive on their Amazon page.

3) Click the 'Follow' button.

Mobile and Tablet:

1) Search for the author's name on Amazon or in the Amazon App.

2) Click on one of the author's books.

3) Click on the author's name to arrive on their Amazon page.

4) Click the 'Follow' button.

Kindle eReader and Kindle App:

If you enjoyed this book on a Kindle eReader or in the Kindle App, you will find the author 'Follow' button after the last page.